HOUSE OF SHIFTERS AND SMOKE

SHADES OF RUIN AND MAGIC
BOOK 3

MEG XUEMEI X

ISBN: 979-8-9891007-3-6
First Edition

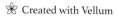 Created with Vellum

HOUSE OF SHIFTERS AND SMOKE

Killian

Soon, I'll have to marry the most powerful queen and rule two kingdoms.

But all I want is Barbie, the new girl in my house and the only thing I can't have.

If I take her for my own, she'll be murdered.

I know I should stay away from her, but I no longer can, even if the kingdoms collapse and the world burns as a consequence.

I might be the villain in the story, but without her, there's no meaning to my brutal, miserable existence.

So, I start to push her to the breaking point so she can survive the bride trials and rise above it all.

Only I don't expect it to hurt so much to see my rivals, the other heirs, swoop in to try to make her theirs.

1

Barbie

Clamor and bustle engulfed me. The mage ringleader barked orders. This sorry lot was desperate to leave the scene.

I grinned viciously even though I was bleeding out. "In a hurry, bitches?"

Agony pounded in my veins, which might burst open if this kept going. I couldn't tell where the pain started and where it ended. Having low tolerance to pain had always been my weakness. And now it became hard to concentrate on even a single thought. Sy was gone, banished or locked somewhere so far away that, for the first time, I could no longer feel her.

Sy! Sy! I screamed and begged for her to answer to no avail. I was utterly alone facing whatever terror waited for me.

The mage ringleader, who was the only magic user in

this group, placed her fingers on my wrist and chanted to try to stop my bleeding, but no healing spells could work on me, even when my power was muted. The woman cursed warily. Someone else stepped up and wrapped a roll of bandages around my stump.

They didn't want me dead, at least not yet.

I gasped at the pain, trying to come up with another exit plan, yet there was none. Wild, panicked thoughts ran amok in my head. Fear iced me over.

They were going to deliver me to my father. What the Shriekers had failed to do, these douchebags might just achieve.

Then I recalled what the ringleader had said maliciously against the iron mask that had swallowed my head. *"This is the first trial of the Brides Selection, and you'll beg for death, Barbie!"*

They weren't Ruin's agents, yet my fear didn't lessen a notch. That woman's threat promised terrible pain. I kicked them. I fought with my one good hand like a caged animal. More hands grabbed me to subdue me, a cold blade slicing into my flesh. I screamed, the sound echoing back to me within the iron mask. My breath was cut short as claustrophobia kicked in. I didn't do well in such a confined space.

I stopped struggling, realizing it was futile. It'd only hinder my logic and observation. I needed to get a good feel of the enemies' operation, and then I'd be able to find a narrow window to escape.

I needed to find the crack among my abductors.

I shoved my fear and panic down to the pit of my stomach and locked them there, alone now without Sy.

"We gotta go before the chaos heir gets here!" the mage barked, her voice tense with fear. "Now!"

I wasn't the only one afraid. I could smell the stench of

my enemies' fear at hearing Killian's name. I smirked, even though agony bombarded me, even though I'd been locked in the cold darkness within the iron mask.

Killian would avenge me, no matter what, even though we hadn't parted on good terms. There was no denying that there was a bond between us. I wasn't a fool. I could see that, underneath his lust and possessiveness, he'd always tried to protect me. What he would do to them would make whatever my abductors did to me pale in comparison.

Of that, I had no doubt.

Find me, Killian! Find me! I shouted out to him silently, hoping somehow it could reach him through time and space.

A foul wind came, summoned by the mage, whipping my exposed skin. Nausea swept over me, icy lead sinking in my stomach as a force hurled me into a damp tunnel.

2

Killian, heir of the House of Chaos

"Where is she?" I roared. "Where is *Barbie*?"

Wild magic pranced frantically along the boundary of Underhill, responding to Hades's power, which roared in my blood. The wild magic had once followed Barbie to my house, curious to learn where she lived. It hadn't interacted with anyone else for centuries, but it'd taken a liking to Barbie. I'd watched, allowing it to survey and weigh the House of Chaos.

Underhill acting in such an antsy manner could only mean one thing—it couldn't locate Barbie either. My girl was no longer on the academy grounds.

My heart sank under a glacier.

A storm rolled over the sky above the academy. Underhill was upset that Barbie had gone missing. Shadow beasts, its sentinels, howled and wailed from within the dark forest, sending chills racing along my forearms.

The beasts were driven by fear, rage, and Underhill's command. If they lashed out and came out to hunt, I'd have to contain them, or even slay a few. It would upset Underhill further, but my men's lives were my responsibility.

My team dashed toward me, flanking me. I could sense their uneasiness, but they held their ground, their weapons drawn.

"Barbie isn't inside," I said, my voice rough as I fought to keep a cool head. "She might've been taken. Search the region. Turn every stone over outside Underhill until we have her trail!"

"Yes, Your Highness!" my men answered as one.

"Whoever took her will regret they were ever born!" Rock growled. Barbie was known to be a pain in the butt, but she had grown on him.

My men divided into three groups and spread out to track Barbie.

Cami stayed with me, worry on her face. She'd been watching Barbie for me in the shadows. She'd reported to me right away when the other heirs dragged Barbie to perform a private dance for them. She'd also texted me when Barbie kicked down the door to the druid's class and ran out like a bat out of hell.

I'd dream-walked to my little scorpion when I didn't see her return to the house. She'd been troubled, but I hadn't paid close attention since I'd let my lust cloud my judgment. I'd thought with my dick. This primal need to fuck her every moment might get her killed one day.

My dragon growled, blaming me again. He hadn't protested but urged me on when I tried to get into my mate's pants last time. But there was no excuse for my neglect of her needs and safety.

I'd thought her anxiety came from being bullied, but

she'd handled it well, better than anyone else. I'd meant to ask her why she'd kicked down the druid's door and if that fucker had crossed a line and bothered her.

Now she was gone.

The possibility of her never returning petrified me, icing over my blood.

No, I wouldn't accept that outcome. Not a fucking chance! I'd find her and guard her.

My dragon bellowed in rage and fear for our mate, wanting to take over so he could fly to every corner to look for her. I reined him in, reasoning with him. It wasn't time for him to be out yet and draw the enemies' attention to us. Plus, he wasn't exactly an experienced tracker.

My cold eyes landed on Rock, my righthand man, and he nodded and stripped at once.

Rock was a werewolf, different than a shifter. A shifter could transform faster. It took a werewolf over a minute to change to their animal form, even a powerful one like Rock.

Indisputably, a werewolf had a better nose than a shifter and was mightier in physical combat, though a werewolf didn't have a powerful shifter's advantage of possessing any elemental magic.

Wild magic touched down on my shoulder as a raven, the form it chose for the moment. Everyone gasped in awe at the sight.

"Underhill demands to assist us in searching for Barbie," I said.

While Rock was still going through the transformation, I dashed toward another path to cover more ground to hunt for Barbie, my heart encased in ice and my throat tight, but I fought back cold panic. I needed my usual icy calm, so I could bring home the girl who no one else knew was my true mate.

A few minutes later, Rock and I ended up in the same spot halfway between Underhill and the House of Chaos. I scented Barbie. She'd been here and battled her enemies not long ago.

I took in the scene. My gaze moved from the newly broken twigs on the ground to the blood that had splattered the blades of grass. Someone had tried to erase the trail with witch magic, but they hadn't been thorough. The abductors had left in a hurry. I bet that they hadn't had a choice. Barbie was never a girl who would roll over. She must've given them hell.

As the scent of Barbie's blood drifted toward my nostrils, nausea shot into my stomach. My dragon coiled in me, thrashing. He'd never been so agitated, his fear for her pounding in my veins, echoing mine.

But feeling afraid and helpless would get us nowhere.

Let me do my fucking job so we can find our mate! I growled back.

Rock in his werewolf form nodded at my silent conclusion before taking off again to double back and track where the trail had gone cold, his shiny black fur vanishing between the bushes.

The raven form of wild magic departed my shoulder and alighted on the spot where Barbie had bled. It raised its head, wailing. A heartbeat later, it was gone, returning to report to Underhill.

I tried to drum out all the panicked noises in my head and focus on the scene, replaying the battle in my head, desperate to find any trace that could lead to Barbie.

They took her from here! my dragon informed me in outrage, sniffing and puffing out a stream of fire and smoke.

They took her to the sky. He snarled. *Let me out to look for her in the sky. I can do what your two legs can't do, princeling!*

My dragon had stayed dormant by choice, especially after my engagement to the Queen of the Underworld. All these years, he hadn't talked to me much. He'd only woken up after spotting Barbie, and now he looked forward to every chance to be in her presence, soaking in her scent. He hadn't exactly demanded to shift in front of her yet, since he was a little shy when it came to her and didn't want to scare her away with his big, ugly lizard form.

He'd been waiting for me to establish a solid relationship with her first, urging me to break up with Queen Lilith, unable to comprehend not only the political repercussions but also that such a rash act would only get our mate assassinated.

You want to wait until your machination is mature, and now she's been taken! my dragon roared at me. *You should've acted earlier. You should've protected her!*

Back off! I snarled back. Maybe he should stay dormant, so he wouldn't be such an opinionated, aggressive asshole. And if he thought he was more dominant than me and tried to take the reins, he'd be in for a world of hurt. I wasn't even known to be merciful to myself. *You won't find her in the sky. They took her somewhere else.*

Where? he demanded.

That's what I'm trying to suss out. Be silent and let me think if you want to help! I said harshly. *The day will come when I need you to be in your beast form. But the day isn't today. So fuck off!*

He huffed out a jet of fire, as if that could unnerve me while I was already on the edge. *I'll give you one day to find our mate!*

I ignored his threat, regretting my bond with this asshole.

A rush of footsteps came my way. The other heirs had arrived at the scene.

"Barbie was taken, wasn't she?" Cade shouted his question, panting from running, his face paling. Usually, nothing could unnerve the high mage.

Louis sniffed, then twin crimson rings formed around his pale blue irises. "They bled her! She shed their blood too. Barbie was taken!"

"I felt her distress while I was in the Jacuzzi in my house," Silas said, his amber eyes glowing. "She and I have a bond too, as she's no doubt a shifter. Her animal called to my alpha wolf for protection!"

"We all felt Barbie's panic for a second before her call was muffled," Rowan said grimly, his silver eyes shining with fury before he stalked toward the perimeter to check around.

I wasn't too pleased to realize that the other heirs were all drawn to her as well. Power called power. That's what it was.

Growling, Silas shifted to a large wolf, bouncing here and there to sniff around before he ran off to find where the trail ended.

I could dismiss the heirs. I had every right to do so, as Barbie was a member of my house, but I didn't. I swallowed my pride, as I needed all the help I could get. I even let Silas participate in our joint effort.

While the shifter heir had always hated me, he also held a grudge against Barbie for rejecting him, so I had no idea why he'd even bothered to come and help. Perhaps he just didn't want to miss out on any chance to show off his power. While he thought he was in constant competition with me,

I'd never really engaged. If he ended up being the one who found Barbie, he'd have bragging rights. If he did, I'd bow to him. I'd bow to anyone who located my Barbie.

Rock returned soon, shaking his head in dismay. Silas also came back to the clearing. The werewolf and the wolf stared at each other for a long second, snarled, then shifted back to their humanoid forms.

"The trail died right here, Your Highness," Rock said. "There's no other trail."

"Guys, look!" Cade called, an incredulous expression on his solemn face.

I tore my gaze from a silver tree, thick blood coating its bark. The blood must've erupted from a severed neck. The enemy's witch magic hadn't erased every hint of a brutal battle in their hurry to leave the scene. A small measure of comfort and relief settled in my stomach, for I knew that it wasn't Barbie's blood. My little scorpion had been fierce, but she'd been outnumbered.

I turned to look at where Cade's wand pointed—a cluster of white flowers sprouted out from the earth where Barbie had shed blood.

Pain stabbed my chest. Acid rage flooded me as I pictured how those motherfuckers had made her suffer. My dragon thrashed within me, bellowing and demanding to slay every single one who had hurt our mate.

I'd have gutted them if they were still here, I said, clenching my teeth, as it was getting hard to leash him. *We have a lot of powers, but neither of us is a tracker. We aren't good at detective work either, so we must cooperate with others to ensure our mate's safe return. Keep watching diligently, so even if I miss something, you won't. Got it?*

I won't even blink! he snarled, peeking out of my eyes in a nasty mood.

"I'm not surprised to see the flowers bloom from where Barbie's blood soaked the earth," Louis said. The vampire prince had drunk from her when she was his squire. I gave him a hard look, a muscle twitching in my jaw. He'd never take a drop of blood from Barbie again. "Barbie's blood is very powerful, as pure as a goddess's nectar."

"There hasn't been any god or goddess roaming for an eon," Rowan said, frowning. All the heirs had returned after they spread out to find the trail, which led back here. "Let's focus on helping find Barbie. The battle started and ended in this circle." The fae heir swept his large hand across the area. "They came to her from all directions to cut off her escape route."

Silas sniffed and nodded. "There must be at least two dozen of them."

Rock confirmed, "With another dozen on the perimeter to make sure she wouldn't get help."

I knew they were trying to be objective, letting cold logic guide them to sort out the scenario of the kidnapping, yet I was still utterly pissed at everyone. Hatred and anxiety lapped at me as I pictured how my foes had dragged my mate off.

"What did they want from Barbie?" Cade pondered. "We know that Barbie is special. But what made someone send a small army to come after one girl? What are we missing?"

"Barbie isn't just any girl," Louis drawled. "She's been around for a couple of months, yet no one knows her origin."

"Don't fixate on her origin!" I hissed, my jaw clenched in fury. "Focus on who the fuck took her!"

"Motive matters, Killian," Cade said. "We want to get her back as much as you."

The other heirs nodded in agreement, but I disagreed

with them. Barbie meant more to me than they could ever imagine. But no one knew what she was to me, and for her own safety, no one could know that my true mate had come. I'd kept her close until she was taken today.

A stray dark thought slammed me in the face. Could it be the work of my betrothed? My heart skipped an icy beat, but I shook my head, rejecting that possibility.

Not even Cami knew about the true connection between Barbie and me, though my cousin saw how much I was drawn to Barbie and was worried about it.

"She killed as many as she could before she was over-powered," Louis said admiringly, plucking a white flower that sprouted from where Barbie had bled and sniffing at it. "She's never one who rolls over and shows her belly."

Silas nodded. Usually, he wasn't impressed by anything. "We underestimated Barbie, but the lot that came for her didn't," he said, his jaw tight. "Which means they know more about her than us, and that her power scale might be close to ours."

All the heirs had witnessed Barbie brushing off his alpha stares.

I traipsed around the clearing as I tried to piece together the entire scene of Barbie being taken from here, not wanting to miss any details that would lead me to her.

"The trail ended here," I called, calculating the odds. "How did they all vanish with Barbie in the blink of an eye?"

Cade flashed open his turquoise eyes after chanting and meditating, whatever a high mage did to get results. His steady gaze was the calm before the storm.

"Teleport," the mage heir said.

Just what I'd thought.

"There aren't that many supernaturals who can teleport," Rowan offered, ice in his silver eyes. "We can narrow it down."

"And round up all the usual suspects!" Silas growled.

"And then we'll drain those motherfuckers to the very last drop!" Louis promised.

"It wasn't teleportation in the usual sense," Cade said gravely. "Whoever they are, they used the 'dark substance.' I can still feel the residue of its foul spell after I deployed the detection spells just now. Dark substance is illegal in all the worlds except—"

"CrimsonTide," Rowan finished for him.

I knew that as well, as did the other heirs.

CrimsonTide, the neutral zone where no house ruled, was a breeding ground for the worst criminals, gangs, rogues, and terrible beings you wouldn't wish to cross paths with.

It was as independent as Underhill. But Underhill didn't bother us if we didn't breach its territory. Yet those dangerous hybrids from CrimsonTide would cross to our five kingdoms, mostly on assassination jobs. They had no rules, no codes, and no morals.

Everyone's faces darkened at the prospect that Crimson-Tide had taken Barbie.

"What the fuck are we waiting for?" Silas pulled his lips back. "Let's march into CrimsonTide now and take back our top bride candidate!"

Something like a kernel of hope sparked in the other heirs' eyes as they answered the challenge. I didn't doubt that in their minds, they all thought Barbie could be *their* mate. She was a wild card when it came to magic, and the heirs would only go for the strongest females.

I suppressed my cold fury, and my dragon growled,

sharing my sentiment and rage. Barbie was no one's but ours!

"What could CrimsonTide want with Barbie?" Cade ran his hand over his face, looking tired and worried, not his usual lighthearted self. "She's new to the realm, a drifter from the mortal world. Even though she's gained some notoriety of late, it shouldn't have attracted such rapt attention from any party in CrimsonTide."

"Who said the interested party is actually from Crimson-Tide?" Silas snorted. "Anyone who has a deep pocket can hire mercenaries from CrimsonTide, so it won't be traced back to them. When Barbie was in my house, she was safe. She became a target after she was dragged to the House of Chaos."

Silas's words were cutting, yet they rang with truth. The instigator behind Barbie's kidnapping couldn't be from CrimsonTide. It would be too easy. But then, who wanted Barbie so badly?

I had enemies. And I was tied to a powerful woman, a queen. I doubted that my overprotectiveness toward Barbie had gone unnoticed. Someone might try to use her to get to me. I'd brought this on my mate.

I contained the terrible storm within me. Seeing my mate's blood soak the earth had nearly undone me, but I must pull it together so I could save her. I'd never accept that it might already be too late.

I'd tear the world apart for her.

"It isn't the time to point fingers, gentlemen," Rowan said. "More importantly, we need to form a good plan to find Barbie."

"I shall go to CrimsonTide alone," I said. "Stealth is the key. We don't want our foes to move Barbie if she's indeed in CrimsonTide."

"We all have spies in CrimsonTide," Cade said, patting me on the shoulder. "Let's pool our resources."

"Happy hunting!" Silas snarled.

For the first time, I didn't find the shifter heir despicable. I needed all the heirs, who had once been my brothers, and their teams to work with me and find Barbie.

"We'll find Barbie, brothers," Louis vowed. "She's one of us now."

3

Barbie

I woke up to piercing pain that had knocked me out cold when I was sucked into an icy vacuum and found myself prone on the hard ground, with no idea of where I was, since I couldn't see with the iron helmet clamped around my head.

I lifted my good hand and realized that my wrist was chained along with my ankle. Even with an iron mask silencing me and a torque heavy around my neck to bind my power, my enemies still considered me a threat.

Rage pulsed in me. Fear fogged my mind. I grabbed the iron helmet, trying to lift it off my head, but it wouldn't budge. An animalistic wail tore out of my throat. I clawed at the iron mask, wanting it fucking gone more than anything. It only pressed tighter against my face, its foul spells and rough edges sinking into my flesh and peeling off part of my skin.

A new wave of pain bloomed in me, adding to the old one. I could feel my face getting wet, not from my tears but from blood. If I didn't stop my struggle, it might just turn my face to pulp. Icy panic sank into my chest, and my panting pounded in my ears within the confines of the iron mask.

Stop! I ordered myself. I couldn't afford to have an episode. I couldn't afford to lose my shit if I ever wanted to escape whatever hell my enemies had fashioned for me.

I forced myself to remove my hand from clutching the iron mask, only to have it fly to the bespelled metal torque around my neck. I gripped it to pry it off. Icy burning shot through my fingers. I jerked away my hand, breathing laboriously, then grasped the torque again to get a feel of it so I could find a way to neutralize it.

It was futile to try to break it with brute force.

Someone besides my father knew about my weaknesses. But how? And what else did they know?

I endured the pain, not releasing the torque until I was certain that it indeed didn't carry my father's dark signature and rotten power. It didn't bear his touch. Did my father have a new ally? But it wasn't like him. He didn't share power, only had slaves.

Yet someone had forged this foul thing specifically to bind my type of power.

A terrible thought coiled in my mind. There was another person who knew about my existence, other than Ruin and his agents.

My mother.

Sy and I had never breached the subject, but any bitch who could mate with an original god had to be able to hold her own. Sy and I had already figured out that I was a three-quarter goddess.

If it was my mother, how had she found out I was in

Shades Academy in Mist of Cinder? Grabbing me in such a manner wouldn't endear her to me. But then, she wouldn't have cared about the rough treatment dealt to me.

A chilling, foreboding feeling twirled in my mind. Would she consume me like my father?

I seized the torque again, hissing and enduring the icy burn. *Fuck!* The torque had a mixed demonic and archangelic signature. From its vibration, I could tell that it was targeting the one-quarter of my genetic makeup that didn't add to my goddess essence.

I had one-quarter mage bloodline. I could easily pass as a human when I tried.

A kernel of hope rose in me. If the spells in this torque grabbed hold of my weaker genetic part, then in time, it'd lose its effect and my goddess genes would overrule the binding spells. But time wasn't on my side when I was being held captive. Whoever was behind this grab wouldn't give me enough time to break out of this bind.

When the burn became too much, I had to drop my hand from the torque, gasping for air from the pain. Yet there wasn't enough air within the iron mask. If it'd been anyone else, they'd have been unconscious or even dead by now from the suffocation and bleeding.

Some animals chewed their own legs off to escape. I'd sliced off my wrist to remove the spellbound bracelet, but I hadn't expected the torque. The one who wanted me had thought of everything, two steps ahead of me.

Think. Breathe.

Rage would do me no favors.

I calmed my pulse and slowed down my breathing to get more oxygen into my lungs.

My trembling fingers groped on the ground to get a sense of where I was. Moss dotted the cracks between the uneven stones. Something scurried across the other side of the room. It must be a rat.

My breathing grew heavy again. All I heard was my laborious breathing and frantic heartbeat pounding in my eardrums within the iron mask. I was heading toward hyperventilation again.

I forced myself to inhale slowly through my nose, then exhale through my mouth, then rinse and repeat, until I cooled off to gather my thoughts.

I'd been dumped in a warded dungeon.

My abductors had teleported me here after they made sure the torque had bound my power, so it couldn't interfere with their teleportation. I could still smell the dark substance they'd used to power the teleportation.

My hand kept exploring the space behind me, the chains on my wrist and ankle making harsh sounds as I moved. Two feet from where I'd been, my fingers touched a concrete wall. Even with my power caged, I could still feel dark spells warding the wall. At my touch, they crawled over my skin like spiders and made me shiver with disgust, but they couldn't harm me.

Which meant even though the torque kept the lethal part of my power at bay and cut off my siphoning, it couldn't completely nullify my magical self. Which meant I could reach Sy if I kept trying.

Sy! I called urgently while I stayed busy investigating my jail to find a way out. *Sy!*

How long had I been here? Had I been dumped in this shithole for a few minutes, hours, or even days? I shook my head. It couldn't be days since my wounds were still fresh. The kidnappers had somehow administered basic treatment on them, not with magical healing, as it didn't work on me, but the conventional way. A bandage had been wrapped around my stump, though the blood still seeped through. There were also makeshift stitches on my side where a blade had slid in during the fight.

If this situation lasted while I couldn't access my power, I wouldn't heal. My wounds would be left open, and then I'd be even weaker. I barely had any energy left, and hunger throbbed in me, digging a hole in the pit of my stomach.

I pushed my hunger, fear, and pain down and pricked my ears to listen, even though I didn't know where the door was. I couldn't see, but I could use my ears and senses despite the iron mask proving to be an obstacle.

As I focused my hearing to a laser point, my kidnappers' voices drifted to me.

"...dangerous bitch...when...deliver..."

"...the messengers will arrive soon..."

My kidnappers were talking outside the door. I held my breath, pricking my ears in that direction to listen, but I couldn't get most of the words, as the iron mask muffled their sounds.

Sy! Sy! I need you! Please, I called again.

I felt her trying to reach me. Severing our connection was one of the cruelest things anyone could do to us. Then, from across the abyss, Sy roared my name.

She couldn't get to me. I had to go to her.

I dove into the chasm. If I shattered at the bottom, so be it. I didn't want to stand alone one more second without her. I spotted Sy surging up to meet me. We screamed each other's names, then our hands clasped, our fingers curling and locking around each other.

I gotcha! I shouted.

Gotcha too, she answered.

I pulled her up, and we alighted on solid ground, huddling and clinging to each other.

I'm sorry, Sy. I sobbed. *I wronged you. Don't leave again!*

I was a bad servant, Barbie. She hugged me tightly. *I won't ever try to usurp you again. I vow it on our father's black soul!*

You were never a servant, Sy! It broke my heart that you put that hat on. You're my other half that I don't deserve. Let's not fight again.

No fight! she promised. *But you need to regain your strength. To get out of here, you'll need to feed. You'll need to let me go. Consume me, and you'll have the strength to break that cursed torque.*

No! I stared at her in horror. *How can you even say things like that?*

It has to be done, Barbie. If I were the primary, I wouldn't have thought twice about consuming your essence. You must do it. You must escape before Ruin comes for you!

Never will I eat you! You die, I die. End of discussion, I said, my lips thinning in disapproval. *Also, your information is outdated. You need to keep up.* I sank into the old habit of criticizing her. *This time, it's not Ruin coming for us. It's someone else.*

She frowned. *Who?*

I don't know yet, but I need you with me.

Always. She paused for a second and said with all her heart, *I love you, Barbie, more than anyone and anything.*

I know, I said, the ache in my chest only deepening. *Like two peas in a pod.*

It'd taken that kind of fight and scare to make us realize how much we meant to each other.

My cruel god father had failed to break me, not knowing it was all because of Sy. I wasn't damaged goods because I had Sy. So, no matter what ordeals I endured, I always got up swinging, and Sy had always been there, shielding me, taking the blunt hits and cheering me up with her endless vulgar optimism.

Tits up! That was her favorite cliché.

No one could take away our love and loyalty for each other, the one thing that made us strong and kept us going. Together, we'd always fight our way out, no matter how dire the circumstances. Like even after all those years under Ruin's thumb, enduring endless torment, he could never truly control us. He could never rob us of our love for life and each other, and our hope for a future without him. And with that, Sy and I had finally managed to escape him.

This time, it was no different. And we'd crush our new tormentors.

It won't be for long, Sy said. *And then we'll eat them.*

I'm not keen on the eating part. Too messy, I offered. *But with your strength, we can snap their necks with one clean sweep.*

Sy couldn't take over since the torque prohibited our shift, but it could no longer keep us apart. She moved as close to the surface as she could, shouldering my pain and trying to take all of it into her.

No, Sy! That's too much for you!

I can take pain better than you, she insisted. *I can carry it for you. You do your thing and get us out of here!*

My headspace cleared as the pain became a dull throb. Sy had absorbed the pain, taking it in her stride and taunting it. *Father did much worse, and we still survived him.*

I heard a faint click from the doorknob outside.

Take cover, lieutenant! Sy ordered me.

When did I become her lieutenant? But I dropped to the ground, pretending to be unconscious and staying in the same position I had been in. Sy, with her superior hearing that not even the iron mask could hinder, sent me all the intel I needed.

The heavy door swung open. Three sets of footsteps entered the cell.

I wondered how many mercenaries waited outside and how many of them guarded this facility. And in my current condition, how many I could bring down.

We can take them, Sy snarled, taking an active role advising me. *We just need to be smarter and faster. Leave it to me.*

"The girl is still out?" a man asked in a gruff voice.

"That torque really knocked her out cold," a woman answered, and I recognized her voice—the mage ringleader. "Our client said it'd work, and it did."

"I heard that girl was more trouble than she's worth," the gruff man said. "She looks small and harmless. Did she really kill eleven pros before you subdued her?"

The third person who entered the room hadn't uttered a word, and my senses told me that he was another magic user and the most dangerous of the trio.

"Pick her up, Brad," the mage ringleader ordered the man. "Our client's reps will be here soon. The faster we get this ticking bomb off our hands, the better off we are."

"Which style? Bride-carry, piggyback, or draping her over my shoulder like a sack of potatoes?" Brad asked. He mistook himself for having a sparkling personality. "Are we going to take the chains off her?"

"The chains go with her," the mage ringleader said.

"And the helmet?" Brad asked.

"It stays with her as well," the mage ringleader said impatiently.

Once I was transported to their client, I'd have less chance to get away.

A large, uncouth hand grabbed me. I kept my heartbeat even and my breathing weak. Then I was half-lifted, a man's hot breath tickling the side of my neck.

It was now or never.

I jerked my head backward with brutal force, smashing my iron helmet into Brad's head, bashing his face in.

Sy giggled at the sickening sound of bones being crushed. Bringing out our bad side never worked well for our opponents.

The big man went down to the hard ground with a thud. I'd killed him with one strike, thanks to the combined strength of Sy and me and that iron helmet.

"Fuck!" the mage ringleader cursed.

"Put her down!" the third man barked.

A mistake on their part. Their voices betrayed where they were. They weren't rookies, but they'd forgotten how dangerous I could be since I didn't look it. I never looked it until I became it.

I leapt and spun forty-five degrees—the weight of the chains was nothing to me—and wrapped them around the mage ringleader's neck in a blurry motion.

Sy's super hearing picked up a movement coming in my direction—the sound of a blade sailing in the air and slashing toward me.

I was faster than a vampire. I was faster than a shifter. Mages stood no chance.

I wheeled the struggling mage woman in front of me as a shield. Her scream came a second later as a blade entered her flesh. Her comrade let out a grim curse.

She'd have been dead soon even without being knifed. She'd be strangled to death. Her friend had only quickened her demise.

There was no better option for her.

She made her bed when she came for us, Sy said vengefully.

One bad decision is all it takes, I told her.

Quickly, I released the chains from around the dead woman's neck, not wanting to be dragged down by her.

I gathered the chains and lifted my foot, since the long chain strung my wrist and ankle together, ready to fling the chains at the last standing man in the room. I planned to disarm him first. My iron helmet would be a secondary weapon when I struck him. It depended on how he moved, and then I'd respond accordingly and aggressively.

Suddenly a series of explosions went off somewhere. The room rocked.

Shit! This place was going to collapse. The last thing I wanted was to be buried alive in a dungeon.

Shit! Sy agreed, staying on high alert.

The sound of rushing footfalls, battle, and more explosions sounded everywhere at once.

I hurled the chains at the remaining kidnapper, only to hit an empty space.

Fuck, that coward had fled.

With no enemy to engage with, I charged toward the door blindly.

4

Barbie

Hell broke loose. I stumbled along what I guessed must be a long hallway like a blind fly, yanking my chains with me.

I tried to run in the opposite direction from all the shouting and battle sounds, but they were all over the place. Someone had broken into the facility, but I didn't know if they were a friendly force or foes.

Sy and I voted for foes, since I hadn't made too many friends.

Barbie! Barbie! Pucker yelled in my ear frantically.

Was my familiar here? The torque had cut off our connection. How could I hear him now? But then, Sy had come back to me, so there was no reason that my link to my ghost familiar wouldn't be restored.

I guessed, with time, my siphon power had finally worn through the spells that fed the torque.

Pucker, find me! I screamed at him with my frantic thoughts, trying to show him where I was, but I couldn't find any reference with the iron mask blocking my sight.

We're here! he called. *I'm here! We set off the explosions.*

Excellent job! I cheered.

Excellent! Sy cheered with me before she snarled. *Someone's heading our way.*

Fight or flight?

Fight! Sy urged.

So I kept going, determined to crack their skulls open with my iron helmet if they tried to grab me. They wouldn't anticipate that awesome and lethal move of mine.

The person rushed toward me, and I charged him/her before he/she could grab me, slamming my iron mask toward the newcomer's face, but instead of hitting the target, I was being lifted into the air.

Shit! This wasn't what I'd expected.

I heaved up my fist, ready to punch down on a head, the chains clanging at my movement. But a large hand wrapped around my fist.

"Barbie, stop!" Killian's deep voice came through my iron helmet.

It's the chaos prince! Sy called urgently. *Cease!*

Killian's power, not of this realm and of this realm at the same time, wrapped around me protectively.

The killer switch in me turned off.

It was him! It was the heir of the House of Chaos.

He'd come for me!

"I'm here, Barbie! You're safe now," he said, letting me slide down to the ground.

"Killian!" I hiccupped, my voice muffled in my ears within the confines of the iron mask, but it couldn't stop me from calling his name. "Killian!"

"Yes, I'm here!" he repeated. "My warriors have surrounded the premises. We have it under control. No one will take you from me again!"

"Take this fucking thing off me, Killian! Take it off! Please!" I cried, my good hand clawing at the iron mask.

"Shush. Easy, little dagger. I'm taking care of it," Killian said. "I'll take care of you."

I stood still, praying for that fucking thing to come off in a second. I could feel the chaos prince's shadow magic that he inherited from Hades rewiring the iron helmet. No wonder I hadn't been able to counter his power when he cornered me in the ice rink. It was death magic, a power that came from the Underworld.

Then the helmet was off my face. Killian shattered the chains that bound my one wrist and ankle as well.

I shook free my golden curls, but a few damp strands were still plastered on my face as Killian tossed the iron mask to the ground with a snarl.

I could breathe freely now without the burden and confinement of the iron helmet, yet my breathing still came in ragged gasps.

We were in a long, stone-walled hallway next to the empty dungeon cells. The only light came from the bulbs hanging from the high ceiling. There were no windows on this level to allow in any natural light. It was damn depressing and creepy here, and victims' screams wouldn't reach outside of these walls.

I was free and safe now. As Killian held me, inspecting me, tears streamed down my bleeding face. All the hurt swirled back, sinking into my flesh and bones, even though Sy had taken most of my pain into her.

Killian's stormy gaze darted from my bleeding face to my stump before he searched for my other wounds. Rage and pain brimmed in his eyes, which shifted from storm-blue to deep sapphire. I could feel his dragon close to the surface, seeking to break out of the chaos prince's skin. Killian's handsome face distorted before he leashed his beast, his eyes returning to cold blue. I didn't want to see him keep wresting with his restless dragon because of me, so I pressed my good hand against his face and peeked into his eyes.

"I'm fine now, Killian," I said.

His beast calmed, yet Killian didn't relax. His throat worked up and down.

"Thank you for coming for me, sir!" I said, gazing up at him through my thick lashes. "You came, Killian! I thought you'd never find me again, and I got scared."

"I'd always find you, my little scorpion. Always!" Killian said, tenderness, fierceness, and cold fury searing his eyes. His rage was reserved for those who wronged me.

The chaos heir was a formidable force. Almost the entire school feared him, but I was never afraid of him. Not even for half a heartbeat.

Pucker materialized beside us, flicking in and out of sight, and I pulled my hand away from the prince's face.

"I helped, Barbie! I led the prince right to you!" he shouted.

"Thank you," I said. "I knew I could count on you."

"Of course," he said, then he noticed my stump and hissed, "They did a number on you, Barbie. I shall skin those motherfuckers!"

Killian gave Pucker a look. Somehow, he could see my ghost familiar even in his phantom form now. It seemed the two had made some kind of deal while I'd been taken.

"Go help secure the perimeter, Guardian Pucker. Make yourself more useful," Killian ordered him.

Pucker nodded reluctantly and faded off into the stone wall.

"Let's get out of here," Killian said. "I'll carry you."

"Take this fucking torque off me first!" I said urgently. "I don't want it to stay on my neck one more second, good sir. When they clasped a bracelet on my wrist to bind my power, I had to cut off my own hand so I could have a fighting chance. The pain was excruciating!" Killian's muscles twitched in his jaw, his dragon peeking out again in wrath. "I miscalculated. I didn't expect them to set a torque around my neck next as a backup plan. This fucking torque drains me—"

Killian clutched the torque with one hand, and I smelled burning flesh. My eyes widened in alarm and terror. "No, Killian!"

I tried to pull away, but he held me, not letting go. His other hand glued to the torque, despite the burn. His death magic and lightning lashed out, crashing into the torque. Then, with a click, the sound pure bliss, the broken torque fell from my neck and dropped to the ground. I stomped on it in fury.

"It's gone," Killian said in a tight voice. "No one will ever put it on you again. I'll cut their hands off before they can even try."

Sy cheered in approval. *So romantic!*

"So romantic, sir." I echoed, then I bit my lip as I realized that I'd said the wrong thing.

But Killian didn't mind.

He wiped away a blood trail from my face, so tender that my heart stuttered. I was already healing now that the torque had been ripped off.

"I can feel you again, little dagger," he whispered.

I also felt the connection between us swirling to life. I

gazed up at him with adoration, gratitude, and desire. I'd never seen anyone more magnificent than the male in front of me, now that the torque was off and nothing could dull my senses.

He pulled me into his arms. "I vow to you, I'll protect you with my last breath."

I nodded, clinging to him. "Let's hope it won't come to that. I don't want you to die."

He dipped his head and kissed me, as if he'd been waiting his whole life for this one kiss. It was merciless and tender at the same time, carrying an unbroken promise. It filled my heart with starlight and lightning, so much so I was falling and kept falling, until we touched down on white sand under red twin moons that entwined with each other.

There was no one else—just Killian and me.

I wrapped my good arm around his neck, and he lifted me, my legs wrapped around his waist.

I kissed him back, a little awkward but full of white-hot passion, as if my whole world was in his palm, as if we'd known each other long before this, before we even existed. It felt like he was always mine, my destiny, and I was his.

"Cousin," Cami warned, approaching us. "Your Highness!"

I hadn't heard her, as my attention was fixed on Killian. She wasn't dangerous to me, so my senses didn't warn me. Sy was mesmerized by Killian's kiss, curling her toes at the secondhand sensation, so she didn't bother informing me of Cami's coming.

Killian slowly pulled away from me, a dragon's growl tearing out of his throat as he turned to Cami, his eyes glowing deep sapphire.

Cami took two steps back, her face paling with worry and shock, yet her jaw clenched stubbornly.

Killian didn't let me go and pressed me against him possessively, like I was his treasure, his dragon's treasure.

"You can't let anyone see you with her like that, Killian!" Cami urged. "You know that."

"Say that again?" Killian snarled. "Barbie needs me."

"If your enemies know that she's your weakness, they'll come for her," Cami said. "They'll hurt her to get to you. It might've happened already."

She meant the incident of my kidnapping.

Killian hesitated, his hold on me loosening. "We killed most of the mercenaries," he said roughly. "The rest self-destructed before we could capture them."

My heart skipped a cold beat. The clues were dead.

"What about your rivals? The prince heirs from the other houses?" Cami asked. "They'll get here any time now. We still have more enemies than we know, and they have eyes and ears everywhere."

Killian swallowed, looking at me, worry darkening his eyes.

It was the first time I'd heard them talking about their enemies in front of me. Who were they? My eyes were on fire as a fierce protectiveness toward the prince ignited in me.

"Rock!" Killian called.

The giant warrior stepped out. He'd been lurking in the shadows.

"Barbie is badly wounded," Killian said.

"Noted, Highness," Rock said. "I'll carry her back to the house and protect her with my life."

Cami let out a breath of relief as Killian finally saw sense.

"I don't like to be carried!" I argued. "I can walk."

Killian arched an eyebrow and handed me to his captain, ignoring my protest. Both men handled me like I weighed nothing. Just then, someone cleared his throat from the end of the hallway. Rowan stepped out.

Had he seen Killian and me kiss? Had Cami and Rock blocked us from view?

"Barbie! It's Barbie!" Cade's voice reached us. And more footfalls followed this way.

"I scented her!" Louis called, and Killian scowled.

"We found her!" Silas shouted.

The princes from the other houses zoomed toward us while Rock settled me carefully in his arms with Killian standing by. They'd finished changing hands.

The princes swarmed around me.

"We need to leave now!" Killian barked. "You four stay with the rest of my team and investigate further. Maybe you'll round up some urchins that haven't escaped, so we can interrogate them and find out who's behind this."

"Fuck off!" Silas snarled. "We don't take your fucking orders. Without our combined powers to teleport here, you wouldn't have located this place. We battled the mercenaries to clear the path for you, and you reaped the reward!"

"What reward?" Killian snarled. "Barbie could have died!"

"Guys, guys!" Cade waved his wand. "We need to keep working together. Remember, this is about rescuing Barbie. Are you okay, Barbie?"

My lower lip quivered at his concern.

"Does she look okay to you?" Killian said while I buried my face against Rock's shoulder.

I lifted my head and turned to the princes, showing them my bruised, bleeding face. They gasped, their eyes widening at my poor condition. I nodded at them and waved my bandaged stump at the ground. They dipped their gazes and spotted the iron mask, the broken chains, and the torque that still emitted a trail of inky smoke.

Horror and rage swept over the princes' gorgeous faces.

"I'm going to stab those dead fuckers over and over!" Silas spat. "I'll find out who is behind all this and claw their hearts out!"

Louis just stared at my stump, as if he thought it was his fault that I suffered.

"Don't worry. It'll grow back," I explained. "Thank you for coming to rescue me, high sirs. I'll never spit on your food or in your drinks."

The princes blinked, then let out low chuckles, even though rage and dismay stayed in their eyes. The tension diluted, so everyone could breathe easier with five high-powered alphas in a cramped space.

"She wasn't joking, idiots!" Killian growled. "Barbie is suffering! We're leaving now."

Before the chaos prince could lead Rock to charge out of the hallway, Rowan stepped into his path.

"It'll take more time to depart CrimsonTide in a conventional way," Rowan said. "Furthermore, anything could happen in this unlawful region. It'll be faster and more logical if we all combine our powers again and teleport Barbie out of here."

I blinked in surprise. I knew I wasn't on the academy grounds anymore, but I hadn't expected to be shipped to the neutral zone where the five kingdoms had no authority. I'd once thought of fleeing to CrimsonTide if things didn't work out in Shades Academy, but it seemed that I had to scratch that idea, since I wouldn't gain obscurity here anymore.

It made sense, though. Whoever had ordered the grab

didn't want the kidnapping to lead back to them if things went south.

"Fine," Killian said. "Let's get the hell out of here."

"You haven't even noticed Barbie's true condition, even though you pose as her caretaker," Louis said, stalking closer and ignoring Killian's threatening growl. "She's depleted. She's too weak to teleport."

The vamp prince was right. The rush of adrenaline had run out after the princes arrived at the scene. I didn't have any juice left, and Sy was in even worse shape. We were most dangerous in our current condition, as we might snap. Without the torque to hold me back, I had to exert every ounce of will I had so as not to suck the magic out of the land and into me.

I trembled. My teeth chattered with effort.

In a blur, Louis got to me before anyone could stop him, pressing his wrist against my lips. Without thinking, I bit into it instinctively. Somehow, my fangs or Sy's fangs slid out, piercing the vampire prince's skin.

His blood, pure and rich and rippling with power, fell on my tongue, and it was surprisingly sweet.

I leaned forward from Rock's arms, my good hand lashing out and grabbing Louis's muscled forearm to prevent him from escaping while I was feeding.

My predatory nature slid out just like that.

"I'm not going anywhere, Barbie." Louis chuckled.

As I peered up, I spotted satisfaction brimming in his pale blue eyes for the first time since we'd parted on bad terms.

"What the fuck?" Silas scowled.

He'd regarded me as a dormant shifter who was under his authority, so he wasn't happy with this little twist.

"Is Barbie a vampire now?" Cade asked in shock and confusion.

"She isn't," Rowan said. "We've never met her kind. Barbie turns out to be able to feed in a variety of ways, and blood from a powerful pureblooded vampire like Louis can give her a faster boost than other energy sources."

I felt a lot more alive after I swallowed two mouthfuls of blood. Instantly, the tiny wounds on my face closed. I was grateful for the vamp prince's donation, so I didn't have to worry about siphoning magic from the land.

Killian growled possessively. "That's enough!"

I hissed in objection, and through the vampire's eyes, I could see my own features shift a little, veins turning visible in the hollows under my bright, two-toned eyes. Louis gazed at me, mesmerized. He was a top predator, and it must be a new experience for someone else to feed upon him.

I could get used to this type of feeding.

"I don't mind." Louis smirked. "I once took blood from Barbie. It's only fair that I return the favor."

I nodded my agreement as I kept drinking greedily.

"I don't want her to become a vampire or addicted to you!" Killian snapped. "She's a member of the House of Chao. And who knows what kind of side effects your blood will cause? I'll let Barbie drink from me."

"But no woman can touch you without being severely burned," Silas said smugly and viciously.

Killian opened his mouth, then shut it, a raging storm in his eyes. He couldn't reveal to them that he could go skin-to-skin with me just fine. More than fine. Yet their quarrel didn't concern me while I eagerly drank from Louis's wrist.

Sy wanted to eat the vampire prince. *His power can sustain us for at least five years if we consume him.*

Louis hissed in pleasure, utterly ignorant that he'd

painted a target on his own back by offering me blood. "I should've known it, Barbie. If I had known it while you were in my house, things would've worked out very differently."

Killian charged him, dragging him away from me.

"What the fuck, Killian?" Louis yelled, fighting the chaos prince. He'd been high from my feeding. "Are you a barbarian now, asshole?"

"I'm still hungry!" I yipped, unhappy to be deprived of my food.

"You shall not turn Barbie into a vampire!" Silas barked at Louis. "She's a shifter, a late bloomer. She shall return to my house, so she'll be better protected."

Cade slammed the heel of his palm to his forehead. "Not this shit again. Let's get out of here before everyone gets even crazier. Do you guys really want to stay in this smelly dungeon and argue endlessly?"

"One more sip from Sir Louis?" I asked Killian hopefully, and Louis was about to fight past Killian to reach me and offer me more of his blood.

Now I thought of it, I shouldn't have been too hard on the vampire prince when he was addicted to my blood. But then, another thought shot through me. Maybe this was all Sy's doing, since she fed indiscriminately.

Sy rolled her eyes, gluing her longing gaze to Rowan. As if summoned by her, the fae prince trained his intense silver gaze on me and sniffed, his eyes brightening, as if he had almost sussed it out. Then he shook his head and dismissed the impossible thought. It was too far-fetched for anyone to link Sy and me. No other beings could shift the way we did.

"No more sips from Louis! He's a bad influence," Killian said firmly, and Cade had to pull Louis back from lunging at Killian. The chaos prince glanced at the other princes. "Let's go! We need to get Barbie to the healers in my house."

"Uh, Sir Killian," I said as all the princes rallied around with Cami and Rock, who carried me, in the center. Cami had collected the iron mask and the torque into her satchel. "Bring me to Underhill. I regenerate faster there." I hadn't wanted to reveal too much of the relationship between Underhill and me, but three princes out of five already knew that I could ease in and out of the forbidden forest. "And no healers in any house can help me anyway."

Killian frowned at me. "Michonne, our top med-witch, healed you last time."

"Uh, I pretended that it worked while I regenerated all by myself," I said.

"Barbie is a lady of multiple layers," Cade chimed in. "If she says Underhill, we take her there."

"But Underhill has to accept her first," Silas said. "It hasn't let anyone in for centuries. You all sure we want to risk its wrath?"

Louis shrugged, then kept quiet as he regarded me.

The princes held hands, their merged power forming a twister full of light with us in the center.

"Underhill!" Killian said.

And the swirling light beamed us up.

5

Barbie

We landed right outside the entrance of Underhill.

A sign on the bark of an enormous black maple read: *Underhill! Enter At Your Own Peril!*

This was the place the supernaturals dared the losers of their drinking games to enter. Most who entered didn't come out, and the few who did could no longer remember their birth names. But to me, Underhill was a haven, the safest place.

A storm twirled over the dark forest, lightning piercing its edges.

"It's been like that since you went missing," Killian said grimly.

"Hello, hello," I greeted Underhill. "I've returned. I need healing, please."

Wild magic took the form of a flaming raven and alighted on my shoulder, its feathers caressing my neck, its beak thrusting into my hair.

Cade and Silas's eyes went as wide as grapes. Louis and Rowan watched with interest. Rock smiled, and Cami blinked. Killian, however, had an unreadable mask on.

"Wild magic!" Cade sucked in a breath. "It's never ventured out of Underhill before, and now it has come out to greet our Barbie."

"I said two hellos politely," I offered, then darted a glance at Louis. Last time I said two hellos here, he'd stalked me.

A gust of dark wind swept out from the forbidden forest, followed by the menacing howls of the shadow beasts. Their quiet paws hit the forest floor as they rushed toward the entrance. They were Underhill's faithful enforcers and first defenders.

Shadows and claws flashed at the edge of Underhill.

"The monsters block the entry," Silas said. "The message is clear. We aren't welcome. We should just bring Barbie to my house, as the House of Shifters has the best healers."

"The med-witches on my payroll are better than yours!" Louis snorted. "I pay them more."

"Underhill will let me in," I cut in before they bickered further. "Lay me at the foot of the black tree, please," I told Rock. "Underhill will take it from there."

He looked to Killian, and the chaos prince nodded. As soon as the werewolf lowered me and put me at the base of the ancient tree, green vines shot out from the ground, blanketing me in their embrace.

The princes, Cami, and Rock watched in awe.

"Thank you, high sirs, werewolf, and Cami." I waved my stump at them, and they winced collectively. "Bye-bye."

"I'm coming in too," Killian said, and stepped toward me.

The other princes followed suit, but a hard wave of shadows and wind slammed into them. The shadow beasts snarled in sync, ready to tear into flesh.

"No!" I shouted. "Don't hurt them! They helped me. They brought me here."

"I'm coming in," Killian snarled back, ready to take on the shadow beasts—shadows and claws be damned.

I'll give the chaos prince five minutes to monitor your healing, so he'll see what I can do, said Underhill. *And then he must let himself out or be thrown out.*

The princes exchanged glances. They all heard Underhill speak for the first time, but they couldn't tell if it was a male or a female voice. It was musical and powerful.

"You should let us in as well, revered Underhill," Louis said. "We're all heirs, and we're nicer than Killian."

Come back for more fangs and claws so soon, vampire? Underhill snorted.

Louis blinked and stepped back.

"I understand you don't like vampires, lovely Underhill," Silas said, not bothering to get into a glaring match with Louis. "No one likes them in the realm. I'm the heir of House of Shifters. We shifters are a lot like your sentinels, the shadow beasts. Allow me in and I shall appreciate it."

You slapped Barbie when she was Little Bob in your house, so you won't have my grace, said Underhill. *I can hold a grudge for Barbie for a very long time.*

Killian turned to Silas, his icy eyes blazing with fury. If not for the sake of Silas also joining the group effort to rescue me, the chaos prince would've charged him and rained down his fists on the shifter prince's head.

These children are testing my patience. They tire me, Underhill said. *I was right to shut them out a millennium ago. Annoy*

me more and I'll rescind my offer to let the chaos prince in. I
allow him in this time merely because Barbie lives in his house.

The shadow beasts growled in displeasure at the princes.

"Don't sabotage Underhill's one-time goodwill for me, fuckers!" Killian warned. "You know what you need to do, brothers. Go, and we'll talk soon."

The vines folded me deep into the forest with the chaos prince in tow. Darkness sealed the entrance, with the shadow beasts standing guard.

As I floated by the copses of ancient trees of all colors, I could still hear the princes bickering outside the dark forest.

"Isn't that discrimination?" Silas shouted, not caring about sabotaging Killian's chance. "We should fight our way in and show them who we are!"

"Show who?" Louis retorted. I bet he was rolling his eyes at his nemesis.

"Don't bother, Silas. You won't win; you'll only embarrass yourself," Rowan said. "Underhill let me and Killian in one time, then threw us both out brutally. It's temperamental."

"Why didn't you tell us about it?" Cade demanded.

"Must I tell you everything now, Cade?" Rowan asked.

"We used to share everything," Cade protested.

"We were children then!" Rowan barked back.

I heard a thud mixed with Silas's groans of pain and snarls.

Had Silas really tried to force his way in?

"That's right, Silas!" Louis applauded. "Try again. You can take them! What can a few shadow beasts' fangs do to you? You're the powerful shifter heir. Put in more effort! I'm rooting for you, man."

He'd once been bitten by the shadow beasts, and he wanted Silas to have it all too.

Misery loved company.

Barbie

Underhill shifted its scenery.

The vines released me and dropped me gently into the lake. The water was warm instead of its usual iciness.

I closed my eyes, soaking in the wild energy freely given by Underhill. Wild magic changed to a flaming ribbon, twirling around me, until I was submerged in the water.

A splash sounded in my ear, the water lapping around me. A large, powerful arm wrapped around my waist and pulled me out of the surface. I blinked away the water and peered into the chaos prince's gorgeous face.

He'd gotten himself into the lake too. He must've thought I was going to drown, not knowing that I could breathe under the water. He knew I was powerful, yet he still treated me like I was made of fragile glass, partly because of the scare I'd given him today—I'd been kidnapped from under his nose, after all, and partly due to his overprotectiveness toward me. He was also a control freak, for which Louis had called him out.

His wet shirt sleeked down his torso, showing off the contours of his taut muscles. I wanted to trace his chest with my good hand, but I restrained myself. I could never be as aggressive as Sy. She was a bad, horny witch with a killer instinct, and I was just me.

Sy growled at my description as she stood sentinel, for the first time not distracted by the high sexual tension and tender moments between the chaos prince and me.

I remained shy as I gazed up at Killian, even though we'd shared a fierce kiss right after he rescued me, even though he'd dream walked to Underhill and given me oral pleasure before he rescued me.

"You came for me, Killian!" I said again, my eyes misty with warmth. "I can't believe you came for me."

"Never doubt it, little scorpion," he said. "I'll always come for you."

My heart fluttered at his fierce protectiveness until Sy started singing and ruined the moment—

Barbie and Killian are sitting in a tree,

K-i-s-s-i-n-g

First comes love, then comes marriage,

Then comes a baby in a carriage.

Fuck off! I barked. *Or I'll sing* Phantom of the Opera *off key when you fuck Rowan next time.*

Sy yawned, but she stopped singing. Her cunning and intelligence shone through. She was different now. It was like she'd evolved overnight, no longer being driven by her primal needs and instincts. Somehow, she'd become well-versed in many things.

Killian dipped his head and slanted his mouth over

mine. A heartbeat later, I realized that it wasn't just a kiss, as his energy poured into me. I clung to him, drinking in his endless supply of starlight. Sy joined the feeding and giggled.

So addictive, she purred.

How did Killian know about my feeding habit? Had he guessed what I was? Maybe he'd gotten the idea from seeing me sip blood from the vampire prince?

A tingling sensation buzzed from my stump, until I could wiggle my fingers. I was regenerating in record time. I pulled away from Killian and stared at my hand, no longer a stump.

"I'm whole again, sir," I said. "I'm no longer deformed. What a relief! What a day!"

"You're beautiful no matter what," he said.

I beamed at him and punched his forearm playfully with my regenerated fist. "You aren't as bad as they say."

See, I was good at flirting too, when given the right environment.

"I don't care what others say, but I'll never be bad to you." He smirked at me, running his hand through my curls fondly.

"Yeah?" My heart stuttered. "And I want you to take me seriously. When your men debrief you on what they find about the kidnapping, I want to be there."

"You'll have to recover fast."

I studied my new hand. "This is a piece of cake. I've had much worse."

His face darkened to a storm. "When? And who else hurt you?"

Even if he knew, he couldn't take on an original god who ate my essence to nourish himself. It'd been a horror show to regenerate only to be his food again.

"Nothing to worry about." I smiled at him and turned my new hand. "It's all in the past now."

I'd focus on only here and now, and this moment with Killian was precious. I wouldn't let anything spoil it. I'd outlived being a victim long ago. But this time, instead of fighting my own way out or engineering my escape, I was rescued. I had people behind me now. I had Killian! How awesome was that?

I came up swinging, babe, so what was there to be sad about?

"I'm good, yeah, I'm feelin' alright
Baby, I'm having the best fuckin' day of my life
And wherever it takes me, I'm down for the ride

Sy hummed with me, mimicking the tap dance I'd done on the heirs' table in the mess hall.

"We'll get them, we'll get all of them, and we'll tear them apart!" Killian vowed.

"I couldn't see their faces, since they wore stupid masks. There were only two magic users, one mage and one something else. I killed the mage, but I think the other one got away by teleporting. They kind of know my type of power. When they got me and put that fucking iron mask on my face, I got scared. Killian, I didn't know you'd come, or anyone would come for me. I got so scared!"

"You're still in shock," he stated, pulling me to him. "But I'm here now."

"I'm in shock." I nodded. "You're here now."

To have an iron mask swallowing one's head could mess up anyone.

He stroked my cheek, sending electric shivers down my neck to my toes.

I leaned into him. "I thought no one would come for me.

But you came! You came for me, Killian!" I repeated, as if I still couldn't believe it.

"I'll always come for you," he said. "But let's not get into the habit of being kidnapped. You'll not go to Underhill alone from now on. I've assigned Rock as your bodyguard."

"I don't need a bodyguard," I argued.

"You do," he said firmly. "And you should learn to be more scared."

I blinked at him. "But didn't you say not to fear?"

He gave me a long look. "In your case, fear is good, so you won't rush into danger. But don't fear too much. You're safe now."

For how long? I still couldn't tell him about Ruin, afraid this cozy and wonderful connection between us would be ripped away, afraid of seeing disgust on his face if he learned about my origin and the curse I bore. Who wanted a girl who could eat magic for breakfast and bring blight upon the land?

They say relationships can't be built on lies, but then, I could never really have a relationship with the heir of the House of Chaos, could I?

Fuck it.

I wasn't going to make my head spin by thinking further.

Live in the moment, I reminded myself.

"I brought this on you, Barbie," he said regretfully.

Yes and no. Even if I'd stayed a boy, trouble would still have come for me. That day in the ice rink, Headmistress Ethel and the druid had planned to take me and put me in a cage, and Killian had saved me, though his method was questionable.

I'd thought I could ditch Ethel, the druid, and their sentinels, but if they had anything to do with the kidnapping, they knew more about me than they'd let on. I shuddered inwardly at the alternative of the druid taking me and holding me captive.

Killian pulled away, self-loathing in his storm-blue eyes, as he thought that I also blamed him for what had happened to me. I'd been snatched under his watch.

I seized the front of his shirt, clinging to him and refusing to let him go, and an electric connection hummed between us.

"I'm here. I won't go away." He sighed, light swimming in his eyes, banishing his negative emotions. He liked to see me cling to him.

"What happened to me was bound to happen sooner or later, sir," I said. "It's silly to blame yourself. I wouldn't blame myself for being reckless either. I'm glad to be in your house, but it seems I'm a little unpopular."

"That's the understatement of the century." He cracked a smile. "You were born to annoy the hell out of people." He traced his thumb over my cheek. "Even so, I'll keep you safe."

Now that her hand has grown back, you need to go. You have run out of uses, chaos heir, Underhill said mercilessly, and the shadow beasts growled threateningly.

On the bank, a bed paved with flowers arose.

Barbie needs to sleep for a full recovery, Underhill added.

"I can watch her," Killian said.

And you don't think that's creepy? Underhill asked. *Get out!*

A black wind whooshed out of nowhere, tossing Killian out of the dark fairy forest.

I opened my mouth but was too stunned to voice my objections.

A moment later, I heard a loud thud outside Underhill,

accompanied by the chaos prince's profane curses and the other heirs' vengeful roars of laughter.

"That must hurt, Killian!" Silas purred gleefully.

7

Barbie

The house magic had redecorated my room as a welcome-back gift.

It had shipped a rocking chair from someone else's room and put it in mine, so I could read a book by the full window and overlook the partial fairy forest. The biggest change was the theme of the room.

The wallpaper was now pale blue with flowery patterns. Tiny golden stars with wings sparkled on the ceiling. The surrounding was devoid of pink. My princess's room in my god father's palace had been all pink. When he deemed that I was a good daughter, I got to sleep in my pink, silky bed instead of the snake pit.

I still had nightmares about my father coming to my pink room to feed on me, gnawing on my essence, my screams rocking the palace walls. After he left, it'd always been Sy who took over our form and cleaned up the mess—

gore and blood all over my pink, silky bed—while I cowered and curled within her, sobbing, fearing the coming of tomorrow and the terror it promised. In those years, she'd always been a solid rock that had carried me through.

The worst thing in my father's care? I couldn't die.

I'd make sure Ruin would never get a chance to feed on me again.

We'll cut him to pieces before that happens, Sy snarled, then peeked at the books on the table, intrigued. *Now what smutty book are we going to read? Are you sure the house can't set up the internet like in human cities? I prefer porn over smutty books.*

I thanked the house, slinked my spoiled butt onto the rocking chair, and picked a book with a discreet cover of roses, dragons, and a crown that the house had selected for me. There were a couple more books that had a manchest on the cover. The house had probably taken those books from Cami's room.

I was glad that the house wasn't a cat, or it would bring dead mice to my feet. But I wouldn't object to the house borrowing things for me to enjoy; I would just make sure not to let anyone in my room, so no one would know what went missing from their dorms. Pucker had also collected half a dozen sexy gowns for me, and I no longer bothered to ask him where he'd gotten them, just to save the headache of keeping track of his shenanigans.

That was why I hung a "Privacy" sign on the doorknob, but I doubted it would stop Killian and his important minions from coming to bother me. When they did, I usually parked myself in the doorway to block their entry, a hand firmly on the door to keep it mostly closed to impede their view and to show them that privacy was important to me.

But they never got the hint.

That was the moral of my story, a new chapter now.

This was the first place that felt like home. I'd never thought that I could have this, not even temporarily. My gaze zoomed in on the two photos that the house had framed on the sidewall—one was a selfie of Bea and me. The other one was me amid the princes with my eyes half-shut in a food orgasm, taken on a date with Rowan in his villa. Cade had sent me the pic.

The house wanted me to be attached to my friends, to the realm, to it. It didn't want me to leave. Ever. And I appreciated it.

I used to think that craving a home and relationships was dangerous. But I'd started to get used to this life, and I wanted them. A wave of shame and guilt washed over me at wanting a life while I'd tried to deny Sy when she wanted the same for herself.

I understand, Barbie, Sy chimed in. *I won't fight you again. I'll take what I can have.*

She'd need to feed soon. She'd see Rowan. But she wouldn't insist on sleeping in his bed and spending a night with him, which she craved.

One day, we'll figure this out, Sy, I vowed to her. *When we're safe and when we take down our father.* Both of us knew that we'd face Ruin eventually, and we should never forget the danger he posed to this realm, to every being on Earth, and to us.

A new kind of fear brewed in my middle, as I was suddenly terrified of being torn away from this place, this life, my friends, and Killian. To distract myself, I started to turn the book in my hands and read. After a page or two, Sy lost patience. She didn't care for the setup. She wanted me to go straight to the smut part.

It needs to build up. When the tension is high, there'll be more flavor, I told her. *Going to fuck right away is erotica!*

Let's read erotica! she cheered.

I propped my feet up on the armchair as I turned another page.

"Hiya, Barbie." Pucker popped out beside me in his solid form, making me jump out of my skin. "Good to see you up early."

"Pucker, do you ever knock?"

"But it's me, darling girl," he said. "We haven't had a chance to have a long talk since your return. I have to tell you that you didn't look too hot in that godforsaken dungeon." He wrinkled his nose in distaste. "Blackened eyes. Left swollen beyond recognition. Pitiful bruises and small cuts all over your bleeding face. And you looked terrified and crazed at the same time. Those motherfuckers put an iron mask on your face. That barbaric practice was banished twelve centuries ago. The princes were all shell-shocked when they first spotted you, and so was I, but I swallowed the sting of my tears." He tilted his head as he studied me before he nodded in approval. "You look peachy now, Barbie. I'm not surprised at your speedy recovery, considering you're basically a goddess."

"Shush. Shush!" I said, cutting him a stern look, as I didn't want anyone, especially Killian, to find out more about me.

Also, I was still pretending to be in an agonizingly slow process of recovery to keep reaping all the perks Killian bestowed on me.

First, I got room service. Second, I hadn't gone to any classes—the boring organized study—for two days now. I considered it a small win and would drag it out as long as I could. I especially didn't have the spirit to attend the druid's divination class. I hoped that the committee or whatever organization they called would void the requirement for me to join the coming bride trial if I could also pull it off.

Everyone thought I was traumatized, which was partly true, so I wanted to keep playing the role well. I put on the look of a puppy being kicked too hard and unable to get up too soon whenever I had an audience. I even put on a show of limping and wincing for good measure while rubbing my side where a blade had gone in when I was grabbed, especially in Killian and his minions' presence.

My performance worked so well that Killian had blocked Mistress Ethel and the druid from seeing me again. He insisted that it was a house affair, and it wasn't their business to keep interrogating me.

That was why he'd gotten me into his house in the first place, so he could shield me and sweep anything that concerned me under the umbrella of house affairs.

"One shush is sufficient." Pucker rolled his eyes. "It's not like anyone can hear us or I'll reveal any of your secrets, as there're too many."

"The walls have ears! Your ghost lady guardian pal might be listening right this moment. We all know she's vicious, and she might have a big mouth as well."

"True and true, regarding her vicious heart and big mouth. However, I rig a muting spell on the walls around your room whenever I visit you," my ghost guardian familiar said smugly. "Even you haven't detected it, since it's a ghost spell."

I blinked at him, impressed, but I was eager to get back to my romance book and read the steamy scene.

Plus, I'd thanked him many times. I couldn't pretend to be unwell, though. My familiar was too smart for his own good, and he didn't care about anyone's PTSD even if it was real. I'd let him take a sip of my goddess juice just to get it over with, so I had no idea why he'd come back so soon.

"This experience changed you, Barbie." He regarded me. "You look more mature than a twenty-year-old now." His voice turned mournful. "Gone is the last of your innocence and the baby fat on your cheeks."

He had no clue that I'd lost my innocence a long time ago in my father's brutal care. All my scars were internal, and nobody would want to peek at those.

When you stare at darkness, darkness stares back, Sy chimed in.

Yet it didn't exactly please me that Pucker did not mince his words. And even though I sat my ass in my room and enjoyed all the perks, I was still jumpy.

No wonder he got murdered, Sy offered gleefully.

"You should go for an early patrol at the Veil, Pucker," I said. "We don't want any Shriekers to sneak in, especially after what happened."

"But it wasn't the Shriekers who kidnapped you."

"It doesn't matter. The point is that we should not let our guard down."

"You're worse than a slave driver, Barbie!" he complained, waving his ghostly wand at the variety of cakes on the desk and the empty ice cream cups piled in the waste bin. "And you're taking advantage of the situation."

I was. I also felt a little guilty at having good things in my life, as if I kept wearing this old mentality that I didn't deserve anything good.

"After being kidnapped and maimed, I deserve a little break!"

He eyed me. "There's no need to be defensive."

"You don't know what it was like to be forced to wear

that foul iron mask and be locked up in a dungeon," I said more defensively.

"Believe me, I know the horror more than you think," he said. "The prince and I will make sure no one comes near you again. Trust us."

I stared at him suspiciously instead of in trust, a half-eaten cake in my hand.

"So you and the prince are two peas in a black pod now?"

He grinned. "We've reached our gentlemen's agreement."

"What gentlemen's agreement?" I demanded. "It sounds bad."

"Well, let's just say, when it comes to your safety, the prince is amicable to some of my terms."

"You must tell me, Pucker. You're my familiar, and I demand your loyalty, even though in your past life you were a cheater, a liar, a conman, an identity thief, and..."

He brandished his ghostly wand wildly. "Drop it!"

I put down my book and gave him a forceful look. "What did you do this time?"

"I want to make sure we aren't exactly exclusive, right?" he asked.

I narrowed my eyes.

"I'm so sorry!" he said, throwing himself, now in his phantom form, onto my bed.

I half rose from the chair. Should I go hug him and tell him everything would be all right?

No! Sy said mercilessly. *We should not believe in his tears or any sob story.*

She was tough.

Then I registered that Pucker wasn't crying. He had tossed himself to my bed to smoke weed, real weed this time. And his form had turned solid again, more solid than ever.

"What the fuck?" I said.

Pucker puffed out a ring, savoring the smell of the weed. "Prince Killian also let me drink his energy in exchange for me being your bodyguard twenty-four seven! His power is amazing, Barbie, and it complements yours."

"Motherfucker!" I shouted. I dogeared the page of my book, tossed it to the corner of the chair, and shot to my feet. "You're getting double pay for the same job?"

"Technically, you use me as an errand boy and a scout, but he uses me as a certified bodyguard. I can multitask."

"I don't need a bodyguard!" I yelled at him. I thought of throwing a book or a cake at him, but it would waste resources. "I don't even need you around me every day. I just want to make sure none of the Shriekers get in so they won't report to—"

Pucker's eyes brightened eerily. He wanted that piece of crucial information, but I'd stopped myself just in time.

"You know what, Pucker?" I threw up my hands. "You can have a gentlemen's agreement with Sir Killian, but I'll dissolve our contract!"

His eyes widened in panic.

I was bluffing, of course. The ghost guardian had two centuries of experience at deception. I had to outwit him.

"I'm so sorry, Barbie!" he cried out. "I didn't mean to hurt your feelings. But I got lonely. In my moment of weakness, I couldn't resist the temptation when Prince Killian offered me a drink of his starlight power."

No one could resist that temptation.

"You should've stayed stronger!" I growled. "And have you learned anything about the investigation on my kidnapping? I hope you didn't neglect your spy duty after you got a full drink of Killian's whatever starlight."

"Not much." Pucker sighed. "None of the princes can agree with one another. Putting all of them in one room is like dynamite about to go off anytime."

I'd given the princes my account of the incident. All we'd learned was that the mastermind behind the kidnapping had hired the mercenaries from CrimsonTide to prevent the trail from going back to them. The mercenaries had been hexed to bind their tongues, so even if we'd captured them, we couldn't get any intel out of them. Only two of them escaped; the rest were either cut down or self-destructed.

It seemed like a dead end, but we still hoped that the princes' spy networks in CrimsonTide could eventually find out something.

I'd also given Killian a long list of suspects—Ethel, the druid, Medea, America...for starters.

"Basically, you included everyone you don't like." Rock had frowned at me when he also reviewed the list.

He didn't get it.

America had predicted that bad things would happen to me from the tarot cards I'd drawn right before I was kidnapped. She must've known the machinations behind my kidnapping.

But before I sprang to call her out, Pucker had stopped me.

"When you suspect your enemies plan to put you in an unmarked grave, you don't go straight to challenge them. You wait for them to slip up. You lurk in the dark, set a trap, and lure them into it. You don't show those psychopaths how brave and clever you are and give them a chance to get away. We can't win in a straight fight. Let's give the bad guys a false sense of security, and they'll eventually slip up, and then we'll pounce. They won't see it coming. That's the way to get them hard. Believe me, I have centuries of experience when it comes to crime and murder."

I didn't point out that in the end, he'd gotten murdered and didn't even see his foes' faces. He was too clever for his own good, but then he also made sense.

I wasn't entirely tactless either. I hadn't included Killian's betrothed on the list of suspects even though it churned in my mind.

I didn't want Killian to think I was crazy due to my jealousy toward his fiancée. And I had to hold back the most crucial information—my origin—during the investigation. But I would keep my eyes wide open.

"Could you make one more round to the Veil while I finish reading the book?" I asked Pucker, then over his look, I added, "Please?"

"Am I forgiven?"

I sighed.

Pucker smiled and faded through the wall.

8

_____

Barbie

Fuck!

This book was filthy.

That romance author, Lauren, overused *cum* and *cunt*. Wait, they fucked her *four* holes? I blinked. Where exactly were those four holes?

Let me read it! Sy perked up and peeked out of my eyes. *An asshole can be counted as a hole,* she informed me like she was some expert.

Fuck it, I needed a break from smut. I snatched another book. *Dark Fairytale: Beauty and the Beast Retell.* Hmm. That sounded interesting, but how many retells could you do?

I flipped the pages and was biting into a sponge cake I hadn't finished when my ghost familiar interrupted me. I didn't know how long I was reading the book, only that I started sobbing.

The door banged open.

I leapt out of the chair with a yip; the paperback flew over the edge of the desk littered with a dozen cakes.

Killian charged in, his storm-blue eyes darting wildly, seeking a threat, lightning twirling on his fingers. The chaos prince was menace incarnate.

When he couldn't find anyone to fry with his bolts, he trained his gaze on me, his menace vaporizing. Tenderness and concern filled his eyes while his brow furrowed.

He zoomed to my side. "What's wrong?"

I stared at him, my lower lip quivering.

He'd scared me for a second, but now that he was here, he provided a shoulder to cry on. It didn't matter who bumped in. Even if it was the things that went bump in the night, I'd cling to them as my emotional support.

I rushed to Killian and threw myself into his arms. He instantly wrapped his arms around me protectively.

Maybe I shouldn't be so clingy. Our relationship was in the twilight zone, or a mine field. But I didn't care when I felt so vulnerable. I had a solid chest to lean on and a nice shirt to wipe away my tears; I wasn't going to give it up.

That dark fairytale romance had left me wrecked!

"Why are you crying, Barbie?" Killian asked again, tilting my chin up so he could study me. "Who hurt you?"

"They broke up, Killian." I sobbed harder.

"Who broke up? And why should you care?" He frowned while wiping away my tears with his thumb, and I lifted my chin to make it easier for him to clean me up.

"You might want to use your silky handkerchief, sir," I suggested.

"I don't carry a handkerchief," he said. "I'm not Rowan, and I've never needed to wipe away a woman's tears until now."

I blinked at him in disappointment. "You're lacking practice, sir?" Then I dismissed the thought and swallowed a wail. "The billionaire dragon shifter heir and the virgin can't be together. They're star-crossed!"

Another tear leaked out of my green eye. My sapphire eye remained dry for some reason.

"Who is the fucking billionaire and who is the virgin?" he growled, confusion in his eyes.

"It's all in there," I said, pointing at the book that had fallen from the desk when he charged in and now lay on the ground, abandoned.

"You cry over a book?" he drawled, letting me go and striding toward the desk.

He gave the comfy rocking chair a suspicious glance, seemingly recognizing it from somewhere. Had the house taken it from his room and brought it here? The house magic had dragged a lot of stuff that didn't belong to me into my room. I ran my lip between my teeth. I wouldn't rat out my ally, but I needed to come up with excuses as to why those things were in my room.

Killian picked the smutty romance up and turned to the page I'd dogeared.

Shit! He had the wrong book.

I froze. Why did I have to dogear that page?

The prince read the line aloud. *"I want to fill your tight cunt with my cum!"*

He paused to ponder it, his eyes glued to the page, before moving to the next filthy line.

My face burning hot, I rushed toward him to grab the book from his hand, my tears drying up as embarrassment vanquished all my sadness. Killian lifted the book higher out of my reach.

"You got the wrong book, sir!"

"I don't think so," he said, his eyes laughing, brighter than stars.

"Give it back to me!"

"Come and get it," he purred, turning the page.

"Don't you dare read any further! It's not a book for guys!"

He arched an eyebrow, then glanced at my flaming face where my tears had probably left a trail—and at the remaining cupcakes spreading over the desk beside a stack of romance books—and laughed.

"How can you laugh, Highness?" I stared up at him. "I don't see HEA in their future. I'll never read any books by Lauren again!"

"How many cakes have you enjoyed while reading a book about a billionaire dragon leaving his cum in a sad virgin's cunt before they broke up?"

My jaw dropped. "That's not what the book is about."

"Should I read the next line to confirm for you?"

He teased, he taunted, yet the heat in his eyes was the most dangerous. It made my heart flutter and my body warm. My pussy throbbed with aching need; it was so wet that I was uncomfortable.

"I need the strength to overcome my sorrow, sir," I said defensively.

He puts down the book. "What am I going to do with you, little scorpion?"

"What do you mean?"

He looked at my lips, the air instantly turning electric, as if an unseen thread tried to pull us toward each other.

"What can I do to make you feel better?" he purred.

Was he flirting with me?

He flirts with you all the time, dummy. Sy rolled her eyes. She never did that before we came to Mist of Cinder. *Every time he sees you, he wants to fuck you badly. You did the dirty deed with him in that space you call dream land. Why not just fuck each other right here, right now? It's so stupid to pretend you two haven't fucked in another reality.*

Sy was her old annoying self again.

Pucker popped out. I jumped, but Killian didn't so much as twitch while slanting the ghost guardian a predatory look.

My ghost familiar darted glances between Killian and me. "Did I disrupt anything?" He brushed off phantom dust from the front of his shirt before giving Killian a small bow. "Princes from other houses are marching toward our house."

"Why the fuck are they still coming?" Killian growled. "I told them to be patient!"

Pucker grinned. "They ran out of patience, it seems, Your Highness. They demanded to see Barbie, declaring they won't leave until she is delivered." He rubbed his hands in excitement. "We're going to have a party, aren't we?"

9

Killian

I had no business hoarding Barbie. I couldn't offer her a future, but neither my dragon nor I could stay away from her, or allow anyone else to have her, especially after we'd just gotten her back.

I was living on borrowed time with her, but while I could still see her, feel her, and cherish her, I'd give her what I could, at least offering her my protection. My dragon and I longed to see her all the time and make sure she was all right. So, before I knew it, I was prowling the hallway outside her room.

I heard her sob and charged into her room. When she threw herself into my arms as if I was her haven, I was more than happy to hold her, cherishing this vulnerable side of her.

The "mating bond" Queen Lilith had forced on me functioned like a magical chastity belt. Should I touch any woman other than the Queen of the Underworld, agony would burn in my veins. It was a lot worse for the other woman who dared to touch me, if she survived.

Only Barbie lived outside any rules. She could touch me as much as she wanted and how she wanted, not because she was more powerful than Queen Lilith, but because she was my true mate.

While Barbie sobbed in my arms, joy and euphoria filled me at holding my mate. When she shivered, I had to fight not to kiss her again.

I wanted to fuck her, stretching her pussy with my cock and impaling her over and over until she screamed my name and begged. My dragon growled his approval, urging me to take our mate and fuck her from behind, his favorite position.

I fought my urge. There should be more man than beast in me. With an arm tightly around Barbie's slender waist, I inhaled her intoxicating scent.

Then she explained to me the reason for her weeping. I couldn't help but laugh. My gorgeous little mate was hilarious and her emotions raw. She hadn't dropped a tear when she'd been gang-beaten, kidnapped, and maimed, but she cried over star-crossed lovers in a romance book.

Before I could rein back my amusement and comfort her, Pucker, the ghost guardian, popped out. He had a penchant for showing up in the wrong place at the wrong time.

Barbie was the one who had revealed his true identity. That ghost was a trickster, but he'd proven useful in helping me find and rescue Barbie. So I didn't kick him out of my house. Instead, I'd made a pact with him. He was now not only my errand boy but also Barbie's undercover bodyguard. I needed to put an extra security detail on my little scorpion.

When those fuckers took her, it'd shaken me. I wouldn't allow that to happen again.

Pucker rubbed his ghost hands together giddily, grinning at Barbie and me. "They won't leave until Barbie is delivered. We're going to have a fantastic party!"

10

Barbie

Cade, Rowan, Louis, and Silas strolled through the courtyard toward the glass-and-steel building, about to lead their warriors and entourages to stomp the House of Chaos.

The house magic played the hologram of their march in front of Killian, waiting for his words.

"Fuck those pricks!" Killian cursed.

Rock bowed half a head at the princes but barred the entrance to the house, his men flanking him. The chaos students outside the house milled around, watching, ready to back up our warriors if the house war started right here.

"Where's Killian?" Silas demanded. "Is he hiding now?"

"My liege never hides," Rock said coolly. "What brings Your Highnesses to our house in such overwhelming numbers?"

"Killian, come the fuck out and welcome us!" Cade

shouted, a smile stretching across his face. "Don't be a fucking drama queen. Or we'll have to stomp your castle!"

"Let's stomp his house!" Louis barked bitterly. "He has no right preventing us from seeing Barbie." He raised his voice for Killian to hear. "You can't block us forever, Killian, you control freak! Barbie still owes me a date. I've come to collect!"

I stared at the four princes in the hologram, my eyes wide.

Killian had blocked Headmistress Ethel and the druid's access to me, but if the princes kept causing a scene, Ethel and the druid would have an excuse to come sniff around and try to get their icy claws on me. The fucking druid had insisted on my returning to his divination class, but no way in hell would I give Ruin another glimpse of me through the crystal balls. If I wanted to meet my father, it'd be on my terms, when I had at least a slim chance of taking him on.

"Killian, be reasonable," Rowan called. "We're here to make you see reason! If you refuse, you'll face the consequences. We'll block your every move in the future. This isn't just your house affair, man. A bride candidate got kidnapped and nearly killed on campus! It's as much our duty as it's yours to—"

"You'll have to give an inch, Your Highness," Pucker chimed in eagerly with a big, ghostly smile on his face. "We can escort the other prince to the common room and have Barbie waiting in the inner room. Each prince can have five minutes alone with Barbie under my supervision. Nothing will happen to our Barbie. The princes want a date? Let's give them a speed date! After that, Barbie will have no obligation to go on a date with any of them, if Your Highness prefers it. The house and I will take care of this, and the other princes won't get a minute longer with Barbie, I promise you."

I squinted at Pucker. He was always full of ideas, but I wasn't sure about dangling myself like a carrot in front of the princes, who were sharks.

"I don't see any benefit for me in doing this!" I protested.

Calculation glinted in Killian's eyes.

"I like how Pucker thinks," he said, and Pucker puffed his chest out. "Let's get it over with, then we can send those pricks on their way." He gave the house a nod and used the house magic to send Rock a message. "Escort the heirs to the common room and tell them that Barbie and I will meet them there."

The chaos prince then turned to Pucker with a predatory grin, all perfect white teeth. "Make sure none of the heirs overstay their welcome."

11

Pucker

It was my time to shine, even though Barbie was a handful.

I picked her a gown that was suitable for the lady of the house, but she gave me shit about it not covering her tits. After tiresome arguments back and forth, I backed off, and she wore a modest flowery dress with no makeup. I pinched her cheeks to give her a rosy hue and received a punch in the jaw.

Barbie wasn't a nice girl. Sy was even nastier. Lucky for them that my specialty was handling high-maintenance ladies.

I walked Barbie to a spacious room and got her settled down on the other side of the table that could easily accommodate sixty-plus folks. A prince would meet her on this side. There would be no crossing over to her side, as all the space was blocked by large potted plants with thorns. Prince Killian didn't want anyone to sit too close to Barbie.

I had the house magic bring Barbie a mug of steaming coffee with a lot of sugar in it and a plate of pumpkin seeds to occupy her. The house hinted at bringing cakes, but I vetoed the idea for fear the princes would enjoy them too much to leave.

Then I phased through the wall to the outer room to eavesdrop on the princes' chats.

"I've set up everything for each of you to have five minutes with Barbie," Prince Killian said.

"Is this a kindergarten or what?" Prince Silas snorted.

The shifter prince was most disagreeable. He ridiculed and countered everything Prince Killian proposed.

Prince Louis narrowed his eyes on the chaos prince. "Five fucking minutes?"

"That's why it's called *speed dating*." Prince Killian spread his arms. He was never patient, except with Barbie, and Barbie wasn't patient either, so the two of them were a match made in Hell.

"It sounds ridiculous!" Prince Louis insisted.

"I'm actually intrigued," Prince Cade said, tracing his jawline with his thumb. "I've never done it. Speed date? It might be my jam."

"We all know about your commitment-phobia, Cade," Prince Silas said cruelly, "even though you try to hide it at every turn."

"I hide nothing!" the mage prince said with anger, his face darkening, unlike his usual self. "Get the fuck off my back!"

"Let's not point fucking fingers." Prince Killian stared hard at Prince Silas. "Which one of us is a role model at commitment? There's no shame in enjoying flings."

Prince Rowan and Prince Louis both nodded. Even though all the princes were racing to find their fated mates to produce the prophesized one so that the successful heir could ascend to the throne of High King, none of them wanted the actual commitment. They were just under unbelievable pressure and had to put on a show.

"Says the man who's engaged," Prince Silas said.

Prince Killian ignored him and turned to the other heirs. "You don't even need to pay for the drinks and snacks for your date. It's all covered."

"You think us that cheap?" Prince Rowan growled.

"I still don't like this." Prince Silas shook his head too. "This whole idea of a speed date is dumb."

I gave him the evil eye, as I was offended.

"Take it or leave it," Prince Killian snapped. "Barbie is in no shape to go on a lengthy date with anyone after what she's suffered through. She's so traumatized that she won't be all right for a long time. Most of the time she trembles in terror, afraid of her own shadow. Do any of you have any sympathy toward her ordeal?"

He was barking up the wrong tree. The princes were known for being heartless and ruthless. And I hoped the chaos prince didn't overdo it, since the description of Barbie trembling in terror just didn't fit with our girl. Barbie shrugged off terror and trauma like old clothes and came right up swinging while eating her favorite cupcakes.

The princes were silent for a second, appearing sullen and musing. They'd all seen the evidence of the iron mask that had been forced over her face, a torque infused with foul magic locked on her neck, and her bloody stump.

"It's my duty to protect vulnerable members of my house." Prince Killian sighed. "I'm doing you all a favor. I had to conjure her out of her fear to meet you all."

"Why does she need to fear us?" Prince Louis barked. "We rescued her! Did you put fear of us in her head since you want to keep Barbie all for yourself? Must you always be such a jerk, Killian?"

Prince Killian narrowed his eyes. "Did you come here to insult me in my house while I try to help all of you out?"

"He's just too bitter as a kept man," Prince Silas gloated. "So he finds joy in derailing our plans at every turn. That asshole is petty like that."

"I'm fucking done!" Prince Killian shot to his feet. "This is the best and last offer I'll give you. Whoever still wants to go on a speed date with Barbie, line up so we have a head count. Make your pitch and get the fuck out, please. Even five minutes with each one of you will wear fragile Barbie out."

Lol! Fragile Barbie? Our girl was all steel and clawed nails.

"Where is she?" Prince Rowan demanded.

Prince Killian pointed at the door to the inner room. "Inside waiting for each one of you to show up. Just don't—"

All four princes shot to their feet from the sofa, elbowed each other out of the way, and dashed toward the inner room, ignoring Prince Killian's warning.

The chaos house slammed its magic into them, tossing them back to their former seats and pinning them down before any of them could get through the door to meet Barbie.

Prince Killian grinned, and his rivals glared at him, cursing.

Even Prince Cade shook his head. "Asshole! I knew you'd pull this stunt!"

"If Barbie passes out due to the fright, the next date will

be canceled," Prince Killian declared, amusement in his eyes. "So, behave yourselves."

"What are you, her pimp?" the shifter prince spat.

Prince Killian bared his teeth. "The door out is wide open, Silas."

"I'll go! I'm sick and tired of this." Prince Louis jumped up from his seat and stalked toward the door. "I need to check on Barbie and make sure a vulnerable bride candidate is well taken care of. If not, she'll be transferred to my house."

"You can dream, Louis," Prince Killian said.

Cami moved into position in tight leather pants and high heels, leading the vampire prince toward the inner room. I returned to my supposed position by the door, just in time to see Barbie roll her eyes.

"Prince Louis, please." Cami pushed the door open.

Prince Louis righted his tie before strutting in like he owned the day.

He'd soon know that it wasn't his show, even though he'd have five minutes.

It was my show.

12

Barbie

I rubbed my eyelids as the vampire prince strolled in, a big smile on his gorgeous face, aiming to disarm and charm me. The door shut automatically behind him to give us some privacy.

I didn't exactly need the privacy. I didn't understand why I must participate in this speed dating, but Killian had promised me moons for doing this and said it was the quickest way to get everyone off our backs and send the other heirs on their way.

I guessed I should show up eventually to thank the other princes for coming for me and rescuing me from that dungeon in CrimsonTide. I owed them a life debt, but right now, the best way to roll was to not acknowledge that debt.

Pucker, however, was beside himself to be a host. Sy perked up as well, and kept criticizing my looks and pose.

Thrust out your chest so the princes can admire your boobs, she advised. *We don't hide our best asset.*

How much effort could I put into it? I only had two tits!

I propped an elbow on the ridiculously large table, resting my chin on my palm, tapping my foot on the edge of the chair. Even the gown couldn't stop me from getting comfortable. This was going to be a long day.

I closed an eye to get some shuteye, since I'd stayed up late to finish a hockey sports romance book. My other eye peered at Louis. He wore a white designer shirt and tight leather pants. That shirt must be new, since I'd never seen him wear it when I was his squire.

Wait! Did I see a bulge in the front of his pants? I almost squinted or opened both eyes to give it a better look, but I resisted doing either. I lifted my gaze, not wanting to give him any satisfaction about the fact that I'd kind of checked him out. It'd been traumatizing enough to watch him star in live porn. But Sy ogled him for good measure and smacked her lips.

Aren't you with the fae prince? I asked.

I'm not dead, she said. *Everyone looks. Rowan looks at other females too. He looks at you.*

Whatever.

Louis grinned at me, heat lighting his pale blue eyes. He had his blond hair combed back like a hot Mafia boss. Dark Mafia romance was popular now, and I wondered how long the trend would last.

"Hello, Barbie," the vampire greeted me with a deep, sexy voice. "I'm glad—"

Pucker chose this moment to pop out beside him, and Louis leapt back.

"What the fuck?" Louis yelped, and Pucker flickered in

and out of view, flashing his brightest smile at the vamp prince. "What kind of fucking game is Killian playing?"

"Greetings, Prince Louis." Pucker bowed. "Welcome to the first date with Miss Barbie in our fantastic speed-dating show."

Louis looked at me then at Pucker again, narrowing his eyes in suspicion. Vampires were as paranoid as shifters.

"He's one of the two guardians of the House of Chaos," I explained in my husky voice while I shrugged. "He used to be Luther. Now he goes by Pucker."

Louis's scowl deepened. "The fucking poltergeist?"

"That's misinformation, or at least it's outdated." Pucker sighed. "I'm the host of the speed-dating show, and I'll be giving scores to all the princes, so you might want to take care not to curse in front of a lady, especially a virgin one. And FYI, you just used one minute of your five minutes of speed-date time."

"Fuck off!" Louis said, zooming over and landing in the chair across from me.

"Minus two points for the House of Vampires for offensive language," Pucker announced.

"Do you have to be here while I talk to Barbie? Well, don't answer!" Louis ordered him, remembering the time limit. The more he scolded the ghost, the more minutes would be taken away from the date.

Louis gave Pucker a threatening glance before turning to me, his expression shifting to a charming smile. I could see him fighting not to look at the veins on my neck. He might try to be a better vampire, but his fangs would slide out eventually.

"Pardon me, Prince Louis, but I do have to answer. And I have to be present," Pucker said dutifully. "As I said, I'm the host of the show."

Louis huffed rudely and shooed Pucker. The guardian looked crestfallen, no longer excited about making his dating show perfect.

I had to cheer him up a little.

"Be nice to Guardian Pucker, please, Sir Louis," I said. "It's tough to be dead, and Guardian Pucker has been doing an amazing job getting this show running so smoothly. If you aren't happy, sir, you should take it up with Sir Killian, but don't take it out on Guardian Pucker, who has shown us only kindness and professionalism."

Louis blinked, then shook his head. "You always have a soft spot for the underlings, which makes you stand out even more than the other candidates."

"It's not a competition," I said, "but I appreciate your understanding, sir."

"You're too polite, Barbie." Louis smiled at me encouragingly. "Does Killian treat you all right? You can always return to my h—"

A tall glass of blood floated toward Louis and landed with a thud in front of him.

"Your drink, Highness," Pucker said, waving his phantom wand. "Courtesy of the house."

Louis lifted the glass and sniffed, his smile morphing to a snarl, his vampire fangs showing and glinting in the light. I leaned back in the chair.

"This is chicken blood. It isn't even fresh!" he growled. "Fuck Killian!"

I wrinkled my nose. It did smell bad.

"Another point taken from the House of Vampires for disrespect toward the heir of the host house," Pucker chimed in. "And you have three minutes left, Prince Louis."

Louis shoved down his temper and pushed the glass of chicken blood away from him. I could see that he put in great effort not to hurl the glass of blood at Pucker or the wall.

He retracted his fangs and smiled at me to show how harmless he was, but a gentleman vampire didn't fit in with his brand. I had intimate experience with his fangs when they broke my skin and pierced the veins in my neck.

"Well, Barbie," he said softly, which didn't sound like his usual self either. "I'd rather go high, even when Killian chose to go low and play dirty. I refuse to stoop to his level."

I looked bored and fought to keep my other eye open to peer at him.

"Good to see you're getting better, Barbie. Have I ever told you that you're beautiful?"

"You haven't, sir," I said. "You only told me that I smelled delicious, then you sank your big fangs into my neck when I was your squire."

He blinked.

"Anyway, Sir Louis, did you bring me a gift?"

He looked confused, so I decided to help him out.

"They say in this realm, a man must give a woman nice gifts when he visits her with intentions. Since this is a date, what gift did you bring me?"

He stared at me, taken aback. "No female has ever asked me for a gift before, especially not directly. I guess they dared not."

"Their loss," I said in displeasure. "But I'm a woman of my own mind. I know what I want, and I go for it."

An incredulous expression flitted by his eyes. For a tick, he was speechless, before a grin broke out on his face. "That's the little Bob I knew. Killian might call you Barbie, but he can never tame you. No one can."

"Now we know what kind of man Prince Louis is," Pucker chimed in, planting his butt on the table near us.

"He didn't bring you a gift, did he? While he's a cheap date, he bad-mouths our prince."

Louis was about to backhand Pucker, but then he dropped his hand, remembering my protectiveness over Pucker.

I thinned my lips. "I just thought it was a custom in the realm to pay respect to one's date."

"Who told you about this non-existent custom?" Louis asked.

"Sir Killian," I lied easily.

"I knew it was that asshole's doing!" Louis growled before mellowing his tone and schooling his expression to gaze at me. "I apologize, Barbie, for my neglect, since Killian didn't inform me that this was supposed to be a speed date and a gift was expected. In fact, he's been trying to block me—"

'My, my, Prince Louis," Pucker cut in. "Since you admitted your error sincerely, I'll let you in on a little secret as to what kind of gifts you should bring Barbie. Do not bring flowers, as flowers are everywhere in Mist of Cinder. They cost nothing. Chocolates won't gain you any favor either. Barbie can have them free in the house. She also secretly raided two bakery shops and hoarded two boxes of strawberry chocolates in her room." I gave him a glare, but he focused on the vampire. "Don't be like those cheap fools who think a single flower can get them into a chick's pants. Times have changed. In today's market, where there are no brakes on inflation, my lady would appreciate jewelry, especially diamonds, for a gift. She'll be in need of them if she has to flee the realm in a hurry."

Both Louis and I stared at him incredulously, though for different reasons.

"When she leaves," Pucker said with determination, "I'll go with her!"

Then, out of the blue, an ear-piercing alarm blared in the room. The vampire prince and I jumped out of our seats. My heart rammed into my rib cage. My foot dropped from the edge of the chair. Louis shot to his feet, baring his fangs and positioning himself in front of me on the other side of the enormous table, ready to take on any threat and defend me.

"Prince Louis," Pucker said with glee, and bowed deeply, "I'm afraid that your five minutes is up. Prince Silas of the House of Shifters is next!"

13

Killian

The alarm blasted. I'd never heard anything that loud. My rival princes dropped their easy chatting, grimaced, and glared at me. Just then, the door to the inner room where Barbie and Louis were having their secret speed date flew open. I didn't like Barbie having to go through this charade, but it was the quickest and most effective way to discourage the other heirs, so they'd quit sniffing around her.

Louis protested fiercely as the house magic threw him out mercilessly. He had no shame as he tried to fight the fair system and stay overtime. I'd been gracious enough to give him five long minutes.

The alarm ceased ringing. I nodded my appreciation at the effectiveness of my house. I didn't even need to lift a finger to drag out the vampire, an old childhood friend and now a rival.

In my domain, none of the heirs could match up to the house magic. If I were in their houses, I'd be at the mercy of their house magic as well, which I tried my best to avoid.

Cami was waiting by the door to escort Louis to our table. She was showing her kindness to save his dignity, if he had any left.

"Prince Louis, please, this way," she said, gesturing for him to rejoin the rest of us.

She wore a revealing gown, but this time, none of the heirs spared her a look. Their minds were fixed on Barbie.

Louis stalked toward our table, flashing me a nasty smile that promised retaliation in the future, and I gave him my dragon smile.

"How was the date?" Silas asked, squinting at Louis in dislike.

"It was great," said Louis. "I'm sure you'll enjoy it, but you'll have to wake up Barbie first, since she's half-asleep after I left."

"You don't need to worry about Barbie being bored. What happened to you won't happen to me," Silas said, raising his chin and strutting after Cami toward the door.

"Have fun, Silas! And good luck!" Louis sneered after him right before the door shut behind his nemesis.

I would review the recording of their speed dates later, even though I was dying to watch the live stream, but I had to be a good host and entertain the other heirs.

"So, how was the date, Louis?" Cade asked in a low voice.

"Fuck Killian!" Louis turned to me and hissed. If I was closer to him, he might spit at my face. I dared him to try.

"What's going on?" Rowan leaned in, wanting the insider tip.

"It couldn't be five minutes!" Louis huffed, glaring at me.

"The house magic is precise. Not a second longer and

not a second shorter," I said coolly. "I also explained the concept of *speed* date ahead of time."

"It was a fucking joke," Louis said. "The room was set up like we were having a funeral for a grandpa, with all the withered flowers around. The low ceiling and black walls were so depressing that they darkened the mood instantly, leaving nothing remotely romantic. The table was so large that I could barely see Barbie on the other side. I didn't even finish greeting her, let alone tell her about my feelings, and the fucking alarm blared. Before I could gather my wits and shield Barbie, as she was also startled like a poor little bird, I was thrown out like a criminal!"

"You're exaggerating, Louis," I said. I didn't appreciate what he'd said about telling Barbie his feelings. My dragon zoomed in on the vampire like a big, bad predator. "And what feelings?" I growled. "You don't have feelings, Louis. You just want to get your fangs near Barbie's neck, which isn't going to happen while she's under my protection!"

"Fuck you!" Louis barked back.

"You want to be escorted out of my house?" I asked aggressively.

Cami and Rock were standing by, ready to show him the door. They both fought to keep a straight face.

"Guys!" Cade said with a sigh. "This should be a fun event. Killian said he even prepared snacks and drinks for the dates."

Louis sneered for good measure at that, as if insulted by the house's generosity. "I'm not leaving! I'll see this through to the bitter end. Wait until it's your turn, and you'll see what I mean. By the way, beware of the poltergeist. I warn you of this because you two are good friends, unlike others." He gave me another hostile look. "That fucking poltergeist will do most of the talking and count it as your minutes!"

"Poltergeist, really?" Cade grinned, interest sparking in his blue eyes. "I gotta meet him!"

"This whole affair makes me wary," Rowan admitted as he turned to frown at me. "Also, Killian, a soft chime to signify that the time is over will be sufficient. There's no need to have the alarm blare like a banshee. You've never been the subtle kind, but this was over the top."

"As I recall, Rowan," I drawled, "you already had a date with Barbie, a really long one."

"You fucking crashed it!" Rowan decided that he no longer wanted to play nice.

"C'mon, man, I can't believe you still hold a grudge over that," I said with an easy smile. "Didn't everyone have fun? We even had a few glasses of 1666."

"That fucking cost me!" Rowan ground out. "My rare collection of 1666 was reserved for a big event, not to waste on you."

"I'll pretend that my feelings aren't hurt," I said. "Well, I just want to know if you still want to proceed and have a speed date with Barbie. You're the most generous among us, a gentleman, so perhaps you will give your timeslot to someone else, or let Barbie have a break?"

"Fuck off, Killian," Rowan snapped. "I won't let you take advantage of my generosity. It's my fucking turn next!"

"Fine, fine! You're so intense." I raised my palms in a gesture of peace. "Have a good speed date with Barbie, then, if it'll make up for last time. I really thought we had a good time in your picturesque villa."

Rowan shook his head in disgust, not one little bit appeased. "So now you just pose as a pimp, since you have her in your house?"

"Nope, I'm not a pimp," I said firmly. "And don't even think about it. Sex is absolutely off the table."

14

Barbie

The shifter prince walked in as if he owned the chaos house and the air I breathed.

I'd resumed my former pose—my cheek on my palm, an elbow on the table, one foot on the edge of the chair. My green eye was shut, and my sapphire eye peeked at him, not impressed.

He seemed to be more muscular. Maybe he'd been spending all his time in the gym. His chest and ten-pack might burst his expensive shirt open. Perhaps that was his intention—to intimidate his rivals or to seduce chicks. Yep, from that smug look in his amber eyes, he must believe all the hard muscles would get me to run into his arms like one of his bitches.

I didn't even bother to force open the other eye, let alone rise to greet him, as he'd expected or would demand later. Surprise glinted in his eyes before anger lifted its ugly head.

But he suppressed a growl and toned down his alpha stare before it came into full effect.

Well, he'd learned not to train his alpha stare on me again.

The house magic had reset everything in the room. The table enlarged, as the house considered the shifter prince a hostile force. I rolled my eyes and told the house that Silas wasn't going to jump across the table to get me, and if he did, I could handle him.

But the house magic danced to Killian's every whim, with my familiar as his enforcer. The trio were mentally linked.

I could counter them and cause a ripple of trouble, but it wasn't worth the fallout. Silas wasn't worth the effort. Plus, I wanted to put the princes in their places for their wicked plans for me that Sy had learned through fucking Rowan. I wondered if their plan of taming me and ruining me was still in place after my kidnapping, since they'd all come to rescue me, which was the opposite of ruining me.

"Welcome to the official speed date with Miss Barbie, our new member in the House of Chaos, Prince Silas!" Pucker rushed to greet Silas giddily.

"Beat it!" Silas snapped. "Who needs you here? This is a speed date for two, not for three!"

Wow, he was far more brutal than Louis. I didn't comment, at least not yet. He might be dead, but he was two hundred years older than me. He could handle himself.

Pucker blinked hard, twice.

Silas reached the other side of the table in no time, his massive wolf peeking out of his amber eyes, giving me his full attention.

"What happened to your other eye, Barbie?" the shifter prince asked, turning the chair around and perching on it.

I'd noticed that he didn't bring me a gift either, so I didn't bother asking for it. Nor would I open the other eye for him.

"Does it still hurt?" he asked, concern in his voice as he remembered how I'd looked in that dungeon.

When Killian fought to get me to his house, he hadn't realized that it only made the other heirs want me more. The rivalry between them was no joke, and Silas always set out to poach what Killian had.

So, no, the shifter prince's new niceness couldn't fool me.

"Mmm," I said.

Earlier, Pucker had tried to persuade me to have both of my eyes open for his show.

"Why?" I'd asked.

"So you can have a better look at your dates."

"What's there to look at?"

"They're all good looking!"

"Can good looks fill my belly?"

He'd shaken his head exasperatedly. But now, after taking abuse from two princes, he seemed glad that I was giving them the one-eye treatment.

I wasn't exactly happy about this speed date chore, since I didn't get any benefit out of it.

Powerful men and their games! And none of them had brought me a gift!

"I'm sorry about what happened to you, Barbie," he growled. "But mark my words, I'll make sure whoever did this to you pays tenfold!"

Would he care if I was still the lowest "shifter" in his house? Would he even have come for me? The princes could show their nice, charming sides all they wanted, but I'd always see the predators beneath, and their predators didn't respect weakness.

I wasn't just any chick who could be charmed easily. I was a monster, though I didn't look it. True monsters seldom did. Adding Sy, we were twin monsters.

Of course, I was grateful that the princes had helped rescue me, but I didn't need to show it and play into their hands. I'd leave no debts unpaid, but I'd pay them on my terms.

"I appreciate it, sir," I said flatly, my tone bored.

"You can call me Silas when we're alone," he said, as if doing me a huge favor.

"That'd be improper," I said. "As I recall, you're very strict on hierarchy, sir."

"We got off on the wrong foot, Barbie," he said, a little disappointed at seeing that I wasn't jumping up and down at having a speed date with him.

"Yeah?"

"We can start over." He gazed at me boldly, his amber eyes glowing with heat. "Have I ever told you how lovely you are?"

My alarm bells started to ring. I trusted this nicer version of the shifter prince even less.

"No, sir," I said. "But you once said that my usefulness was limited to shifting to a chihuahua if I ever shifted. You said, I quote, 'But do we need a house pet who's more a pest? Everyone in this house must contribute, even a street urchin. You don't work, you don't eat!' After that, you wrinkled your nose and said, 'Now beat it. You stink, Little Bob! You need to take a bath.' Before that, you backhanded me. If I hadn't been nimble, I'd have sprawled on the floor, or even cracked my skull. Oh, you also forced me to carry rocks before Sir Killian got me out of your house."

After Killian had exposed me as a girl, the shifter prince had been so pissed off at my deception that he used compulsion to make me suck his cock to publicly humiliate me. He'd failed, though, so the joke was on him.

He looked stunned before he blinked hard. Asshole didn't even remember all that.

"The list is long, sir, if you want me to continue," I added.

"I didn't know you were a girl back then," he said, rubbing his jaw, calculation glinting in his eyes as he pondered how to turn my thoughts in another direction.

Right on cue, Pucker popped up beside us, flicking in and out of sight.

"Why are you still here, poltergeist?" Silas scolded, taking out his frustration on my familiar. "I told you to fuck off, and I meant it! Barbie and I deserve alone time and guaranteed privacy."

"Nothing is guaranteed in any corner of the universe, Your Highness," Pucker said, puffing up his ghost chest in outrage. "And I can't fuck off. I'm the host of this speed-dating show. Only Prince Killian can fire me from the job. Anyway, the show must go on, and we've prepared snacks for you, courtesy of the house."

The house had taken away the glass of chicken blood that was served to Louis. He'd rejected it, though. Now a plate of cubed bread materialized in front of Silas.

"What is this?" He narrowed his eyes as he inspected the bread, then he picked up a cube, squeezing it between his thumb and forefinger, but the bread remained intact. "This is harder than a rock! Does Killian intend to break my teeth?"

"But you have shifter fangs, Prince Silas," Pucker offered. "I'm sure you can handle it."

"Take it away!" Silas ordered him. "You, begone too. We

don't need to have a third wheel, or Killian's spy, hovering over us!"

Pucker turned to me, looking miserable and angry. "I quit! I don't need all the abuse! There's no respect for the dead in this realm."

"Take it easy, Pucker. Deep breaths." I shrugged. "Just know that they don't even respect the living."

"Before I leave the show," Pucker said, lifting his stubborn chin, "I must perform one last task."

The ghost guardian waved his wand, and the house whisked away the rock-hard bread cubes and deposited a pot of steamy tea in front of Silas, leaving the lid open.

"Enjoy, Prince Silas of House of Shifters!" Pucker offered with a professional bow. "And you have two more minutes left."

And he was gone.

Instantly, Silas started to sneeze. I sniffed the air and widened my eyes. The house had brought him strong wolf-bane tea. Shifters were extremely allergic to wolfbane, and if you didn't want a wolf to be on your tail, the best way was to spread wolfbane on the trail while carrying a bag of wolf-bane powder on your person.

Killian must have had the house magic brew the most potent wolfbane he'd illegally gotten from the black market.

"What the fu—?" Silas couldn't stop sneezing.

"Are you all right, sir?" I asked in fake concern, my voice husky.

The scent of wolfbane spread through the entire room in no time. Silas's eyes turned bloodshot from the allergy, then he bent over and sneezed nonstop.

He had it bad!

"Whadd...the fu—fu...?" he tried to curse.

"I don't follow, sir. Fu—fu what?" I asked, but now he

could barely open his eyes. "Should we call Guardian Pucker back? If you have a cold, sir, I gotta get out of here! I don't want you to pass the fucking cold to me. I might not be immune to shifter sicknesses, since I haven't fully recovered from being kidnapped and tortured!"

You aren't a human, Pucker chimed in my head. *You'll never catch a cold.*

You can't know that! I scolded him. *And I don't want Silas to know that either. Why are you still here? I thought you quit.*

Silas tried to gaze at me, tried to speak, but he was too busy sneezing and fighting off the virus at the same time. A new plume of wolfbane steam floated into the air from the teapot. I had no intention of covering the lid though. It wasn't my business.

"It's not a cold." He finally forced the words out.

The alarm blared in the room, and I clapped my hands over my ears. The door flew open, and the house hurled the shifter prince across the room and tossed him out while he was still sneezing like a monkey from Hell.

15

Pucker

When Prince Cade strolled out of the dating room of his own volition instead of being thrown out by the house magic, Barbie followed him in a lovely gown I'd picked for her.

She was gorgeous, even with her two-toned eyes narrowing, her bottom lip jutting out in displeasure, and her golden curls bouncing.

Every eye was trained on her with varying levels of desire. My mistress always commanded the room without trying. Pride beamed in my chest.

"That coffee was fucking awful," Prince Cade said, running his teeth over the tip of his tongue to try to get rid of the taste. "I can't believe Killian keeps that brand of coffee in the house."

"Believe it, sir high mage," Barbie deadpanned. "I drank

a different kind. The coffee the house served you expired years ago. It must've grown mold."

The mage prince looked incredulous before he spat out the taste and glared at Killian. "Asshole!"

Barbie nodded without sympathy. "Sir Killian wants to make sure none of you have a good time. If the coffee is good and fresh, you might never leave."

"You should not tell Cade that, Barbie. That's a house affair," Prince Killian said, his storm-blue eyes shifting to sapphire, full of heat. "And why are you out? You have one more date to go."

"Yeah?" Barbie lifted her chin in defiance. "Who's going to drag me back to the funeral room that smells of stale chicken blood, moldy bread, pungent wolfbane, expired coffee, and dead flowers? The other sirs only needed to suffer for five minutes, but I had to sit through it all!"

Cami, Rock, and the other attendants all fought hard not to laugh.

"That bad?" Prince Rowan winced, and the other heirs all glared at Killian.

Prince Silas was still reeling from his sneezing fit. Served him right for being nasty.

"People go on dates to get to know each other," Barbie said, eyes on fire. "Yet none of you asked what kind of food I like or what my favorite color is."

Barbie had been lowkey when she first came to Shades Academy, but she'd had enough. Other bride candidates dared not take this tone with the heirs, but Barbie's birthright gave her the right, even though she hadn't realized it. No one could keep her at the bottom of the food chain. She was an apex predator, an almost-goddess, which could be one of the reasons that the heirs were all drawn to her without understanding why.

Power called to power.

They tolerated her while they wouldn't do it for anyone else. The challenge from Barbie was so refreshing and entertaining that none of them seemed to be angry, but rather mesmerized by her outrage.

"These dates were poorly managed and one-sided," Barbie continued. "The Guardian of the House was so discouraged at the lack of respect toward me that he had a meltdown before he quit!"

I blinked. That wasn't why I'd quit, and I didn't melt down. I might be a dead guy, but I wasn't a pussy.

"Only Sir Cade brought me a gift—two jars of raw honey from China." She flashed two bottles of nicely wrapped honey in her hands, and Killian shot an annoyed look at Cade. He was possessive toward Barbie, even though he couldn't have her.

"The size is very small," Prince Killian commented.

Barbie dipped her gaze to the bottles. For a second, she wasn't sure, but then she lifted her golden head and nodded at the mage prince. "Yes, the size is small, but it's the thought that matters. Sir Cade got them for me from China."

"It was made in China and imported here," Prince Louis shouted. "Everything is made in China!"

"What's the difference? The label says China, so I got it from China symbolically for Barbie," Prince Cade defended himself.

"And you secretly brought a gift for Barbie to upstage us," Prince Silas accused, and sneezed again.

Prince Cade threw up his hands. "This is what I call paranoid. This competition isn't healthy."

"I gotta get the fuck out of here instead of listening to all this on an empty stomach and wobbly legs," Barbie complained.

Empty stomach? Barbie was a pathological liar. She'd never had an empty stomach since she got into the House of Chaos. In fact, she was always eating, like her stomach was an endless pit. Did it have to do with her goddess brand?

"If you even care, you should know that I haven't even fully recovered from the terrible trauma," she kept whining. "The good guardian of our house's suggestion of gifts like cash or diamonds has fallen on deaf ears. I'm tired and hungry, so I'm just going back to my room to finish that smut book."

"What smut book?" all the princes asked.

"It's about shooting cum into a cunt," Prince Killian said with a smirk.

Barbie flushed, gave the chaos prince a baleful look, and shot out of the door, full of spirit and energy, which contradicted what she'd said about wobbly legs.

Heat seared in every prince's eyes. The vampire prince stared at where Barbie had disappeared, lust and longing heavy in his pale blue eyes. He was probably picturing shooting his vamp cum into Barbie's goddess cunt. Killian might have detected the same thing as me, since he growled at Prince Louis threateningly.

Prince Silas frowned. "Why do women want to read about cum when they can have it?"

He'd finally ceased coughing and sneezing. Well, even though I didn't like him, I had to give credit to his strength, endurance, and power.

"Smut is always popular with ladies." Prince Cade chuckled. "Men are visual animals, but chicks have different needs."

"What about me?" Prince Rowan demanded, annoyance flitting across his handsome face. "I haven't had my five minutes! I'm the only one who's left out."

"Well, if it's any comfort," Prince Louis said, "Barbie isn't in good enough shape to go on another date. As I said, she was half-asleep when I walked in. Killian obviously hasn't taken good care of his newest member. He shouldn't have dragged her here and forced this speed dating on her."

"At one point, she almost fell off the chair." Prince Cade shook his head. "Until she smelled the honey I brought her."

"No girl has ever fallen asleep in our presence," Prince Silas scowled, "which says—"

The prince of House of Chaos chuckled darkly. "Which says she isn't interested in dating you. So, respect her wish and stay the fuck away from her."

16

Sy

Rowan had been waiting outside Underhill. As soon as I appeared in his view, he darted toward me like a shark, and then I was wrapped in his strong arms.

He held me to him so tightly that it almost hurt, as if he was afraid that I'd get away or just disappear into the air the next second.

I was pleased at his eagerness and possessiveness.

"Hello, stranger," I purred. "Miss me?"

He growled. "Quit playing games!"

"What games?" I grinned wider, a full mouth of fangs on display.

He stared at me, dazed by my wild beauty. I wasn't afraid to acknowledge my stunning looks. Why pretend? I had this asset, so I was going to flaunt it in front of the fae prince and daze him even more, though my fangs had scared a few human men when I fucked them. They'd passed out, their cocks going limp in me. Barbie had been even more upset due to the feeding being undone.

"Are you going to keep playing hard to get?" he asked.

I blinked at him in confusion. "But I'm not hard to get. I'm easy. I come to you as soon as I'm able because I need to fuck you urgently. I'm thinking of fucking you all the time, sugar. It was the most amazing feeling to have your big cock embedded deeply within me, thrusting and thrusting."

He studied me intently as his anger and frustration seemed to fade. Lust rolled off him in their wake.

"Do you always talk this way?" he asked as he brought me to lean against the black tree, our usual spot. My back pressed against the bark with his large hands on either side of my head.

"Only to you. You're special." I grinned at him, cupping his bulge.

It was huge, and it needed to dip into my wet heat. I was more than happy to help it out while reaping the benefit as well. That was why I came to him, wasn't it? He hissed in pleasure and pure male need, his silver eyes turning brighter than the summer sky while lust flashed in them like lightning.

I was giddy to have such an effect on him. Every time we fucked, he only grew more hooked. I wanted this physical relationship to last, since I wanted him as my sole feeding source. After having tasted the fae prince, I didn't want any others.

"I barely talked to my other targets—I mean other males," I continued. "I went straight to fucking them, hard and brutally, until they nearly passed out, then I—"

"Stop! I don't want to hear about you fucking other males!" he snapped.

"But you asked, sugar," I said, giggling.

His anger turned me on and amused me. I was telling him the truth about how I'd dealt with other males in the past. With Rowan, everything was amazing. It was a brand-new experience, and I was a happy repeat customer, but I also promised Barbie that I wouldn't go too far again after our last fight.

That fight had sunk me into a deep depression, so much so that I'd neglected my duty to protect Barbie. If it weren't for Killian arriving in time, she might've been taken to the one who had orchestrated the kidnapping. I shuddered at the possible horrible outcome.

"I've never met anyone like you," Rowan said.

"Of course, my sugar Rowan," I said. "I'm one of a kind. We should fuck now, since I don't have all night."

"Fine," he said. "After fucking, you'll need to answer some questions. I won't let you lead me on a wild goose chase forever."

"So demanding," I purred.

My pussy was soaking wet. Rowan could barely contain himself either, even though he wanted answers.

"I hope this time that asshole Killian won't pop out," he grated, darting his silver eyes around to check for an unwanted intruder while I slid my hand into his trousers and freed his massive erection. "He can't get this, so he resorts to watching others fuck. He wants to fuck that new girl in his house badly, but he can't."

I smirked as I felt Barbie perking up, all flushing and hot and upset.

"I feel bad for the chaos prince," I said. "Let's not be too hard on him if he comes to watch."

"He's bound to another," Rowan continued. "I don't think he's thrilled about it, even though Queen Lilith is a great beauty. Maybe males just want what they can't have. Forbidden fruits always taste better."

Barbie bristled at the mention of the Queen of the Underworld.

Let's break them up, I told her. *I got your back.*

"So you're saying that Barbie is the forbidden fruit to the chaos prince," I purred. "What am I to you? Do I taste better than forbidden fruit?"

He palmed my slick pussy. "You're my little monster, and my little monster is so wet for me, so ripe and ready to be fucked."

He nudged the head of his cock at my entrance, brushing open my plump folds, fooling around, before he thrust in powerfully. I gasped at the sensation, half-shutting my eyes, as I savored the feel of his cock sheathed deeply within me, filling me and stretching my inner walls.

"Many women need to be prepared, since I'm bigger than other males," he said. "But with you, it's always easy. You don't even need foreplay. Not that I don't like foreplay. You're just so responsive and ready all the time. With you, I don't need to hold back. I don't need to be gentle. I can just fuck your delicious cunt however I want."

Can you tell him to refrain from using the c-word? Barbie grunted. *It's disrespectful. When I was younger, I was traumatized by the inmate shouting, "I can smell your cunt," in* The Silence of the Lambs.

I'm not going to listen to your negative review in the middle of fucking, I said.

Rowan let out a low groan at the pleasure as he kept fucking me hard.

I dipped my gaze and watched our joined flesh while he gave me a moment to marvel at our coupling. My pussy gloved his shaft seamlessly. It was a gorgeous sight. Too bad no one was filming us. I'd love a close-up.

Barbie rolled her eyes. *Don't take too long, Sy. We need to get back to the house in an hour, and my bathing time in the lake should be factored in as well. Killian has me on a tight leash. Somehow, he'll know if I stay away from the house for too long.* Barbie no longer used a sharp voice with me. She'd mellowed out after our last brutal fight. *I'm going to take a nap while you're at it. Oh,* she added. *I talked to Underhill. You and Rowan can go inside the forest to bang. Don't go deep, though. Just behind the tree so you guys can have some privacy, though Underhill will be watching. There's a flower bed prepared for your unholy copulation.*

I wrapped my legs around Rowan as he thrust into me, powerful and demanding. In and out. In and out. Hitting all the G-spots. I threw my head back and giggled at the pleasure.

"Enjoy how I fuck you, don't you?" he asked. "Want me to go harder?"

"Later, sugar," I purred. "Let's fuck inside the forest, since I want you to bang me in a nice bed for a change."

"But Underhill—"

"It'll oblige," I said. "Trust me."

"If you say so," he said. "I don't want to see Killian and his cronies show up here at any time."

He carried me, our flesh still tightly locked, and stepped through the entrance of the forbidden forest. There was no resistance or dark wind slamming into Rowan's face. No shadow beasts snarling or even around.

A flower bed rose from the forest ground behind a row of bushes and pink blossoms.

Rowan took in the scene in appreciation. He grabbed my

butt and propelled me to ride his massive length a few more times before he stalked toward the bed.

"Just don't venture deeper into the forest and we'll be fine," I said, moaning at his thrusts. "We have to respect Underhill's boundaries."

He laid me on the bed and thrust deep into me, his weight delicious. "When it comes to fucking you, I respect no boundaries."

I giggled, showing him my fangs, and arched my back to receive him even deeper. He pounded into me brutally, and I writhed in delight.

"Little monster, one day you'll be the death of me!" he growled above the loud, erotic sound of flesh slapping flesh.

I wrapped my legs around his waist tighter. Whenever he plunged down, my legs clamped him harder, and my pussy squeezed his cock mercilessly, as if it owned it.

"That's how you want to play, is that it?" he hissed in pleasure.

He pulled out and flipped me to make me lie on my stomach, driving into me from behind. He pinned my hands above my head, heaving his hips up and down and plunging his hard shaft into me, every thrust powerful and delicious.

We fucked in that position for a few minutes before he got me on all fours to pound into me. I loved his domination, as no one had ever dominated me before.

My breasts bounced at his every vehement movement. He gripped my hips as he pounded into me again and again, bruising me. My breathless moans grew louder and louder as the pleasure kept building up in me. Rowan gave my butt a few hard slaps while fucking me at a blinding speed.

In the distance, the shadow beasts finally growled.

"I can't get enough of this hot pussy," Rowan groaned.

His next long, hard, and rapid thrusts made me see stars.

A wave of orgasm swept over me, dragging me under, and I roared my release.

Rowan cursed, his cock growing harder, and came with me, pumping his seed into my womb. His hand came around to brush my clit roughly to offer me more pleasure. I cried and screamed and giggled. I didn't think I could take it anymore, yet I wanted more. Rowan kept pounding into me even after my waves ebbed.

"Good job!" I grinned, licking my lips.

"I'm not done with you, little monster," he said as I dropped my belly to the flower bed, sighing happily as I fed on his bountiful energy.

He pulled out of me, his cum dripping down my thighs. The fae prince turned me around to face him, spread my legs wide, lifted my butt, and plunged into me.

"My fae stallion!" I meowed.

My well was already full. Now Barbie was busy procuring energy for herself. That greedy little eater!

"Now's the time to tell me where you live," Rowan demanded, stilling even as his cock throbbed deep within me in pure male need. "Or you won't get any more."

Barbie tensed, pausing her feeding. *Don't tell him! Don't be dumb, Sy. He thinks with his dick, but you should know better.*

You think I'm just going to roll over and show him my belly for a couple of good fucks? I hissed back. *You're the dumbass for saying I'm that dumb!*

Even though we'd made up and had been careful with each other ever since the last fight, she still didn't have confidence in me. And it hurt more than I thought it could, as if the trust was still broken somehow.

"Are you sure I won't get more?" I purred, propelling my hips forward aggressively to ride his length and slamming into his balls.

My strength matched his in every way, and he fought not to roll his eyes back in pleasure.

"I'm serious, little monster." He gathered himself and hissed, restraining himself from thrusting to show his resolve. "I need to see you as often as possible, not just sneak here to fuck you. I want more than just a physical relationship with you. And if you won't reveal your residence, then come to stay in my house."

"It sounds appealing, but I can't do either," I said regretfully, my chest aching.

"Then we're done," he said, hesitating for a beat, and pulled out of me.

My heart went cold, cracking.

I told you men are fickle, Barbie chimed in. She never wanted me to get attached to Rowan. *Let's go, Sy. We're filled, so it's not a total loss. We'll just find you another feeding source that doesn't ask too much. We can go back to the way it was before. You were perfectly fine before.*

Barbie was terrible at emotional support.

And I didn't want to go back to before, to those dark, mindless years without Rowan.

But then, if he was done with me, I wasn't going to beg.

I sat up and flattened my short skirt. His seed still streamed down my thighs and dripped onto the flower bed.

"Get out," I said. "I'm going to take a nap."

"Just like that?" He stared at me incredulously. I bet he wasn't used to women not begging after being dumped.

"You said we were done," I said harshly. "So what else is there? Get the fuck out before Underhill tosses your bare butt out. You'll fall, your face planting on the dirt, which won't be a pretty image, princeling."

Excellent, Sy! Barbie cheered. *Kick him out! We're done with the fae dude. There're plenty of dicks around.*

Yet my heart broke a little more. Maybe my other half was right. Maybe men were all flaky. It was stupid to fall for men, to think that they'd hold our hearts gently in their hands.

I fought to keep my tears at bay, and my eyes hurt from the pressure. I hoped that Barbie hurt as well! This was a quarrel between Rowan and me, but I was mad at her too. She was so insensitive.

"You'll just toss me aside as if I mean nothing to you?" Rowan growled, anger and hurt darkening his silver eyes.

I shot to my feet, my face a couple of inches from his. I pulled my lips back in a snarl, my mouth full of sharp fangs that were about to give him a bite!

"You dumped me, fae!" I said hotly. "Be grateful I let you go! If you think I'm like the weak-ass females you used to fuck, think again. I don't care if you're a prince. I don't care if you're rich. Your status and rank mean absolutely nothing to me. Get the hell out of my face!"

He grabbed me. "You don't command me, little monster! I'm not done with you."

He tilted my head back and kissed me hard.

I hadn't meant to, so I was confused when I opened my mouth eagerly for him. He thrust his tongue into me, sweeping my hard palate and sending tingles of pleasure to my nerve endings. His rock-hard cock pressed against my front.

I bit his tongue to punish him for his former attitude, tasting his rich and powerful fae blood. He hissed in pain and pleasure and kissed me more aggressively. My lips felt bruised and swollen, yet I felt delicious.

When we finally broke away from each other to take air into our deprived lungs, he laid me on the bed again. He shoved up my short skirt. His weight fell on me, and then he was moving inside me, on top of me. The moves were gentle and purposeful, as if he was making love to me.

I moaned, my gaze bright as I took in his handsome face and the lust in his eyes.

What the fuck happened? Barbie demanded. *I thought we were getting out of here, but you landed yourself in another fucking session.* She threw up her hands in exasperation before she went back to feeding.

"I won't let you go, little monster!" Rowan vowed. "I didn't realize how much I need you until I realized I could lose you."

"Next time, when you deliver your threats, mean it, princeling," I purred viciously. "For I won't give you another chance to play me. I'm not the kind of woman you're used to. You haven't seen my true monster face yet." I meant Barbie. I paused as I savored his long thrusts before adding, "If I can give you more, I will. But my hands are tied, and I can't explain. So don't ask more of me. It's hard for me too, but we both can still get something out of this physical relationship. At least we can feed from each other to our great satisfaction. I won't ask you for exclusiveness." Rage, sadness, and resignation washed over me. "I won't ask anything of you. If you want to stop this, if you can't make it here to fuck me in the future, I won't have hard feelings toward you either."

"Will you be exclusive to me?" he asked, driving into my molten depths so hard that I gasped in approval.

"Why should I?" I asked while giggling at the incredible pleasure. "Isn't this an open relationship?"

It wasn't even a relationship, but I'd accepted what I could or couldn't have.

"You don't fuck anyone else!" he hissed, his silver eyes glowing with jealous fire. "I won't fuck another either. We can meet here as you prefer, but I want to see you more often. There should be a way I can reach you."

"Fine, sugar," I said. "If you can always deliver—"

"When haven't I delivered?" He pounded into me with punishing force, and I threw my head back in delight.

"—and stop being so demanding, I can make compromises," I promised.

We moved together fiercely.

Tell him to send private messages to me on Spinchat and I'll get them to you. Barbie paused to bite her lip. *This one is high maintenance.*

That can be said about you, I retorted.

"Here's the deal, sugar Rowan," I said. "You can ask Barbie to get messages to me."

"What's your relationship with Barbie?"

"We're acquaintances," I said. "She owes me a couple of old debts, so she'll help me out now and then. Don't expect too much from her though. She's fickle, and she can be a cunt."

Barbie bristled, and I smirked.

"Tell me about that girl. We need to make sure that we can trust her," he said, grunting, thrusting into me, hitting my G-spots, and I moaned blissfully.

He picked up speed as lust hammered us. We weren't the tender kind. We were savages.

I slid my hands up and down the flexed, hard muscles on his back as he moved in me relentlessly. My fae male was so powerful. When his next thrust hit home, I cried out at the force, my fingernails finding purchase and leaving a long blood trail along his back.

He growled in approval, fucking me with abandon, all short, rapid thrusts before one drove home. My pussy clenched around his length. And then we both came at once, his cum flooding my depths.

Afterward, I rested my head on his hard chest now that we had a bed.

"Your friend Barbie has got an attitude issue," Rowan said. "But I don't blame her. Who wouldn't under Killian's tyranny?"

"I heard that she ditched only you during a speed-dating show." I aimed to provoke.

He cursed. "Everything leaks these days, and bad news travels fast without context. I just wanted to ask her a simple question—where I could reach you—and I was rudely denied my five minutes. On second thoughts, I was spared from the unpleasant experience the other heirs suffered through. The alarm blared at the end of every speed date, and then the heirs were kicked out like criminals. It was outrageous. Killian stooped so low as to hire a poltergeist to do his fucking dirty work."

I giggled. Neither Barbie nor the heirs had had a good time during the speed dates. It'd been hilarious.

Rowan gave me a look and kissed my cheek. "I don't usually curse, since it isn't the fae way. But this speed dating trend? It was a fucking sham! That jerk, Killian, was getting off on screwing with us. I've been watching Barbie due to her unique power, even though she's unknown. She's more than an Echo, though I don't exactly know her power source, which makes her even more intriguing. Killian knew it when he first laid eyes on her. Now that he's finally gotten her under his roof, he's controlling her in order to use her. Take advantage of her naïveté, even. He hoards her like a dragon guards his treasure."

"Do the other heirs agree with you?" I asked, urged by Barbie.

Rowan nodded, threading his fingers into my long, lush hair. "We've formed a pact. We'll free Barbie and bring the heir of the House of Chaos to his fucking knees."

Barbie bit her lower lip, brooding, cooking up her own schemes. I left her to her own devices.

"So you and the other princes are in business now?" I asked. "But everyone says that Prince Silas and Prince Louis hate each other."

"They still do, but they formed a temporary alliance in order to go after Killian," Rowan said. "But they don't see what I see. When you get to the bottom of this, it's not about Killian. Somehow, Barbie is the source that turns the heirs against each other."

Barbie bristled. She just couldn't handle criticism.

I lifted my head from my lover's chest and beamed at him. I liked this—talking after fucking. Very nice!

Rowan smiled back at me. "Let's take a nap, little monster."

Get him to leave! Barbie shouted at me. *I got you a bed to let you have some privacy, not to let him sleep over here. We need to get back to the house soon, or Killian will come looking. Do you remember it took us a while to even get out of the building, since Killian has doubled the security detail? If Killian deems me a security risk, you might not get out to fuck the fae next time!*

Chill your small tits! I barked back. *I'll handle it. And you need to get Killian to chill.*

I'd once thought the chaos prince's overprotectiveness and possessiveness toward Barbie was cute, but when it inconvenienced me, it grated on my nerves.

"Don't fall asleep, princeling." I let out an exasperated sigh as I tugged at Rowan. "You need to go."

"After a nap," he said with a charming smile. "It's always nice to have a nap."

"Next time, sugar," I said gently. "C'mon, I told you we couldn't stay long."

He got up reluctantly. "I'll see you home, then, or at least escort you to a more crowded place. It's not safe in this area. Barbie got grabbed last time. I'm not taking the chance of letting you be kidnapped as well."

"They wanted Barbie, not me," I said. "I'm nobody. No one knows about me. There's no target on my back. You go now, prince. I'll leave after cleaning up."

"But—"

A sweep of dark wind rose from the ground and threw Rowan out of the forest in the blink of an eye, and then walls of shadows sealed the entrance.

There's no need to be aggressive, I told Barbie. *He was just leaving.*

"You know how to reach me," I called toward Rowan, who was on the other side of the wall of darkness.

"I'll send Barbie a message," he shouted back.

Tell him to bring gifts, Barbie said. *I'm not the kind of chick who works for free.*

"Uh, Rowan sugar, you still there?"

"Yes?"

"You need to bring Barbie gifts next time you see her," I said, "or she won't pass your messages to me."

"What should I bring her?" he shouted.

Diamonds! Barbie barked urgently as if I were deaf. *Pucker said diamonds are the best. We need to accumulate a fund in case we have to flee at a moment's notice.*

"Diamonds," I said. "She likes diamonds!"

A long silence. Then—

"You're kidding, right?" Rowan asked drily. "A few hookup messages for a diamond?"

17

Barbie

I told Killian that I hadn't fully recovered, but he said that if I could run that fast when I overheard that there was a special dinner in the house, then I was in better shape than almost every student. He'd also pointed out that I'd forgotten to limp on two more occasions.

"But I'm still afraid of my own shadow!" I protested. "I'm not ready to go to class, since everyone looks like a kidnapper to me."

Killian shook his head at my whining while his men laughed.

"You don't know a werewolf can smell lies, do you, Barbie?" Rock asked.

So, I started to go to class, as it was mandatory, and the prince's cronies made sure of it. However, Killian allowed me to attend fewer classes. He went through my curriculum personally and cut out one-third of them, despite some professors' protests, especially from Headmistress Ethel and her druid.

I was overjoyed that I no longer needed to go to the druid's divination class. Killian told the druid to fuck off, since I was still going through intense "therapy" after being kidnapped and maimed. He emphasized that he needed me to be mentally available for the benefit of the ongoing investigation into the campus kidnapping.

Headmistress Ethel had opened her own investigation and summoned me. Killian had insisted on being present, and the other princes had as well. I had to recount the events over and over until Killian put a stop to it.

The other heirs also backed up Killian on my attending fewer classes, and offered to let me have private lessons with them when they practiced advanced dark magic that was exclusive to the heirs. The princes were no doubt rivals, but they always presented a united front when facing any outsider forces.

I limped into Professor Longweed's magic conjuring class.

Instead of a confined classroom like the one I'd stumbled into while trying to lose the vamp prince on a blood hunt, the class was set in an open space with warded fences on three sides. The fences were spelled to withstand magical attacks, which the students would carry out soon by throwing their elemental magic and swinging their dicks around.

I could rip off the spells on the fence, but I didn't want to stir the shit. I was going to turn over a new leaf.

Students hung out with their cliques, their chatter filling the space. I recognized half of them, since they'd tossed their magic at me last time I crashed their class.

A group of students who struck superior poses and

shared important looks gathered around Professor Long-weed in the center, and her sultry voice pierced the open space.

I spotted Bea, Wyatt, Jinx, and two other geeks from the House of Chaos in the far corner. They were my crowd now. Wyatt had officially become a member of the chaos house after I'd put in a word for him to Pucker and Killian.

I rushed toward them in glee.

"Stop, Little Bob—Barbie!" Professor Longweed's shriek cut through the room.

Shit!

How had she seen me while being surrounded by her favorite elites, especially America? It helped that America was also Headmistress Ethel's niece.

I forced myself to halt while all I wanted was to join my friends.

The crowd in front of Professor Longweed parted, and she stepped out, a shawl wrapped around the shoulders of her pink dress. The fae professor narrowed her sharp gaze on me. Why were her pale silver eyes so wide apart? Maybe I should ask her so she could do something about it?

"Hello." I smirked. "Professor Weedlong, right? Long time no see!"

"It's Professor Longweed!" she hissed, her accent growing thicker, her lips pursing into a thin line. "You're the most dishonest student!"

"Pardon?" I blinked at her innocently. "How so?"

"You pretended to be a servant boy and fooled everyone, especially the esteemed princes!" she accused. "It was distasteful and unforgivable!"

"But I didn't fool all the princes. Prince Killian singled me out and humiliated me in a scandalous manner!" I cried out. "Also, it wasn't my fault. Prince Louis named me 'Little

Bob' and made me his squire in the first place. The whole affair was unfortunate and distasteful." I nodded at the professor. "But all the esteemed princes have forgiven me. If you don't believe me, you're more than welcome to check with them, and I'm sure they'll vouch for me. Prince Cade even gave me two jars of honey made in China as a get-well present. He's too kind. I don't know if you heard about my kidnapping or not?"

I waved my new hand at Professor Longweed. "It grew back, but the tragedy left more scars inside than outside. Anyway, let's go back to the matter of the jar of honey. Prince Killian pointed out, accurately, that the size was too small." I spotted fire in the professor's eyes. "Longweed, no, My Lady Longweed, if you're worried about my going back to being a boy, you can rest your mind." I shook my head in dismay. "That's not going to happen. Prince Killian has strict house rules."

"Silence!" Professor Longweed ordered me.

"Okay, I'll comply." I lifted my hands. "I'll go silent now. Happy?"

Professor Longweed's eyes only spat more fire.

"Barbie never takes responsibility for anything!" America said, her lips also thinning, but her glare had somehow lost its usual sharpness. Her friends' glares were more acidic.

"That's not true," I said, then I consulted Professor Longweed humbly. "May I have your permission or blessing to speak and explain to My Lady America, Professor Longweed? Or would you like to place a silence spell on me?"

It wouldn't work, but I was trying to be respectful and responsible.

"That's unnecessary!" Longweed barked. "Remember to behave. I won't allow any shenanigans in my class!"

She shooed me away like I was a bothersome pigeon perching on the lunch table. I gave her a smile and dashed to my friends before she could change her mind and stop me again.

My friends punched me on the arm, big smiles on their faces, to welcome me. This was my first class since the kidnapping. Not that I cared about any organized study and strict schedules, but hanging out with my friends made up for all the bullshit.

"Class!" Professor Longweed clapped her hands to get everyone's attention. "Today, you'll practice conjuring your elemental magic." Her piercing gaze found me in the far corner, and her lips thinned again. "For those who are of a lower status, you'll need to improve your skills fast if you want to progress into next year's program or have a better chance at employment after your graduation, even if you fail at the Brides Selection. Go join your group practices."

I didn't have their type of magic. There was no such thing as a learning curve when it came to my power, as it was innate.

This class wasn't for me, but Killian insisted this was a lowkey class, and that if I kept cutting back my class schedule, I might just drop out of Shades Academy and go sleep on the streets. In the end, his tone was harsh and sarcastic, and I knew when to stop pushing his buttons. He wasn't a patient man.

No way could I explain to him or anyone that I wasn't a builder. I was an eater.

I couldn't create spells, but I could eat them or siphon them and turn them around to send them back to the original casters. The others mistook me for an Echo, who could nullify magic. That had been Professor Longweed's first diagnosis of my power, and others took it for granted, except for the druid.

The princes also suspected that I was more than an Echo.

My dormant core power had nothing to do with my siphon ability. I didn't know what it could do exactly, but it must be dangerous even to my father, since he'd gone to great pains to spellbind it. I needed to figure out a way to break my father's spells so I could access it before Ruin came calling.

The students spread over the practice field. The same houses stuck together, but there were a couple of mixed groups as well. America and Medea's minions joined forces, throwing fireballs and brandishing wind, water, and ice as if they were the shit.

Our small group was the other mixed one. Bea, Wyatt, Jinx, and their geek friends from other houses formed a horizonal line and let out their magic.

Every student possessed one form of elemental magic, a requirement to be accepted into Shades Academy.

Only the heirs were powerful enough to hold two elemental magics. Killian's magic, however, was of another caliber. He'd confessed to me that he was Hades's grandson, so he owned death magic, but he was careful not to show it to anyone else.

Vampires could summon wind. Shifters were affiliated with water magic. Fae took for them the earth magic. Mages mostly used spells to push out their elemental magic due to their weaker elemental power.

I slid beside Bea, engaging her in a hushed conversation while I watched others wielding their magic. I was trying my best to blend in and lie low until the class was over.

Fire, water, and wind flew around. Vines shot out of the ground.

"The princes still haven't found the bad actors behind your kidnapping?" Bea asked in a low voice.

I bit my lip. "All the clues died in—" I motioned Bea closer. She leaned toward me while moving her wand in a circle, pretending to be hard at work on her magic. Her wind stirred our hair. I cupped my mouth near her ear and whispered, "CrimsonTide." Bea's eyes widened at the name. "Prince Killian isn't giving up, and nor will the other princes. They've set a plan to lure—"

"Barbie!" Professor Longweed shrieked.

Bea and I jumped. I whipped my head in the direction of the snobby professor.

"This isn't a gossip class!" Longweed snapped. "And since you've whispered your poisonous lies into that witch girl's ear, care to share with the rest of the class?"

Many students stared daggers at me, and some snickered at my being singled out again. Bea's face paled. She wasn't a good liar, and she hated confrontation, but I had her covered.

A few students pulled out their magical tablets, ready to record another "Barbie being humiliated" livestream, but Longweed darted them a stern look, prompting them to pocket their devices.

"I wasn't gossiping, Professor Longweed. I followed your instructions to the letter," I offered. "And my teammate's name isn't 'witch girl.' Her name is Bea. I was trading tips with Bea on how to level up. Her magic caliber belongs in a mage's rank, but she's unfairly treated as a low-ranking witch."

"And *you,* of all people, know how to fix it," Longweed retorted, "by recategorizing and recalculating Bea's magic caliber that was evaluated and scored by the magic committee in Mist of Cinder upon her registration?"

Medea and America's minions laughed mockingly.

"I think so, Professor Longweed," I said humbly and sincerely.

"Really?" Professor Longweed's thin brows rose with her tone of ridicule. "Why don't you share your miracle tips so the class can also benefit?"

Shit! Longweed was being sarcastic.

My friends darted nervous glances between the professor and me. They felt bad for me, but they didn't want to lose their places in the academy by taking a stand against a professor.

Bea's face paled further. She'd been flying under the radar, but for my sake, she'd been pushed to the front over and over. She sent a pleading look at Professor Longweed, but fae weren't known for being merciful, and Longweed was like a bitch who wouldn't let go of a bone.

No one, except me, had seen that Bea's mage power had been spellbound.

In the House of Mages, druids and mages perched on the top, with Cade ruling them all. Sorcerers stood on the next rung, and witches were shoved to the bottom. Among the witches, there was a strict hierarchy in their covens as well.

Bea's humanity didn't help her case, only made the supernaturals push her around. She'd been mistaken as a low-powered witch, and today I would right a wrong, and then those coyotes would bow to her—including Fake Blonde, now Fake Silver, since she'd dyed her hair silver after I pointed out her dark roots to Cade.

I was planning to find the right time to talk to Bea about her magical block since it might shatter her world if it was her family that had bound her magic, but Professor Long-weed had forced my hand, so I had to push the schedule up. Since there was no gentle step to guide Bea now, I'd have to make a loud statement, as loud as American tourists.

With a bang! Sy cheered.

As I unleashed my siphon power, a black wind entered Bea, sending her bending over. She struggled to raise her head and stared at me with wild eyes.

It has to be done, but it'll be over soon, friend, I promised her silently.

My power sank its merciless teeth into the elaborate spells that bound her and swallowed them. I was an eater of magic, spells, curses, and the world after all.

A ray of light swam in Bea's eyes. I knew she felt it, the difference, the heaviness in her gone.

"They say show, not tell, Professor Longweed," I said. "How about we let Bea demonstrate it?" I patted my witch friend on the shoulder. "Fly, little Bea bird, fly. You're free now."

Bea raised her wand, hesitated for a second, and flung its tip forward.

The wind she conjured, stronger than any student could summon, crashed into the fence, chipping away a portion.

Gasps choked out through the field.

None of the other students could fucking achieve *that*. Even their strongest fire couldn't scorch an inch of the fence warded by top-tier mages and fae. But of course, I'd aided Bea a little by weakening the spells a notch.

"Turn the tip of your wand toward the ground, Witch Bea!" Longweed shrieked.

Bea obeyed, lowering the wand to her side, and turned to me, tears in her eyes, a smile on her quivering lips.

"She faked it!" shouted Fake Silver.

"It had to be a fluke," America agreed.

"Bea is the weakest witch in the House of Mages," Fake Silver shouted louder for everyone who was willing to hear her, jealous anger tainting her eyes. "She shouldn't even have been accepted into this elite school." She recycled her fae boyfriend's mean words. "She's from one of the exiled families!"

"Yeah? Fake Silver, a.k.a. former Fake Blonde, right?" I said. "You just can't stand that Bea is the real deal and ten times more powerful than you. I suggest you lick the bottom of Bea's dirty shoes to make amends."

"My shoes aren't dirty," Bea murmured.

Fake Silver's face reddened in rage. "How dare you, Fake Servant Boy! Fake Little Bob!"

I laughed. "That's a good one. Keep going, Fake Silver."

"That's enough!" Professor Longweed barked in her shrill voice, and pointed at Bea.

Bea panted nervously at all the pointing fingers and accusing glares. I laid a hand on her slender shoulder to give her strength as she'd done for me, and Jinx laid her hand on Bea's other shoulder. Then all our geek friends laid a hand on her person to support her. Wyatt couldn't find a spot to lay his hand, so he glanced at her butt, likely debating if he should press his hand there.

"Try it again, Witch Bea. I won't tolerate cheating in my class!" Professor Longweed ordered Bea while shooting her long finger at me. "Stay away from the witch girl, Barbie, so you can't help her fake the results."

I reluctantly stepped a pace away. "But Bea needs my moral support."

"Come running!" Professor Longweed barked. "And stay by my side so I can keep an eye on you."

I had no choice but to zoom to her, causing the wind to

flap her hair. The professor gave a yelp, not expecting that I could sprint faster than a vampire. One second, I'd been with Bea and our friends, then the next, I stood by the professor, shifting my weight from my left foot to the right.

She gave me a hard stare full of distrust. "Stay right here, and don't you dare try anything." She gave America a fond nod. "Lady America, watch Barbie. If she tries to cheat, stop her!"

America puffed up her chest. "I will, Professor Longweed!"

Longweed gripped the ruby charm hanging around her neck and spewed incantations in an ancient fae tongue. A minute later, a new ward rose up in front of the fence a few yards away from the partially shattered one. Professor Longweed's fae spell was potent, since she'd used her fae artifact to strengthen it. It wouldn't matter to me, as I could eat it in my sleep, but I wouldn't want to anger my pesky professor.

Also, this was the time for Bea to truly shine in front of the coyotes.

"Go ahead, Witch Bea." Longweed pursed her lips, her eyes gleaming with confidence at the ward she'd put up in front of Bea.

Bea waved her wand, and everyone stepped back to be out of her striking range in case her spells went awry. Some students raised their shields.

"Now! Don't waste more of your classmates' time," Longweed called.

Bea's spell, boosted by her new power, lashed out. This time, her wind carried a spark of fire. Her blue hair flew in the current. Her wind speared through the professor's ward and shot into the fence, breaking it in two.

Silence fell over the practice field. Longweed turned to narrow her eyes on me.

"I didn't do anything." I spread my arms. "It's all her. Should we call her Mage Bea instead of Witch Bea, Professor Longweed?"

Our geek friends rushed to Bea to hug and congratulate her. I was about to shoot toward her too, but Professor Longweed flung her arm in front of me.

"What have you done for that girl, Barbie?" Longweed demanded. "Don't you lie! I can tell, and you don't want the lowest grade from me!"

I sighed. "My good friend little Bea must be from a powerful mage bloodline, but someone put a magical block in her without her knowledge. All I did was remove it."

Longweed widened her eyes. "Spellbound?"

"Now you're paying attention." I nodded. "Even you didn't see the hidden spell, did you, professor?"

She narrowed her eyes at me in displeasure. "I don't think you're exactly an Echo. How dare you keep up the act and put on another deception?"

A school of students rushed to me, wanting me to make them more powerful as well. A few of them even offered to pay me for a private lesson. Sweet!

Professor Longweed shooed them away and turned to stare down at me again. "I'll have to report you to Headmistress Ethel, and Prince Killian as well."

I blinked at her. "But you were the first one who said I was an Echo. Aren't they going to hold you responsible too, Professor Longweed?"

Speaking of which—Headmistress Ethel in her impeccable pantsuit appeared at the entry of the class, her light gray eyes like shards of ice snagging on me right away.

Shit!

My heart rammed into my ribcage. I calmed down a little when I didn't spot her creepy druid in tow. The headmistress and the druid hadn't been thrilled that Killian had blocked their access to me. The chaos heir had almost come to blows with the druid by refusing to let him take me away under the name of investigation, and countered that the druid had scared me so much that I'd fallen right into the trap of the kidnappers.

I tried to duck behind Professor Longweed at the sight of the headmistress, but the professor held my elbow firmly, as if she had a sixth sense that could detect my intention of bolting.

"What did you do this time, Barbie?" Longweed asked in a low voice, her gaze glued to the headmistress.

Headmistress Ethel was a middle-aged beauty and one of the sternest women I'd met. But this time, she didn't have a squad of sentinels rallying around her, but half a dozen horned students.

I smirked. "They aren't coming to arrest me, which is nice for a change. And look, the new students have horns!"

"Silence," Professor Longweed ordered me, and dragged me along with her to meet her boss.

"Headmistress Ethel." She bowed.

"Professor Longweed." Headmistress Ethel nodded. "I'm bringing the new students from the House of Underworld for an orientation."

Professor Longweed gasped. "So, it's true, then?"

My heart skipped a beat. I pricked my ears to absorb the information.

"We don't want to make a big splash due to the resistance in the realm, as you know," Headmistress Ethel said, and Longweed nodded gingerly. "So I'll introduce the new students from the House of Underworld to each class instead of holding an assembly. We can always announce it when the House of Underworld is officially acknowledged as the sixth house in the realm. Shades Academy has to make a stand first by accepting the students from the new house. Diversity is the goal. We'll add over a hundred new students, including the ones banished by another house unfairly, from the House of Underworld."

Headmistress Ethel shot me a scathing look, obviously blaming me for the banishment of Bellona and other former chaos house members. Well, what an interesting development. Killian had kicked out those delinquents, but his betrothed took them all into her house. I tried to hide the glint in my eyes as I planned to run back to Killian and tell him about this news. Maybe I should find every chance to drive a wedge between them?

Pucker had been gathering intel for me besides his duty of patrolling the Veil. He'd warned me about Queen Lilith bringing her House of Underworld to Shades Academy. The campaign for establishing the House of Underworld as the sixth house in the realm had been going on for a while, and the queen's engagement to the heir of House of Chaos had played a big part in her gaining a footing in Mist of Cinder.

"Of course," Professor Longweed said. "Queen Lilith of the House of Underworld is the biggest donor to Shades Academy."

"It's not about the academy fund, Professor Longweed. Though with it, we can upgrade all our facilities." Headmistress Ethel gave the professor a sharp look. "It's about fairness, and it's time the sixth house has its rightful place in Mist of Cinder!"

So Headmistress Ethel was either Queen Lilith's ally or her pawn.

I surveyed the six new giant students who stood behind the headmistress. Their skin varied in shades of light or dark. Four of them had scales along the sides of their necks, and all of them had twin horns protruding from their heads.

They were pure-blooded demons from the Underworld.

The demons stared at me openly. Two of the alpha types sniffed at me, and their eyes glowed a menacing crimson.

My nostrils flaring, I pulled my lips back in a silent snarl, challenging them back.

The largest demon, whose arms were bigger than my thighs, smirked nastily.

My heart pounded. This shit had become real. Killian's betrothed, the Queen of the Underworld, would come to the academy soon and stake her claim not only on this realm but also on Killian.

My head suddenly swam, and my mouth tasted like ash. The rest of the headmistress's words flew through my ears, and the rest of the class passed in a blur.

Thoughts of Killian and his betrothed filled the dark space in my head.

Would he still shield me when she was here? Or was I a toy he'd toss away?

We'll drag down the bitch queen by the hair and stomp our foot on her face, and Killian will see who is more beautiful and powerful! Sy said. *Should he refuse to see sense and still choose her, we'll dump him. You can hook up with Cade, or another. There're plenty of big dicks in Mist of Cinder.*

18

Barbie

The House of Underworld set up their establishment between the business district and the Veil. It was on the south side of the campus, so at least it'd be a long walk for Queen Lilith to stroll to the House of Chaos.

Yet it offered me little comfort. My stomach felt queasy at the prospect of their reunion, even though Queen Lilith hadn't made her appearance while her demon boys settled down.

Several demons had been in the same classes as me. They always stared at me, as if I were fresh meat and they wanted to take a big bite. Vampires stared at me all the time too, but they wouldn't dare touch me. I was under the protection of the meanest chaos prince, and even though I was no longer in the House of Vampires, Louis had extended his command—anyone who drank from me would experience a brutal death. But he himself glued his hungry eyes to my neck every time he saw me.

I was always the monsters' favorite.

I expelled the thoughts of demons, vampires, and monsters and looped my arm around Bea's as we headed toward Clockwork. Bea was going to help me study for the midterm. She was a grade-A student. I was a grade-D. I didn't feel too bad, since there was only B and C between A and D. But I didn't want Killian to puff his mean, royal breath down my neck, so I needed to get a couple of Cs at least.

I surveyed the lime-colored building that curved around the campus street. Sy had first fucked the fae prince here, or more precisely, she'd gotten fucked while he pressed her against the brick wall of Clockwork.

Sy grinned at the memory, a dreamy look on her savagely beautiful face.

Has Rowan texted you yet?

He hasn't brought any diamond as payment, I said sharply. *I'm not giving you to him for free!*

Sy pouted. She'd be brooding over it for a while, leaving me alone with my friend.

We strolled into the building of Clockwork. The study hall was enormous. Rows of desks stretched to the end of the hall, one-third of them already occupied. A dozen lanterns made of fae light hung above each desk, even though the afternoon sunlight was shining through the windows.

Bea led me toward a corner table where no one would notice us. Before we put our butts on the chairs, clamor broke out across the hall.

I looked on, but Bea tugged my sleeve. "It's not our business. Let's just lie low."

"Okay. I'm in no shape to stir shit," I agreed.

I sat down and pulled out a textbook titled *The Origin of Magic.*

"Move!" Bellona's shout instantly caught my attention. "My friends and I want to sit here."

I turned my head in the direction of her voice and stood up. "It's Jinx! Bellona dude is bullying Jinx!"

Every house was divided into popular chicks, minions, outcasts, and geeks. Popular chicks were royals and nobles, like Medea, America, Dixie, and Cami. Minions were Fake Silver, Fake Silver's fae boyfriend, small-eyed Javier, Bellona, and Imelda, among many others. I was the number one outcast, and Bea was both an outcast and a geek.

"But we were here first," Jinx said. "We're in the middle of studying."

Jinx was a geek from my house. Seven other geeks from the House of Vampires, the House of Fae, and the House of Shifters shared a long desk, with Jinx near a window that provided a view of a line of blue jacaranda trees.

Bellona's new friends were three giant demon students from the House of Underworld, and they wanted the seats that came with a beautiful view. As a new member of their house, Bellona was eager to impress them.

"You think my friends and I are inconveniencing you?" Bellona drawled.

Her demon friends sneered. They were itching for a fight and to make a statement in Shades Academy.

Medea perched on a long desk two rows away with her minions, drinking tea and looking on. Bellona had been her attack dog before Killian kicked the dog out, and she remained loyal to Medea. It was probably Medea who'd gotten her into the sixth house, since the princess of the House of Chaos had claimed a close tie to Queen Lilith.

"Look, we want no trouble," said Drusilla.

Drusilla was a dhampir, half-vampire and half-human. Her kind's social rank was lower than a pureblooded vampire. She'd once told me that powerful vampires could breed with humans in this realm, even though it was rare. In general, it was harder to even make a vampire, since magic had become so watered down in Mist of Cinder.

She hadn't been impressed with me when I was Little Bob, and she'd joined Medea and America's small army to beat me up in the Ring, her retribution to me for stabbing Prince Louis. She'd been in love with him, and I bet that he hadn't shared with her or anyone else why I'd put a knife in his chest. He'd never looked at her with desire, instead had her bring him blondes to feed on and fuck. When I was in the House of Vampires, she'd been his love-sick assistant.

I wondered why she had jumped ship and now hung out with the geeks.

"Let us finish studying for the midterm, please," Drusilla continued. She didn't cower like the witch geeks or even the shifter geeks, who mostly shifted into smaller animals. "We won't sit here again if you like this spot."

"She said *please.*" A light-skinned demon snickered, and the others joined him.

"It takes time to remove our textbooks." Wyatt gestured at the desk, where a stack of books was piled in front of the geeks. "Be reasonable, man. You can have this desk next time. How's that?"

"How about we help you remove your stupid books?" a bronze-skinned demon barked, lashing his clawed hands out and sweeping the bundle of textbooks that belonged to Wyatt to the floor.

Wyatt shook in anger, but he froze in place as a third demon got in his face, sneering.

"Leave!" Jinx shot to her feet.

Her friends also stood but passed hesitant glances between them. They weren't fighters. They couldn't win if a fight broke out. In this realm, it was the right of the strong to take from the weak.

Hellfire sparked from the demons' fingertips and horns. Bellona smirked like their bitch, even though she was several inches taller than them as the descendant of a frost giant.

For the first time since I'd been dragged onto the wagon of bride candidates, it wasn't me who was being targeted. It was kind of nice for a change, but Jinx and Wyatt were my friends. I couldn't just sit on my ass and watch them be bullied.

Bea looked conflicted. She wanted to help our friends, but she was afraid. Even though her power had upgraded, she didn't believe that she could take on Bellona and the demons. And we both knew that if we interfered, especially if I helped, Medea would lead her army to attack us. It was her personal mission to see my ruin.

"Make us," Bellona purred.

"You guys are from a new house in the realm. Know your place!" Drusilla clenched a fist.

Vampires only bowed to their king and prince, and in Shades Academy, they obeyed only Prince Louis.

"How are you going to put us in our place, then, human?" Bellona sneered at Drusilla. "You shouldn't even be in this school. Now let me show you how to know your place." She swung her massive arm at Drusilla.

The dhampir ducked, then drove her fist toward Bellona's jaw. Bellona was equally fast, despite her size. She grabbed Drusilla's fist to pull the dhampir toward her and headbutted her. Dark blood trickled from Drusilla's nose.

The demons sniffed, getting more excited at the smell of blood.

Shit, it was going to escalate.

"Screw the one-by-one rule!" Jinx snarled. "Let's take down the giant bitch!"

The geeks rushed Bellona as one. Jinx had ice magic, and her ice slammed into Bellona to encase her opponent.

Bellona laughed. "Playing ice with me? You're a joke."

Ice had no effect on Bellona.

Our geek friends traded determined looks and tossed their wind, vines, and fire at Bellona. The three demons lunged, insanely fast. The light-skinned one grabbed Wyatt and slammed him to the ground. The other two demons had Jinx and a shifter girl by the throats, choking them for fun.

Bea let out a terrible cry. "No!"

I sprang toward Jinx and her group, leaving Bea behind. Students gathered in groups, blocking the aisles, so I had to leap onto a desk. Then I was jumping from one desk to another, ignoring gasps and shouts and keeping going, until I had vaulted over a big crowd that had gathered to watch the fight.

I touched down in a crouch on the desk where the dispute had started, planting one fist on the wood. That was one of my favorite martial arts postures. I slowly raised my head, letting my golden curls bounce a little.

"Hello? Hello!" I smirked at Bellona and the demons. "Why wasn't I invited to the party while you're giving my friends a nice massage?"

The demons snapped their attention to me, hunger in their eyes. I managed not to shudder, but I couldn't maintain my smile any longer. My facial muscles were tired.

"This is *Barbie*, the bad actress I told you about!" Bellona said loudly.

I frowned at her. "Dude! You just spoiled the surprise. You're a party pooper, do you know that?"

She snarled.

"Barbie, Prince Killian's new pet, right?" the biggest demon asked, swaggering and still holding Jinx by the throat while she tried to throw magic at him, to no avail. "He had other pets before you. You should ask His Highness where they ended up."

Everyone who wasn't on my side laughed on cue, though some laughter sounded a bit nervous and accommodating.

"Hmm." I tilted my head. "I see, your queen sent some small-time demonic comedians to Shades Academy. I don't think you'll make it in this business. The market is very tough now."

Shocked gasps rose from the crowd. No one dared to disrespect the Queen of the Underworld, even if she wasn't around.

"Watch your fucking mouth, little cunt!" the demon bellowed, slashing his claws toward me.

I had already dropped to the desk, my hands planting on the smooth surface as anchors, my feet kicking out and making hard contact with his jaw from the side to avoid booting Jinx.

The demon boy had to drop Jinx as his head snapped back from the impact, a shocked look flashing in his dark red eyes before rage clouded them.

Jinx rolled away.

I flew into the air—an impossible acrobatic move for the untrained—and grabbed the horn of his bronze-skinned friend. While the bronze-skinned demon shrieked in pain, since horns were one of the most sensitive parts of a demon,

I used his brown horn as a prop for a roundhouse kick to the throat of his pal.

They might be strong and fast, but I was better.

The third demon crashed into the crowd, which parted in time to let him fly by, thanks to their supernatural reflexes. He collided with a desk, shattering it, and dropped to the ground, groaning in pain. No dignity.

These demons, though tougher than other supernaturals, were easier to hurt than their beastly brethren due to their humanoid forms. But then, their queen wouldn't send beasts to Shades Academy, would she, if she cared about public opinion?

The supernaturals in Mist of Cinder might be savages, but they still wanted to maintain the appearance of civilization.

Two demons lunged at me, their prolonged claws slicing toward my neck for the kill. I leapt away, but the third demon got me with his fangs, piercing my left shoulder.

I pulled back and rolled to the other side of the desk. Pain bloomed in me. Sy hissed, sucked the pain into her, and pumped her strength into me.

The other geeks rushed to help Jinx, Wyatt, and Drusilla get to their feet and then brought them to stand on the other side of the desk, flanking me.

Everyone tensed and sniffed as I bled; my blood was powerful, and its potent scent permeated the air.

Drusilla jumped to the desk and stood by my side. I turned at an angle, not wanting to give her my back while I still faced the demons and Medea's goons. If she used this opportunity to lunge at me, I'd kick her harder than she could take and return her to her former demon captor.

"I'm not your enemy, Barbie," Drusilla said over my wary

glance. "I never was. I'm sorry for joining them to beat you up last time."

She tore off the sleeve of her uniform and jerked her chin at my wounded shoulder. There were vampires in the room, and she knew how enticing my blood was to them.

I gave her a thankful nod, and she moved closer to me and wrapped the makeshift bandage around my shoulder to stop the bleeding. With her vampire speed, it took her a couple of seconds to get the job done.

Drusilla nodded at me and slid off the desk, not wanting to hinder my fight.

The demons' stunned, enraged looks never left me. This was our first fight. They hadn't expected a doll-looking chick with ridiculous golden curls to have that kind of speed and strength.

A goddess versus demons. It's barely a fair fight! a voice chimed in my head, then my ghost familiar appeared by my side, though no one could see him.

He scanned the hall, grinning ear-to-ear, loving all the bloodlust and anger and fear in the hall.

I haven't come to Clockwork for two centuries, he said. *Not much has changed. Immortals!*

I'm busy here, Pucker.

I can see that, my dear girl, he said. *I had to zip here in fast and furious style.*

You should've brought my Deathsong, I said.

If I'd gone solid, I wouldn't have been able to get here in time to watch this, he said. *That sentient blade gives me the creeps. The other day it told me it needs to murder more people.*

Let me wrap this up, I told Pucker.

"Bellona, my dude friend, how's going?" I flashed a sharp smile at Bellona, her big bosom, which could suffocate a man to death, rising and falling as anger and frustration seized her.

"How many times must I tell you that I ain't your friend?" Bellona spat.

"Don't worry, big dude," I said. "Your secret is safe with me."

"You think you're untouchable because you're an Echo?" Bellona sneered before she turned to her demon pals. "Amon, would you do the honors and wipe that stupid smile off her face with your hellfire?"

My eyes widened as I spotted hellfire twirling on all three demons' fingertips. Would hellfire burn me?

We won't know until we take it, Pucker said expectantly.

It wasn't him who was going to take it!

The demons smirked evilly at me, their hellfire dancing on the tips of their claws.

"It's forbidden to use hellfire on students!" Bea shouted. She'd come around and stood with our geek friends.

"Barbie started the fight, and we're merely defending ourselves," Amon said.

So, it was true that demons were all liars.

"Let's talk about this first, dudes," I said. "We can still solve this conflict without resorting to violence. Violence should be the last resort, don't you agree?"

They stared at me in distaste. Demons loved violence and always rushed toward it without thinking twice. All three demon students raised their hands, their hellfire at the ready.

I put up a finger. "Wait! I still have a couple of questions."

"Don't listen to her!" Bellona called. "She's stalling. If you give her time to think it through, she'll trick us!"

"Bellona is speaking from rich personal experience." I smiled knowingly. "But you aren't her bitches, are you? You don't seem to be the type. She says shoot, and you say where? You're demons, fierce and nasty demons! My question is simple. Is Lucifer your boss? The textbooks say Lucifer took Hell for his domain after he was cast out of Heaven. Does he still hang around, or has he abdicated, so there's now a new queen in town? Or was the Underworld divided, so Lucifer and your queen split Hell between themselves?"

"Lucifer left a long time ago!" a second demon said. He was a bit shorter and looked younger than the others.

"How come?" I squinted. "What happened? He couldn't just disappear like that, right? It was irresponsible, since he had people depending on him!"

The second demon opened his mouth to answer, but Amon smacked the back of his head to stop him.

"Do you know that your prince will soon be our queen's consort?" Amon smirked. "Soon the entire House of Chaos will bow to our queen."

My heart skipped an icy beat.

"I see you're a curious little thing, aren't you?" Amon said. "There are rumors about you. Other houses are warned not to touch Prince Killian's pet, but we're from his betrothed's house, so Prince Killian will be more than happy to share you with our queen however she wants."

He threw up his palms, eager to shoot a jet of his hellfire at me, and the other two demons followed suit.

"Wait, demons! Wait!" I called urgently.

"Make her bald first!" Bellona hissed. "I hate her full head of golden curls!"

"Stop, demons!" Bea screamed.

From her table, Medea smiled, watching the scene over

the brim of her teacup. She hadn't said a word, but I knew that she had orchestrated this.

I sat down on the desk with my legs crossed, resting my hands on my knees in a lotus posture.

"Now go ahead, demons," I said. "Shower me with your hellfire. I'm a bit thirsty here."

"Barbie, get out!" Bea shouted. "Hellfire is the most destructive fire!"

"Are you sure?" I asked.

A stream of hellfire hit me in the face, then another stream followed.

My geek friends cried and shrank back. They shouldn't worry. My shield had them all covered, and Bea had thrown up her mage shield in front of me, which was unnecessary, though appreciated.

The hellfire, warm and naughty, sank through my golden curls. I closed an eye, swimming in the dark red fire.

"It's a bit weak, demons," I called out. "Don't hold back. Do better."

The demons snarled, their hellfire now engulfing me, sparks dancing on my curls and arms.

Are we getting a sauna? Sy asked. *It's a bit ticklish, though.*

Pucker's here, I told her. *We can have him suck away the ticklish part of the energy. We should've known that demon energy isn't all friendly, like its owners.*

No, thanks, Pucker said, floating between the demons to study them closely, as if to check if they had pimples. There hadn't been demons in Shades Academy for centuries. *When you can take a sip from a goddess or Hades's dragon grandson, why would you want to drink from much lesser beings such as demons?*

You're so snobbish. You promised to be a better man, I said in disapproval.

I'm picky, he countered.

"Can you give me more fire, demons?" I asked, struggling to keep my other eye open. "I'm getting a bit sleepy here."

"What the fuck are you?" Amon demanded.

Seize this chance to build an army, your army, while all see what you can do, Barbie! Pucker shouted in my ear. *Rally the oppressed around you. A thousand ants can take down an adult elephant.*

I blinked. *Are you serious?*

How did Superman fall? Pucker asked.

How? I asked.

He smiled. *He fought alone.*

Fascinating. Sy leaned forward in the backseat. *Maybe we should listen to your familiar.*

Numbers win! It's all a numbers game, Pucker explained, puffing his chest out in self-importance. *In human history, powerful kingdoms fell all the time. When the weak banded together, they brought down the strongest. In this realm, the strong have the birthright to prey on the weak. But you can have the weak. Rally them and they'll be your army. They'll walk over hot coals for you, as no one has spoken up for them before. Be their leader, so they won't cower again. Shake things up. You aren't passing through here. It's your home now. A power shift in Mist of Cinder is long overdue!*

Let's turn the sheep into monster sheep that aren't afraid to bite! Sy howled. *We got this.*

I bit my lip. They were probably right. I had to go profound now. Mist of Cinder was the last patch of pure magical land. Darkness and corruption roamed in the human world now. I wondered if it was because Ruin was closer than ever.

Even as the hellfire warmed me, I trembled at the

sudden flash of memories of my father feeding on me, worse than being eaten alive by a pride of lions.

I expelled the dark memory and swallowed, surveying the hall of prey and predators.

I'd always told myself that I was no one's hero and that I couldn't even save myself. I carried the shame and terror of my birth and past, hoarding my darkest secret.

Pucker was right about shaking things up.

With the demons from the sixth house joining Medea and her army, they would be unstoppable. If they won this fight, they'd pick on anyone they wanted. They'd hurt my friends to get to me.

So let's make a fucking stand.

I wouldn't just rally the weak from my house. I'd gather every sheep from every house, and I'd be the baddest shepherd dog that fended off lions and wolves.

The demon Amon had opened the floor for me by asking, "What the fuck are you?"

"What the fuck am I?" I laughed, shooting to my feet. The hell energy gave me a surprising boost, as if it was part of my genetic origin. "I'm the new voice for the underserved, the good, the smart, and the worthy. I'm the defender of those who can't defend themselves. I'm one of the underdog bride candidates!"

I looked into the crowd, making eye contact with those who hunched their shoulders. They'd been repressed for so long as the bottom feeders that they didn't even know how to straighten their spines.

"Listen up, chicks and dicks," I shouted. "You've been sheep all your life, but you don't have to stay sheep. You've been told that you're weak and everyone can stomp on you and take away whatever little you have. Even in Shades

Academy, you're treated as second and third class. Today, I say, enough is enough!"

Silence. Everyone just stared at me.

Then a shriek rose behind me.

"Enough is enough!" Bea shouted.

"Enough is enough!" Wyatt echoed, then all our geek friends joined them.

Then shouts of "Enough is enough!" rocked through the hall as many more voices joined theirs.

"And today, we're mad as hell about all the shit we put up with!" I roared. "Today, we say: No. More. Shit!"

"No. More. Shit!" Even more voices added to ours.

No shit! Pucker shouted into a demon's ear.

"Yes! That's it!" I pumped my fist into the air. "Rally behind me, my friends! Today, we have a voice! Who's with me? Who's rooting for the underdogs?"

"We are!" Even more voices shouted across the hall.

I cupped my ear. "Who's rooting for the underdogs?"

"We are!" they roared, their pent-up anger carrying them.

"Who are the underdogs?" I roared back.

"We are!" half of the crowd roared.

The demons stared at me, shocked. Medea and her army shot daggers of hate at me.

A hologram that was streaming live on Spinchat appeared in midair. At the bottom, hashtags—*#RootforUnderdogs, #UnderdogsArmyisBorn, #BarbieleadsUnderdog, #TeamUnderdogBrideCandidates*—flashed by.

Jinx smirked at me, typing furiously on her tablet. Her geek friends followed suit.

Hundreds of comments appeared at a rapid speed.

Medea's army countered with *#PutdownBarbie, #StompUnderdogs, #ExpelBarbie...*

A social media war broke out in the middle of our fight.

Pucker threw his phantom head back and giggled like an evil mastermind.

"Who the fuck am I?" I laughed at my opponents, sweeping my predatory gaze over them. "I am the one who fucks all your magic! I'm the one who never fucking bows, kneels, or bends!"

"You bowed to Prince Killian!" Medea shouted furiously, standing now, surrounded by her minions. "My brother stripped your power in the ice rink, and thousands of us witnessed your shame. You can't fuck his magic, can you? Look again! Look at how pathetic you are!"

"Behold the pathetic loser Barbie!" Bellona bellowed.

Another hologram streamed, playing the scene of Killian stripping off my clothes with his darkness and starlight and showing my utter humiliation.

"Pathetic Barbie! Loser Barbie!" Medea's followers chanted.

"Underdog Barbie! Brave Barbie!" my crowd chanted back.

I giggled with Sy's lung capacity, and my laughter drowned out the noises in the hall. "Princess Clown is spot-on!" I pointed at Medea and roared. "She and her army make us look powerless and helpless, then call us pathetic. I say: No more bullshit!"

"No more shit! No more bullshit!" my crowd roared after me.

I nodded, kicking up a classic tap dance on the desk to go with my campaign. Pom-pom. Dong. Tar-ta!

"We say *stop* today!" I called, letting my voice carry to every corner. "They beat us into submission in the past. That stops today! We aren't weak, even though we might look it, even though we might act it, even though we might appear to be loners. But we're not weak. We have got strength inside! Now let our steel come out and let our bravery guide us. We. Are. Underdogs! Together, we're stronger than ever! Together, we don't bow down. If they pick on one of us, they pick on all of us, and we push back as one!"

All for one, one for all! Pucker tutored, grinning.

I pumped a fist into the air and roared, "All for one! One for all!"

I might just let Pucker come up with all the campaign lines. He'd do it for free anyway.

Clockwork Hall divided into two crowds. The underdog crowd gathered to the left, getting into a glaring and shouting match against Medea's army on the right.

"Hit one of us again, and they hit all of us!" I called. "We'll fucking push back. We'll fucking punch them back double hard!"

"Solidarity, underdogs! We're one!" Bea screamed.

Wow! I didn't know she had it in her, but she always came through for me due to her loyalty. She didn't have my lung capacity, but she made up for it with an amplifying spell. She was a powerful mage now.

My crowd stomped the ground. "We're one! We're the underdogs!"

I howled, and my new army howled back.

I broke apart the hellfire that had gathered on me and sent it into the air. It exploded into fireworks. The demons stared at the fireworks, then at me, and growled. But there was nothing they could do.

My crowd cheered and applauded.

Jinx, Bea, Drusilla, Wyatt, Charlie (a fae girl), and Mila (a shifter geek) jumped onto the desk and stood by my side, lifting their chins high.

We had representatives from five houses.

"Today, we have a voice," Bea shouted. "We're no longer the weaklings!"

"Join Team Underdogs! Sign up with us," Jinx called. "Every underdog will get a token that serves as your protection. If they beat one of us, we punch back as one!"

My seven friends clasped their hands together and raised them into the air.

Medea landed on the desk facing ours. "Today is the day we put down pathetic Barbie and mark her as a dead underdog!" she roared. "I, Princess of the House of Chaos, claim the right to cut off Underdog Barbie's head and quell this rebellion!"

19

Barbie

I knew it would eventually come to this—me versus Medea in a showdown—but I hadn't expected this conflict to rise to be a political issue. And now Medea would use this opportunity to finish me off, a perfect crime, but some might call it making an example of me.

I watched my geek friends' faces go white with shock and fear. This was unprecedented, and who could fight a princess and win? My crowd went quiet, waiting for me to make the next move, which was pivotal to the fate of the underdogs campaign.

If I failed, they'd all suffer. They'd be stomped.

The opposing crowd cheered, shouting Medea's name like religious fanatics, Bellona the loudest. A dozen more demons stalked into the study hall, pushed to the front, and rallied behind Medea.

"I've suffered you long enough, rat," Medea sneered at

me. "You think yourself worth two cents since my brother took you in as his new pet?" She kept referring to Killian as her brother, even though he rebuked her for riding his coattails. "No matter how shiny your hide appears, you're nothing but a rat. Soon, you'll be one of Queen Lilith's squeezing toys. Don't you know that my brother shares everything with Her Majesty, the greatest beauty and power in the realm, not just her bed?"

Rage, red and hot, shot to my head. I did not just see red. I saw death! My control slipped, and Sy's rage rose to join mine, urging me to kill Medea brutally.

"You must really be dying for them to share you, Princess Clown," I said viciously. "But from what I see, Prince Killian treats you like dirt even though you're a princess. And I wonder why."

Medea snarled amid the deathly silent hall, dozens of tiny snakes entwined with her hair hissing at me.

"How dare you! You're nobody, and you'll be a dead nobody, or a dead rat, today."

She took a deep, confident breath, ready to jump over to my desk, impatient to end me.

"Hold!" I called. "Let me come to you."

I didn't want to ruin my friends' textbooks that were scattered on the desk. Some of them were from poor supernatural families. They couldn't afford new sets.

I leapt and landed on Medea's desk, facing her. Hooking two fingers, I beckoned her to come swing at me.

Medea lunged, kicking her leg out toward the side of my face, devil's consort style. Shit, she was fast. I ducked, narrowly missing being dented on the cheek. That vicious princess wasn't fooling around. She aimed to kill. She kicked her other foot up as well, going for my soft throat.

I twisted my torso and dropped to a crouch, letting her

foot slide past. She wheeled to kick my head. I rolled away. Her stomp shattered part of the wood. Yep, she'd meant to kick me to death. If her boot had landed on a weaker supernatural, their skull would have cracked open.

I could feel my geek friends holding their breath a desk away, but Medea's supporters cheered, even though I'd avoided that lethal kick from their princess.

"Coward Barbie! You're a disgrace!" Bellona shouted in rage, blaming me for not willingly taking the hit.

"Brave Barbie! Go, Underdog Barbie!" Bea shouted back in support of me.

"Go Underdog Barbie!" my supporters bellowed.

I raised a fist into the air. "Oh, yeah! I'm getting there, guys! Thanks."

Medea jabbed a fist toward my eye socket, swinging her other fist in a slashing arc toward my temple. It would be hard to avoid both blows while I rose to my feet. It was too late to stop the momentum.

I pressed my palms together and thrust them up. When they separated from each other, my armguards met Medea's strike. The impact forced her to stumble back. Surprise, pain, and anger flickered in her jade eyes.

I'd been fed well in this realm. I'd even gotten some good shuteye during the daytime when nightmares plagued me less. Being kidnapped and temporarily losing a hand was child's play to me. In the House of Chaos, my strength had grown exponentially.

With a hiss, Medea lunged at me again. Her kicks and fists flew at me faster. I slipped away from her, playing cat and mouse with her, albeit with narrow margins.

Then it occurred to me that Medea seemed able to anticipate my moves as if she could read my mind. I didn't feel her magic brushing my mind, so she probably had an innate ability that I couldn't counter. I could siphon physical magic, like spells, curses, or elemental magic, but not someone's inner gift.

That was why she was so confident in this fight. But even with her advantage, I still stayed one step ahead of her. Surprise, surprise!

Surprise! Sy said viciously.

When I registered that Medea could anticipate me, I no longer formed thoughts on my next moves.

Watch her tell! Pucker shouted. *She's got a weakness on the left. Punch her left, Barbie, then drive a fist into her jaw. You can knock her out in one strike, like you did with that ice giant's brat.*

We need to humiliate the princess first to let everyone see who's superior, Sy argued. *Claw her face bloody!*

Two backseat drivers argued in my head as if it were their forum. While I was distracted, Medea rammed her knee into my gut.

Fuck, that hurt! I nearly doubled over. Bitch was so mean!

Bitch's so mean! Sy pouted, her lower lip quivering in rage.

Shut up, everyone! I yelled at them. *I can't think, let alone land a hit on my foe, when you two use my headspace like it's your own Facebook page.*

What's face book? Pucker asked.

But the two quieted after that. Sy took the pain into her, dulling the ache in me.

Medea's army gave cheers. Bellona jumped up and down, which lifted her shirt up and exposed her middle.

I dodged to the side when Medea swung at me. Her fingernails glanced off the top of my ear while I slowed down to shout, "Stop jumping up and down, Bellona dude! Your belly button is showing, and it has long, thick hair sprouting out. It's disgusting! I need to go home to wash my eyes."

Bellona stopped cold, and many students winced at the disturbing image as well.

As I stepped left and right to avoid being smacking by Medea again, my crowd shouted, "Fight back, Barbie! Fight back!"

"I'm trying!" I barked back, a bit annoyed. "You think I'm sleeping or eating cakes? I can't believe you guys are so aggressive!"

I jabbed my knuckles into Medea's kidney under the peer pressure, and the princess hissed in pain. I allowed her to leap back to nurse her wound. I'd given only half of my strength, since I didn't want to punch a hole in her kidney.

Why not? Sy demanded.

We don't want to kill her, unless she tries to kill us, I said.

She aims to kill each time! Sy said. *I'm going to eat her.*

A lot of supernaturals were on her to-eat list.

Medea did a wheelhouse-style kick and swung her leg toward my head.

I dodged it. "You try to be fancy, but you're lacking creativity. You aim for brilliance, but you often come up short." I tilted my head and smiled at the pure hatred in her eyes. "Despite your royal title, you aren't even good enough to live in Prince Killian's shadow. No wonder he doesn't want you to call him *brother*."

I kicked my leg out in a feint. Medea sidestepped to the left, just as I'd expected. Before she could counterattack, I dropped low, hooking my foot around her ankle, lightning fast, and then slammed her in the knee hard with my other foot.

She went down, and I pressed the advantage and landed on her, pushing my left foot down on her heaving chest.

"Hello, princess." I smirked at her. "How are we doing so far?"

My crowd went wild.

A group of Medea's goons tried to jump on the desk to fight me off, but my team moved forward as one and blocked them.

"This is a one-on-one duel!" Bea shouted. My meek friend was turning into a bulldog. "Princess Medea started it!"

Medea snarled, whipping her head around, and a dozen snakes emerged from her hair.

"Don't let them bite you!" Jinx shouted. "Those snakes are her power. They're poisonous. Their venom can—"

Three snakes led the attack and shot toward me. I quickly grabbed the necks of all three snakes and tossed them away with a groan of disgust. Their cold skin made my skin crawl.

Then dozens of snakes swarmed me. I looked on in horror, frozen for a long beat, before jumping off Medea and scrambling back. Anyone would freeze if their father had tossed them into a pit of snakes as a child. You didn't just get over the fear overnight.

A snake sank its fangs into the corner of my left eye. Pain pierced me. I cried, snatching that snake and smashing its head into the edge of the desk.

I shall get Prince Killian! Pucker said, and then he was gone.

"Healers!" Bea screamed in panic. "We need healers! Barbie was bitten by Princess Medea's snakes!"

My friends rushed toward me, but the demons blocked them from reaching me.

Swaying on my feet, I stared at Medea in a dreadful realization.

The old Greek gods might've gone from our realm, but they'd left their hybrid offspring on Earth. Medea was Medusa's descendant. If she'd inherited Medusa's full power, I wondered if she could turn me to stone when I stared back at her face.

Her snake had bitten me.

That was why Killian hadn't allowed Medea to challenge me when I first entered his house. If she'd fought me back then, while I was shaken from being stripped in front of thousands, I might've been defeated and denied entrance to the House of Chaos, even if I survived.

And Killian wouldn't be able to shield me if I wasn't in his house. Well, he had to let me go now. I'd been bitten by the most venomous snake. I could feel the magical poison flowing in my veins.

Asher was assigned to shadow me for the day, but he didn't follow me to class. He had other errands to run. And a fight had never broken out in the study hall of Clockwork before.

Pain burned in me from the poison in my bloodstream, and Sy gasped as she took it into her, absorbing the venom as much as she could. I didn't even have the strength to thank her, as nausea filled my head.

You have my strength! Sy hissed in pain. *Take the bitch down!*

I growled, my hands turning to claws, partially shifting. But I wouldn't dare to go for a full transformation. I lashed out, lightning fast, and my blade claws beheaded several snakes at once. Their severed heads rained down around me.

Medea widened her eyes, fury and hatred burning in them. Shocked gasps spread across the hall, and the shouting increased. The crowd hadn't been so stunned when I was bitten, but they appeared uneasy at seeing my hands turn into blade claws.

Medea shouted, raising her hands to summon more snakes, as if she had an endless supply of them. I stood my ground for the coming snake attack.

"Stop!" a harsh voice boomed from the far entrance of the study hall.

Clockwork rumbled, and the students shrank from the raw power of that voice.

Killian had come.

Then I sensed more powers rippling in the air behind him. The other princes had also arrived. A heartbeat, and they all zoomed to our desk where I still faced off with Medea.

Shit!

They'd seen me get bitten by a mystical snake. And they'd seen my claws as well. But I couldn't dwell on it while facing a vicious foe who was hellbent on putting me down.

"Medea, cease!" Killian ordered her as he concealed his fear for me, but his pale face betrayed his emotion.

"Stop it, Princess Medea! Barbie needs treatment as soon as possible after your snake bite!" Silas shouted, his amber eyes glowing with rage and worry.

Ever since my kidnapping, the heir of the House of Shifters had made sure my wellbeing was also his business.

Medea tilted her head to the side, a cruel smile tugging up a corner of her lips. She ignored Silas and focused on Killian. "You want me to spare your pet, brother? Will you say please? She has already been bitten by my snake, but she still has one more minute to sink into a coma, a suitable punishment for this low commoner who doesn't know her place."

"A weaker supernatural would've perished by now at

such a bite from Princess Medea's snake," Cade said. "Barbie is strong, but she still needs immediate care!"

The other princes had called for the healers, and they were coming. I was touched, even though I knew their former plan of taming me.

"Thank you for your concerns, high sirs, but I'm fine," I said, trying not to sit down at the dizziness. "I can handle it. I have experience. I got lots of bites from snakes when I was a kid."

"Medea's snakes aren't the ordinary kind," Louis said, worry in his pale blue eyes.

"Even if Medusa had come herself, her power wouldn't work on me," I said, letting the fact that I knew about Medea's heritage sink in while trying not to wince at the left-over pain. Sy had taken most of the burning agony from the venom into herself. My heart was full of love and gratitude for her. Without Sy, I wouldn't be standing here today.

"I'm good, sirs!" I had to calm Killian as I watched him fight back his panic at seeing me bitten. I couldn't let anyone know the depths of how much he truly cared about me. I could tell from the cold, murderous rage in his storm-blue eyes that he was set to kill Medea. One more push and he'd lose it and do it, and the consequences would be dire, even for the heir of the House of Chaos.

I needed to do all I could to protect him back.

"I'm good." I repeated my lie. "But I need to sit down for a minute, since it's been a long day."

Before I could sit down, I spotted Headmistress Ethel pushing to the front of the crowd, her eyes widening in surprise at my resilience before she quickly schooled her expression to her usual stern and haughty look.

"I knew it would be you who made headlines again!" she snapped, carrying the rigid winter wind in her voice.

"Uh?" I darted a nervous look at the headmistress and the sentinels who flanked her. "What headlines, Madam Headmistress Ethel?"

I smiled at her when I didn't spot that awful druid and his crystal ball.

She didn't care for my smile and speared me with a disdainful look before turning to Killian. "You can't interfere, Prince Killian. This is a duel between two bride candidates, though one is lowborn."

Lowborn? Pucker sneered. He'd returned with Killian. *That old crone isn't worthy to lick the bottom of your butt. If only she knew you're a goddess!*

"A new member of my house is wounded!" Killian growled.

"As long as Princess Medea doesn't kill Barbie, at least not intentionally," Ethel declared, "it's within Her Highness's rights to continue the duel and teach a lowborn a lesson, one that other lowborn should also learn from. If it was Barbie who started this fight to challenge a royal, she'll be punished according to the laws of the five kingdoms, starting with detention and solitary under my authority."

Which meant that she and her druid would finally get their hands on me, since I'd be out of Killian's reach and protection.

"You're not taking her anywhere," Killian said coldly, and the rest of the princes rallied behind him.

"I know it's hard to believe, but I didn't start the fight," I said, my voice bright and clear. "We geeks, outcasts, and the underserved were studying quietly and diligently and devotedly for the midterm. Then the three demon boys, who are Princess Medea's new best friends"—I thrust two fingers to point them out—"jumped us. The hell boys were very aggressive. They tossed hellfire at me to toast me but failed, because I don't back down from any fire." Killian sent them a chilling, murderous look, and the demons averted their gazes. "And I, one of the underdog bride candidates, had to fight back to show all the nasty bullies that we aren't weak." I pumped a fist into the air and roared, "Team Underdogs!"

My geek friends behind me bellowed with our supporters on the left side of the hall, all pumping their fists into the air. "Team Underdogs!"

I cupped my ear to encourage them, and my crowd thundered, "Team Underdogs!"

The princes started, stared at me, then darted their puzzled glances at the divided crowds. The right side of the crowd booed against the left side that now stomped the ground while chanting, "Team Underdogs!"

The two sides were ready to come to blows with their fists and magic.

"Hear us roar! Don't forget to add the hashtags, peeps!" I shouted with my crowd, kicking the desk hard in a tap dance to add some spice.

"Silence! Stop this madness now!" Headmistress Ethel shrieked, her power lashing out and beating the masses to silence.

I smirked at her with an innocent expression. "Are you against FOS, freedom of speech, Headmistress Ethel?"

"You shall be expelled for causing a disturbance!" Headmistress Ethel called.

"Expel Barbie," Killian said lazily, "and I'll just pardon her and take her out of the pool of the Brides Selection."

"Unacceptable!" Silas barked. "It's not for you to say who can stay out of the Brides Selection."

Louis narrowed his eyes at Killian. "Every eligible female should be included in the Brides Selection."

"You won't get our votes," Rowan said, "and it'll be your one vote against our four, Killian."

They didn't want Killian to have exclusive rights to me.

Headmistress Ethel darted her glances between the princes. "Then let Barbie concede her defeat and beg the forgiveness of Princess Medea."

"I can't surrender, though, ma'am," I said. "It's against the order of nature, since I'm a lot stronger than Princess Medea. The strong rule the weak; this is the foundation of our society, isn't it?"

"How dare you?" Headmistress Ethel scolded. "Not in a million years can you be stronger than a royal!"

"You aren't happy that I'm still standing tall instead of collapsing like Princess Medea's other victims after being bitten by her snakes," I pointed out. "You're worried since you don't know what to do with me, aren't you, Head-mistress Ethel? So you keep barking, but you're barking up the wrong tree."

The princes chuckled, settling in to watch the show.

"Watch your mouth, or I'll send you packing!" Head-mistress Ethel snapped.

"Barbie is absolutely right about being superior to Medea," Silas said, still supporting me. "Nobody strong shall surrender to the weak."

"It's common knowledge that Medusa's power runs in Princess Medea's veins," Rowan chimed in, "but even Medusa's poison couldn't subdue Barbie."

Medea flashed a vile smile at me, not concerned about my claws that had beheaded a group of her snakes. I'd retracted them as soon as I spotted the princes heading my way. Now an unnerving confidence glinted in the princess's eyes, as if she knew she could still bring me down, as if she had an ace that no one had discovered up her sleeve.

"A rat thinks she can usurp me," she sneered, and lunged at me.

I acted too, no longer concerned about revealing my strength and top speed in front of everyone. It was time for me to step up and make a statement for all the underdogs in front of the top dogs. It was time to make a difference in Mist of Cinder.

I punched Medea straight in the face, shattering her cheekbone before she could get to me. The sickening crack fell on the silent hall.

Medea yowled in pain and stumbled back, and I pursued her mercilessly, driving my fist into her neck in a flash. Another kick, and she tumbled and fell onto the desk.

With her venom flowing in my veins, I could still take her down in one bout.

That was my fucking message.

"What is Barbie?" I heard whispers rise across the hall.

"I'm one of you!" I roared, my foot on Medea's chest, my fists on my hips. "I'm an underdog like you!"

20

Barbie

"Stop the freak show!" Ethel screamed at me.

I made a show of cupping my ear and smiling at her. "What did you just say, Headmistress Ethel? I can't hear you over the cheers. You need to roar!"

And I threw my head back and howled.

Headmistress Ethel's eyes spat cold fire, but all the princes laughed, heat in their eyes that made my heart flutter.

I had no title or land, but I had enough power.

And power called to power. That was why the heirs all responded to me.

A hint of a smile ghosted Killian's handsome face. He hadn't stopped me from going after Medea. I could see that he was pleased and relieved that I'd brushed off the effects of her snake bites. I could also feel his radiating pride, which made my body hum and heat for him.

My crowd howled with me.

"Have your last laugh, you whore!" Medea shouted as she pulled a chainlock from around her neck, revealing a metal lock at the end of the silver chains.

Shit! Shit!

It was forged from the same dark material as the torque that had bound my power. Someone who knew a lot about me was using Medea as a pawn to get to me again.

Digging deep into my genetic knowledge and memories, I recalled my father's saying. He'd mentioned that only rare metals forged in both Heaven and Hell could counter or lessen our powers. He'd also warned me of the celestial beings from other realms, our ancient foes.

Rumor had it that Queen Lilith came from the fallen stars. Could she be behind all this?

I stared down at the chainlock in Medea's hand, chills slithering up my spine in waves. Medea flung the chains toward my ankle, faster than a dark flash.

Run, Barbie! You can't let it touch you! Pucker screamed. *It'll enslave you!*

He went solid and flung himself in front of me to shield me. The chain cut him in half. He howled in pain.

"Pucker!" I screamed, pouring my energy into him to sustain him just before he faded out.

Everything happened so fast.

My heart rammed into my ribcage; cold sweat dampened my armpits. I was afraid of losing my ghost familiar. I wasn't sure if he could hang on to me and this realm as a ghost after he'd taken the blow that was meant for me.

Shouting broke out everywhere.

Killian and the other prince tossed their powers at Medea to stop her from getting to me. They'd all felt the foul magic from the chainlock, a weapon meant to harm a god.

"Medea, back off!" Killian roared.

Medea cast the chainlock at me again. Something rumbled in me and surged out before I could react. I registered a second later that it was my core power, the power that had slumbered in the vast void, bound by Ruin's commands and his ancient spell. I'd tried to access it for a decade and failed, but now it roared to life and unfurled all on its own before I could control it.

It had felt the ultimate threat and wouldn't allow any weapon to unmake me.

The darkest flame, hotter than hellfire, hotter than heavenly flame, alighted on the chainlock, burning through every metal link. Medea's eyes widened for a flicker. Her mouth opened, yet no sound could come out.

The darkest flame shot toward the princess of the House of Chaos, engulfing her and consuming her. A blink, and the flame vanished without a trace, as if it had never appeared, as if it hadn't blasted out of me and incinerated a descendant of Medusa in a heartbeat.

I searched inwardly for the dark flame, but all I could feel was a dull ache and vast emptiness. And I was bone tired.

Sy ran her tongue over her fangs, stunned and speechless as well.

I stared ahead. Where Medea had been, nothing was left. Not even a mote of dust. My dark flame had erased her completely, as if she had never existed. The only evidence was a few inches of the chains that hadn't been melted, courtesy of my power. It wanted to leave a reminder to warn everyone else.

The hall sank into shocked, horrified silence until Bellona wailed like she was having hiccups.

"Murderer!" Headmistress Ethel's shriek was unbearably

piercing. "Barbie murdered Princess Medea cold-bloodedly in front of everyone! Arrest her!"

The academy sentinels moved forward to seize me, but Killian's power of darkness had already lashed out, hauling them away from me. His lightning followed, flashing across the wall of darkness to create an unbreakable barrier between Headmistress Ethel and her sentinels. Anyone who dared cross it to get to me would risk being electrocuted.

I hadn't noticed when the druid appeared. He now stood by Headmistress Ethel, his hooded, dark eyes fixating on me. I hadn't met anyone creepier than him, though my father was a lot scarier.

"No one touches a member of my house," Killian drawled lethally.

"Princess Medea was a member of your house too, Prince Killian, in case you've forgotten," Headmistress Ethel said icily, her voice trembling with rage and fear. "Despite your fondness toward that girl, she'll be hanged for her atrocious crime!"

The hall rioted. The princes were shouting, and everyone else was telling their versions of the unfortunate, terrible incident.

My mind went numb. Blood drained from my face.

All I could think was that my dormant core power had shown up at the worst time. But if it hadn't, that chainlock might've damaged me irrevocably.

I bet that Medea hadn't planned to use it on me in public, but she couldn't stomach being defeated by me in front of everyone. She couldn't bear to see Killian watch her being humiliated.

"This is a house affair, and I'm taking Barbie back to the house," Killian said, his power drowning out the shouts in the hall.

"This is no longer a house affair when a royal bride candidate was murdered!" Headmistress Ethel countered. "You aren't above the law of Mist of Cinder, Prince Killian. Even you can't harbor a murderer without suffering the consequences!"

"Whom are you pointing fingers at as a murderer, Lady Ethel?" Killian sneered. "That's a severe and irresponsible accusation!" He gestured at the other heirs and my geek friends. "Let's hear what others saw."

"Everyone saw Barbie burn Princess Medea to death!" Headmistress Ethel hissed, then, as if remembering something, she stepped back a couple of paces to put more distance between her and me.

I could see apprehension coating many supernaturals' eyes. They feared me now, as if I was an abomination. Well, I was afraid of my own powers too, considering that I couldn't control this dark flame.

"You saw what you wanted to see, Lady Ethel," Rowan said in his deep and firm voice. "Barbie didn't kill Princess Medea, though it was no doubt a tragedy that Princess Medea perished under such befuddling and suspicious circumstances. Of course, we need to investigate this incident and get to the bottom of it, but we shall not make any rash conclusions or accusations without solid and uncontested evidence."

"Are you defending a true murderer?" Headmistress Ethel called in dismay. "Has Barbie gotten to you too, Prince Rowan? What kind of spells did she put on you?"

"It's funny you mention spells, Lady Ethel," Cade chimed in. "We all know Barbie is an Echo. She doesn't have her own magic. She can only cancel out others' elemental magic and neutralize spells. So, I have to agree with Prince Killian that Barbie didn't burn Princess Medea."

"Then where did that black flame come from?" Headmistress Ethel demanded in a sharp tone that she usually didn't use with the heirs. "Princess Medea didn't carry that kind of unholy fire magic. And we've never tested Barbie's power. She hasn't even registered!"

"Though that girl is an unknown, she's dangerous," the druid claimed. "We must dissect her power and see what she's capable of. The headmistress and I will take measures and test her to decide if that fire that's even more powerful than hellfire was generated by her or not. She'll have to answer for her horrible crime if she conjured that unholy fire. Ever since she came, she's caused unrest in Shades Academy. The realm is no longer safe because of her. It's time you all detach from her, heirs of the five houses. This girl is full of dark deceptions while she bats her two-toned eyes and shows you her innocent, pretty face."

Fear and rage lit my eyes.

The druid sounded so convincing. My unholy flame should've burned him and his crystal balls.

"Take down the barrier, Prince Killian," Headmistress Ethel ordered him. "We need to take Barbie into our custody. But I promise you that we'll give her a fair trial for the murder. I'll see to it in person."

Evil delight flashed in the druid's eyes as he and his mistress prepared to take me away. When he laid his hands on me, I'd burn him. But if he was behind the kidnapping, he'd have a device to bind my power, and he could do whatever he wanted with me.

I shuddered at my fate, as I could tell that he didn't even seem too concerned about my dark flame.

"You forget yourself, druid. Over my dead body will I allow you to take Barbie from this spot, from my house," Killian said without an ounce of emotion before he turned to the other princes. "Will you be with me on this, brothers, or should I stand alone when it comes to protecting an innocent, vulnerable member of my house?"

Silas looked at me, his amber eyes glowing. "I'll stand with you for Barbie!"

"I will too," Rowan said. "Innocent until proven guilty. Barbie can be a pain in the butt, but she's no murderer. She doesn't have it in her."

Sy peeked out at the fae prince in approval and lust. *But we have it in us! Too bad I can't eat her.*

Louis sidled up to Killian's left side. "This is a house affair! No one shall take Barbie except Prince Killian, though all the heirs shall supervise the investigation to get to the truth."

All the princes posed to defend me, their magic ready at their fingertips.

"Wait a second!" Headmistress Ethel called in outrage. "This can't be happening!"

"You want an excuse to get your hands on Barbie by framing her as a murderer?" The chaos prince cocked his head, his storm-blue eyes turning to merciless sapphire, a predator dragon peeking out. "I'll give you the true murderer. Look at that chain, or what's left of it, which Medea deployed to try to kill Barbie."

"Fuck me!" Cade said, inching closer to inspect the chain and sucking in a breath. "It's not an ordinary chain-lock but a forbidden, dark artifact, the same make as the torque the kidnappers used on Barbie."

Finally! I'd been waiting for the princes to catch up, since anything coming out of my mouth would be discredited under the circumstances, as Ethel and her druid were hellbent on crushing me.

Louis snarled, his white fangs showing. "Princess Medea

must've been working with the kidnappers from Crimson-Tide all this time!"

Cade nodded grimly. "This artifact is beyond her power. She had no idea what she was playing with. One doesn't play with fire they don't understand and have no control of and expect to get the fuck away with it. When she tried to take out Barbie with the chainlock, she ended up setting fire to herself."

The mage prince produced a satchel and flicked his wand. The remaining chains rose from the desk and clanked into the satchel. The mage grabbed the satchel and turned to Killian with a look of challenge. "I'll take the evidence of the crime to my house for further examination."

Killian shrugged. "I can send that torque and the iron mask to your house so your mages can compare notes."

"You will?" Cade asked.

"Of course, brother," Killian said.

Cade's face lit up. He seemed to be the kindest of the heirs, yet he was also merciless to the bone.

Medea's death hadn't shaken any of them.

"For all we know," Headmistress Ethel said, her face white with anger, "the kidnapping could be one of Barbie's own machinations!"

Killian snapped his head at her, his smile so chilling that the headmistress stepped back, her lips quivering.

"Are you also accusing us heirs of conspiring on staging the rescue as well?" Silas snarled, his amber eyes glowing menacingly.

"What I meant is—" Headmistress Ethel stammered.

"Everyone knows Medea, the fucking traitor, is your star pupil!" Killian snarled. "Was she under your influence or instructions to harm Barbie, Lady Ethel?"

"You're out of line, Prince Killian!" Headmistress Ethel's

eyes widened in fury and fear. "I won't put up with this! I shall bring this matter to the kings and the Council."

"Run back to them as their puppet," Killian said coldly. "Even they can't protect you. If you're the mastermind behind Barbie's kidnapping and torture, I'll tear your throat out!"

I blinked. Killian had openly declared war on the headmistress and her organization for me.

"I can assure you that I had nothing to do with Barbie's abduction," Headmistress Ethel retorted. "And you, my dear prince, will have your father to worry about. King Vasiliy and his beloved new queen won't take kindly to their daughter being brutally murdered in broad daylight."

Chilling dread twirled in my middle. If the kings and the Council came after me, the princes wouldn't be able to protect me. And I wouldn't want to put them in the spot of being at odds with their sovereign parents.

I needed to have a plan B.

I bit my lip. I'd started this underdog campaign, but eventually I would let down all the underdogs by fleeing, and they'd be in a worse state than they'd been because of me.

I surveyed the hall and looked over my shoulder at Bea and our geek friends. They nodded at me with respect and support in their eyes. They had faith in me. While warmth swam in my chest, icy dread also squeezed my heart with its claws. The last thing I wanted was to drag them down with me.

Every action bore consequences.

"Stepdaughter to my king father," Killian said. "And if Medea had lived, she'd beg for death."

He turned to the princes, nodding his thanks, before he called, "Rock, escort Barbie back to the House of Chaos."

The air rippled, then Rock and the team suddenly appeared and rounded the desk where I stood. Rock held out a hand toward me. I nodded my thanks at him and slid off the desk by myself, lithe as a cat.

Instantly, the warriors from the House of Chaos formed protective ranks around me. I let them. I needed this protection, not for my sake but for everyone else's. I was spent and jumpy and hungry. If anyone attacked me now, I might lose control and drain the realm's magic to fill my depleted well, if my dark flame didn't kill indiscriminately first.

Killian strode toward the exit with all four princes by his side. They might be rivals, but they always presented a united front when any outside force went after one of them.

I trailed behind them, lowering my head and trembling inside. The chaos warriors walked with me, forming a wall around me.

Right before I stepped out of Clockwork, roars rose behind me. "Team Underdogs! Team Barbie!"

Tears brimmed in my eyes, and the fear in me lessened.

They'd risen now, even without me.

Tits up! Sy reminded me. *Let's show some manners.*

21

Barbie

Killian's shoulders relaxed as soon as he got me into the steel-and-glass building of the House of Chaos.

He ordered Rock to stand guard outside my door. "No one goes into her room, and make sure Barbie stays in."

I swallowed my usual line of, "But I didn't do anything wrong," and instead asked sheepishly, "So I'm under house arrest, high sir?"

"Hole up in your room until shit calms down," he said. "Boredom won't kill you, but many beings outside our house will want your head. I need to meet up with the other heirs to hash things out."

"Shouldn't I attend as well," I asked, "since it concerns my fate? Also, I'm good at brainstorming. I assure you that I always come up with bright ideas."

"Do you?" He snorted, yet heat flashed in his eyes. "As

much as I admire your spirit, you've had quite a day. You can barely stand up straight."

I straightened my back and snapped to attention while looking at him head-on.

A faint smile ghosted his carnal lips. "Stay out of trouble for two seconds while I'm not around. That's all I'm asking."

Cami watched us silently, but Rock chuckled. "Asking Barbie to stay out of trouble is like asking a scorpion not to sting anyone."

I scowled at him.

"Then it's your job to make sure that little scorpion doesn't sting anyone," Killian said coolly. His gaze fell on me again, alighting on my lips. I remembered the delicious feel when he'd kissed me last time. I wondered if I would get another kiss. "Promise me you'll stay put in your room, Barbie."

I nodded.

I wouldn't break the promise, but Sy would. She'd need to feed soon after what we'd gone through. She was more than anxious to see Rowan, to fuck him.

"I need to hear you say it before I leave," Killian demanded.

"But sir, I need to find Pucker first," I said. "It's an emergency! I need to make sure he's okay."

"I'll find him later," Killian said.

"No, sir," I said. "He's in bad shape after he took that blow for me. He saved me. I won't rest until I find him!"

"He's a ghost," Cami chimed in. "What's the worst that could happen to him?"

I furrowed my brow in worry. "His existence could be erased. His soul could be erased."

A look of horror passed over Cami's face. "Who has the power to do that?"

I, my father, and probably the one who forged the torque and the chainlock in Heaven and Hell could harm Pucker beyond salvaging, but I didn't tell her that.

"Find him then and get him settled in your room until I come back," Killian said. "Don't do anything stupid."

"I won't." I gazed up at him and said with feeling, "Thank you, sir."

He didn't need to stand up for me and defend me. It'd be so much easier to just give me up. I'd made his life a lot more difficult ever since I got into his house.

I remembered every kindness in my heart, and Killian was more than kind to me. He was my protector.

Does that mean that you've totally forgiven him for showing your perky tits in front of everyone in the ice rink? Sy asked hopefully.

"Help her find that ghost guardian," Killian told Rock. "And have someone bring food to her room."

The chaos prince sent me another lingering look before he departed, as if he couldn't bear to leave me, as if he wanted to pull me into his arms to make sure I'd stay safe.

I swallowed, my eyes full of feelings.

Shit, it felt good to have someone worry about you, even though that someone was overbearing.

I FOLLOWED THE FAINT, familiar bond that flickered on and off and found Pucker cowered in the corner of the basement boiler room, as if he needed all the fires to warm him up.

My heart ached as I saw that even in his ghost shape, he was deformed. He'd gone solid to throw himself in front of me to save me, which nearly erased his essence. And now he was trying to piece the two parts of himself together to no avail.

"Wait for me outside, please," I told Rock, who had followed me into the basement.

"I can't leave you alone here," Rock said. "His Highness's orders."

"You're welcome to do a security sweep, then you must step out. Guardian Pucker is here. I need to help him, or he'll fade."

Rock frowned.

"You can't see him," I said. "But you saw him go solid to take the blow from Medea that was meant for me. When he's in his phantom form, only Prince Killian and I can see him. Trust me, please. I need to help him." I fought back a sob. "He's suffering."

Rock hesitated for a second and stepped out.

Pucker turned to me, trembling.

I rushed to him, crouching by him and hugging the two severed parts of him to me. My goddess energy pulsed into him, infusing into his soul until his two parts meshed and he became complete again.

"Mistress," Pucker sighed, coming back to himself.

"Just Barbie," I said. "You always called me Barbie."

"You came for me."

"Of course," I said. "Even if you didn't save me, I'd still come for you. I'd come for you even if you stayed an identity thief and a bad actor."

He smiled. "I didn't take you for the sentimental type."

"Yet you threw yourself in front of me to shield me. You were nearly erased by that nasty blow."

"It was very nasty," he agreed before he shrugged. "I'm a dead man, but you've just started."

"Dead or living, I don't want you gone," I said, offering my wrist. "Take a few more sips. You've earned it."

"Nay," he said, standing up. "I'm going to drink from everyone else in the house. You need to keep your energy, as you're depleted."

And then he was gone.

When I came out of the boiler room, Rock was rubbing his forearm, which had goosebumps all over. With his superior werewolf hearing, Rock had heard the conversation between Pucker and me. He darted his gaze left and right to detect the presence of the ghost guardian, wondering if Pucker was sucking his energy at the moment, since he was the closest target.

"You look ashen," Rock said with a frown. "How much did he take from you?"

"Minimum. I'm fine."

"You should've let him take some from me," Rock said. "I don't like it, but in this case, I'd allow it."

"Only Sir Killian and I could put him together after he was almost—" I shook my head as fear of losing Pucker coursed through me. I'd have a word with him and warn him not to sacrifice himself again.

"Take it easy, Rock." I smirked. "Pucker will go to you tonight after you fall asleep, since you've volunteered to offer him a drink."

His bronze face paled. "Didn't he already drink from you?"

"The more, the merrier! Guardian Pucker is as insatiable as Guardian Lady Magenta. Guardian Pucker never asks when he saps energy from any of you in the house. He's only polite to me, and of course he learned to stay away from Sir Killian unless he has permission to approach him."

Rock growled. "No wonder sometimes I felt exhausted even when I was fully rested."

I nodded. "You're one of his favorites, since you're more powerful than others. Both guardians can get a good, satisfying boost from sipping your energy juice."

Now that Pucker was fine, I felt lighter inside, even though more trouble would be waiting for me, brewing on the horizon even as I spoke.

One step at a time.

Sy preened. *Next step is for me to see my sugar Rowan.*

Next step is to have food, then nap for an hour or two. Killian will want to interrogate me when he returns.

He'll go easy on you. He always does, Sy said with a yawn, and went to sleep.

Rock cursed. "Tell them to stay away from me!"

"I don't like to tell other people what to do, you know," I said, then over his glare, I added, "Don't you worry, Rock. You won't feel a thing other than tired after Pucker takes a swig of your energy. It's similar to donating blood to Prince Louis. Only that Pucker is like a spiritual vampire. Ghosts need to suck energy to stay sane and positive. You know what I mean? Pucker has many flaws, and he's morally gray, but he isn't too bad compared to many other vicious beings."

Rock shook his head in disgust. "This can't continue in the house! I'll have to bring the issue to the prince. We must put a stop to it!"

"Well, you should scratch that idea," I said. "Or the ghost guardian will visit you more often when you fall asleep at night."

"Hello, werewolf." Pucker materialized between us on the staircase, grinning. He looked much better now, even younger. "Talking about me?"

"Fuck!" Rock jumped.

Pucker flickered back to his phantom form and followed me back to my room.

I sprang toward the table, where plates of food threatened to weigh it down. Pucker threw the door shut in Rock's face.

"Maybe you should go listen to Killian and the princes in their meeting," I suggested, "now that you're energized."

"Prince Killian can see me," he said.

"You can hide in the wall."

"There's no hiding from him," he complained. "He can sense me anywhere. The last thing I want is to spy on him. I don't want to get on his bad side. You don't even know how ruthless he is. And I'm still traumatized from being sliced in two!"

He was still worried about me, so he wanted to stay close to me.

"Fine, stay," I said.

"That's stress eating, Barbie," Pucker commented, watching me devour the food.

It was more than that. I had this endless void in me. I consumed as much food as I could and let Sy feed her way, so we wouldn't turn into the eater of the world like my father.

"You shouldn't feel guilty," Pucker continued, as he could feel a wave of renewed anxiety lapping at me. "She'd have killed you without an ounce of remorse. Medea had been seeking every opportunity to get rid of you. If she had lived, I bet all my money that she'd murder you in the arena as soon as the first bride trial started."

"You don't have any money," I said, biting into an egg and cheese burrito.

What's wrong with you? Sy chimed in, jerking awake

from her nap. *When was it an issue, especially if it was to kill or to be killed?*

"I was caught off guard," I said, going for an onion soup cooked by Killian's personal chef. I was familiar with the taste since I'd raided his private kitchen a couple of times. "I didn't mean to kill her. I didn't expect her to just go up in flames."

"Would you feel better if you decapitated her instead?" Pucker asked.

You'd feel better beheading her first, then setting her on fire. Sy nodded her understanding.

These two didn't have a single empathetic bone in them. I might not have had empathy before I came to Mist of Cinder, but ever since I'd taken the role of its protector in secret, I didn't like to take a life in this realm unless it was absolutely necessary.

"There'll be hell to pay for killing a royal," I said, musing.

"Prince Killian will protect you," Pucker said.

"I've brought him enough shit," I said, my appetite gone. "The king and queen will come after me, and there's nothing he can do. They outrank him. The queen will want my head since I killed her daughter. The Council will back up Head-mistress Ethel and the druid. Killian can't fight on all sides."

"He isn't alone. All the princes will fight for you," Pucker said. "We all saw how they defended you against that old bitch Ethel and the evil druid."

"In the end, they'll cave when all the kings and queens condemn me." I sighed. "And I don't want to put the princes at odds with their parents because of me. I've caused enough problems. I want to be a blessing instead of a curse for a change."

"You need to think of the big picture, Barbie," Pucker said softly. "In the end, who'll be able to defend this realm?"

My heart skipped a beat. Had he figured it out? I couldn't hide all my secrets from him, since he was my familiar, even though I hadn't told him a thing about Ruin.

Everyone saw the darkest flame, Pucker said. *But we can't let anyone know that it came from you until one day you can reveal your true power. Now everyone is only speculating on the flame. Killian insisted that it was generated from the dark magic in the chainlock, and then it incinerated Princess Medea who activated it. It's good that no one understands your power and they all think you're an Echo. We need to keep it that way.*

I swallowed hard. *That's what I am afraid of, my own power. I lost control. I couldn't contain it. I didn't even understand it, as it just came roaring out and burned people. It was supposed to be my ace in the hole, but if I can't harness and leash it, what good is it to me?*

Can you feel it now? Pucker asked. *Let's practice. Hold a drop of it and lift it slowly.*

I peeked inside, and the abyss stared back.

We'll practice in Underhill, Pucker said. *You must tame it if you want to survive the giant shitstorm that will eventually roll our way.*

I nodded. My ghost familiar had thrown all he had in with me, and it was time for me to truly trust him.

So I told the ghost guardian about my father, the God of Ruin, the eater of the world, and that he was coming.

22

Barbie

Killian had been summoned to the court of the Kingdom of Chaos. He'd have to face his king father, his queen stepmother, and the Council for questions on my duel with Princess Medea that ended up with her being burned to nothingness.

He wouldn't have to deal with this shit if he hadn't shielded me. He could still wash his hands of me by offering me up and letting me be hanged.

Everyone had seen the livestream of the duel before it had been banned and taken down from Spinchat, the supernaturals' main social media site.

Killian left his entire team to guard me, except for Cassius, the Silent Blade. I'd met him once. Cassius had been Killian's personal bodyguard since his childhood. He went where Killian went, like his shadow.

Cami had offered to go with her cousin, but Killian

needed her to stay as the mistress of the House of Chaos while he was away.

"Anyone comes to take Barbie from our house by force, kill them," Killian had told Cami and Rock before his departure. "You have my killing order. I'll be back as soon as I can."

I'd bitten my lip, vowing that it wouldn't come to that. I wouldn't let the House of Chaos go to war with the entire realm for my sake. I would flee before the conflict could escalate out of control.

Out of sight, out of mind.

If I took myself out of the equation, no one else would get hurt.

An hour after Killian left, Cami came to knock on my door. When I opened it, she slid in and shut the door behind her. Then she opened a fist, revealing a small pink diamond on her palm.

"Prince Rowan wanted to give you this in person," she said. "But Killian said clearly that no outsiders are allowed before he returns. Prince Rowan said this would be payment for ten messages and asked you to check his urgent messages in your Spinchat inbox."

My face stretched into a big smile as I snatched the diamond from her palm. "Tell him it'll be payment for six text messages."

Rowan was loaded. Who didn't like to take advantage of the rich and privileged?

Cami narrowed her eyes. "You forget yourself, Barbie."

"Pardon me," I said. My smile didn't drop. "I'll remember myself next time, My Lady Cami."

"Don't My Lady me," she said.

Sy peeked out to inspect the diamond. She'd asked me a hundred times if Rowan had messaged me.

I guess he really wants to get laid, I said. *I'll message him in a minute and tell him tonight is on!*

Sy beamed at me. *You're the best pimp, Barbie!*

You're welcome. I grinned, my mood improving dramatically. *We won't do it for free anymore. Live and learn!*

Live and learn, Sy cheered.

Cami stared at me with open suspicion.

"I'm giving Sir Rowan private lessons via text message, Lady Cami," I lied.

"About what?" she demanded.

"Uh, well," I said. If I fended her off, she'd keep coming back or even get Killian involved. Rowan must be really desperate to see Sy to ask Cami to bring me the diamond. Desperation drove people to do stupid things, and I bet Rowan was lovesick. "Everyone knows about my knack of neutralizing spells, and the fae prince wants to study my ability."

She narrowed her eyes further. "Are you trying to con a prince heir?"

"Shush, Lady Cami!" I said, darting my eyes around wildly, even though it was only her and me, plus Pucker in his ghost form, in the room. "I don't have a trust fund, unlike you, and a girl has to eat. I don't have any other gifts except that no spells work on me. If Sir Rowan finds it in his generous heart to offer me a small fortune to study my gift and satisfy his academic curiosity, I'm not going to turn him away."

"I can smell your lie a mile away." Cami snorted.

"Fine, I'll come clean." I spread my arms. "He pays me to be his pimp, and he has a type."

"I don't get what the princes see in you." She shook her head. "Personally, talking to you is like talking to the wall most of the time." She gave me a wary look. "Just be careful when it comes to the princes. They're charming, but they're top predators." She paused for a beat. "You can trust only my cousin."

She'd softened a lot toward me after she saw Killian kiss me and observed that I could withstand his lethal touch just fine.

We didn't hit it off, but I liked her.

I smiled. "But I'm not sure if I can trust Sir Killian either. Men are fickle, and I was born with trust issues, Lady Cami."

"Just tread carefully, especially in front of Queen Lilith. She'll arrive at Shades Academy anytime now."

She didn't say "Killian's betrothed" this time, probably for my ears, but the mention of the Queen of the Underworld instantly sent me into a foul mood. Even the diamond in my hand didn't cheer me up as much. Cami turned on her heels, made a beeline out of my room, and closed the door behind her.

Pucker eyed the diamond on my palm in approval. I strode toward the closet and put it in a shoebox. There were a few more pieces of jewelry inside. Either the house had given them to me, or Pucker had stolen them for me.

After the servants came and removed all the empty dishes from my room, I put the privacy sign on the outside doorknob.

In the drawing room, Rock and his team were playing cards while staying guard. They were eavesdropping but pretended otherwise. Now they narrowed their eyes at me. To them, "privacy" from their charge was a dirty word.

"Gents," I said. "I'm calling it a night."

"You okay, right, Barbie?" Rock asked.

I whistled at him. "Yeah. Why shouldn't I be?"

The warriors shook their heads. Well, they thought I'd

still be shaken like a little leaf. I'd done that, though, and now I was over it, and Sy needed to go.

You're up, Pucker, I told my familiar.

He would distract the warriors for a few hours and keep them at bay so they wouldn't come knocking on my door and find that I was gone.

Pucker cracked his neck before he went solid and materialized by the card table. Everyone jumped out of their chairs, shouting in alarm, their weapons drawn. Cami flung her magic, but it passed through Pucker like a bubble.

"Hello, girls and boys." Pucker grinned evilly. "Don't be rude. I'm Guardian Pucker, and I'm more than happy to show you a trick or two on the card table."

23

Sy

I jogged toward my lover, swaying my hips.

The fae prince leaned against the maple tree under the moonlight, his silver eyes tracking my every move, the hunger and heat in them making my cunt wet instantly.

Get him hooked! Barbie urged. *You must do a good job, so he'll give us more diamonds.*

I hissed at her, silencing her. I couldn't get rid of my third wheel, since we shared the space, but I did not need her constant negative comments.

And now I was just hungrier, so I gave up my swaying and sprang toward Rowan.

I didn't run into his arms but leapt over seven feet to get to him. Surprise flitted by his eyes, but he caught me with strong hands, and I clamped my legs around his waist. If he were a human male, I'd have driven him to the ground. But Rowan stood firm, gripping my butt cheeks possessively.

I rubbed my cunt against his front, soaking his pants, for all I cared.

Without exchanging pleasantries, he slanted his mouth over mine. I parted my lips and thrust my tongue into his open mouth.

I might not be a proper lady by society's standards, but I liked to let my man know what I wanted so he'd deliver the way I wanted. No need for subtlety. I was here for a fuck, not to play games.

Our tongues tangled in a mating dance, primal lust boiling in me. While I kissed him back hard, I slid my fingers into his trousers, going for his huge erection, pumping its hard length up and down before pulling it out of his trousers and freeing it.

Rowan didn't miss a beat. He growled in pleasure at my touch and lifted me to position my entrance against his crown. One powerful thrust, and he was sheathed deeply within me.

I could tell that he'd missed me just as much as I had him. He thrust into me hard and fast without giving me a second to adjust to his massive shaft, venting his pent-up lust and rage. But I liked it. I could take anything he threw at me, and I loved rage fucking.

I shoved my hands into his shirt, raking my fingernails across his muscled back. He hissed in approval. The princes all liked a little pain mixed with their pleasure. At least, I knew three princes were like that.

My heavy breasts bounced up and down as Rowan pushed me to ride his cock. I moaned against his lips, starting to feed.

Barbie sat in a corner, smiling and thinking about

diamonds while taking the potent sexual energy Rowan and I created into herself without doing any of the hard work.

"Like me fucking you, little monster?" Rowan broke our kiss and growled. Lust twisted his handsome face. "Missed my cock, didn't you?"

Tell him yes! Barbie turned to us. *And ride him faster, Sy! He likes you wild. Try a different angle. Make him more excited and get him to come asap. We need to harvest more juice.*

Shut up! I spat at her.

I didn't want my lover to come so fast. No woman liked a man with a reputation as a three-second wonder.

"I want your cock all the time, my sugar Rowan," I offered. "After you make me come hard thrice, I'll give you a blowjob."

"You will, my little monster?" he asked, thrusting into my molten core vehemently.

I smirked at him and lied easily. "I'm the queen of blowjobs."

Barbie rolled her eyes. *That's a terrible title.*

Rowan hissed, "You'll give no one blowjobs but me!"

"Possessive, aren't you, sugar?" I purred.

"You're my woman," he said.

Barbie peeked out. *Good, he's hooked!*

I met his brutal thrusts beat by beat. We fucked like two beasts.

Underhill has a place for you, Barbie said. *I don't want anyone to see you two fuck without shame. We talked about safe sex, remember?*

Safe sex means condoms. I corrected her. *Supernaturals don't catch STDs, except for witches. You should worry about your friend Bea.*

"Let's go inside Underhill, princeling," I said.

"Like last time?" he asked.

"Like last time, sugar."

"Underhill likes you too."

He didn't know it was because of Barbie's connection. The wild magic loved *her*. Underhill had been lonely for so long, and finally, it had met another pure magical being.

To my delight, Rowan delivered three more long thrusts before he carried me into the forest, putting a shield around me, and our bodies remained locked together.

In front of us, at its inner border, Underhill had erected a small cabin, with vines and flowers draped over the wooden walls.

My eyes widened before my face stretched into an appreciative smile. Underhill had made us a lovers' lodge.

More like a whorehouse, Barbie barked. *So don't get too comfortable. When it's time to go, you'll need to leave.*

I grinned wider. *You whore me out for diamonds now, don't you, little pimp?*

I was only glad that Rowan couldn't hear the internal chats between Barbie and me. He'd freak out even more if he knew Barbie and I cohabited, like two peas in a pod.

Rowan let out a whistle as he saw a flower bed well-placed in the middle of the cabin under a mirrored ceiling so we could watch ourselves while we fucked.

"Thanks," the fae prince said to Underhill, and kicked the door shut.

Now that Underhill and I have provided a good working place for you, Barbie chirped, *get to it. Do a quickie. I need to glean more energy. And tell your lover boy if he brings bigger diamonds next time, Underhill and I will make the whorehouse even nicer.*

She hadn't done a damn thing for Rowan and me. She just got Underhill to do all the work while she reaped the reward—diamonds. But then, I got something out of it too—

I got hot sex! There was nothing in this world better than fucking. I'd take getting fucked by Rowan over diamonds any second of the day. What could diamonds do for me?

"Now that I've impressed you by getting us a nice cabin, my sugar Rowan," I purred, taking credit as well, "it's time you serve me and make me come. Will you make me come hard?"

"Is this a role play?" he asked as he laid me down and followed me to the flower bed, thrusting into my depths.

I watched his gorgeous buttocks flex in the ceiling mirror in fascination as he heaved up and down, plunging into me over and over. Then I lifted my head to stare at his cock driving deep into me. My cunt gloved him tightly. He was made for me!

He groaned. "So wet, little monster! Your juice coats my length."

The wet sound of flesh slapping flesh echoed erotically off the walls of the cabin. I clamped my legs around the small of his back, feeling his hard muscles rippling beneath as he fucked me vehemently.

I moaned loudly as his thrusts became more powerful and brutal, pouring his energy into me. Barbie lunged to take it into herself while fanning her face.

I moved on top of Rowan, riding his length. I rocked my hips, although I barely had any room to maneuver since his cock stretched my tight passage to the limit. Yet I managed to heave up and down, swirl, and slam into his base.

I fucked my man with abandon. Rowan rolled his eyes back in ecstasy, cupping my bouncing breasts in his large hands.

"Fuck me, little monster," he called, bucking his hips up to drive into my molten core.

"I *am* fucking you, sugar."

Our speed became a blur, our hard breathing mingled, and our flesh locked tightly and erotically.

This was the best coupling ever!

"Your cunt squeezes me so hard!" he growled in approval.

"Will you fuck only me?"

"Yes, little monster. I haven't fucked anyone else since I started fucking you."

His thumb brushed my swollen clit, and my legs jerked at the sensation.

His cock drove so deep within me that I gasped at the slight burning pain that mixed with the incredible pleasure. He pounded into me faster and harder amid my breathless gasps and moans.

I exploded on his cock at his next brutal thrust and roared as I came. He bellowed as he arrived a second later, pumping his bountiful seed into me.

We both fed on the potent energy we created together, and I sighed in satisfaction.

He lifted me off him, got me on all fours, and thrust into me from behind while we were both still high and riding through our climax.

I cried at the new wave of pleasure, and my claws slid out to their full length.

Rowan stilled behind me, his muscles stiffening.

Shit! Barbie cursed, and tensed, pausing her feeding.

"Barbie showed the same claws when she cut off the heads of Medea's snakes," Rowan drawled.

My heart pounded, or more likely, it was Barbie's heartbeat roaring in my ears. I was always the cool one. I understood Barbie's reason why our dual identity couldn't be discovered, though I didn't exactly agree with her. I'd longed to live my own life ever since I'd met Rowan.

But she kept saying that there wasn't anyone else like us and that we'd not only be labeled as an abomination; we'd be regarded as a threat. It wasn't just humans who feared the unknown and were known for eliminating different species. The supernaturals weren't that much different when it came to genocide.

"That's how Barbie and I became friends." I huffed a peal of laughter and slowly retracted my claws. "Do you know that girl with golden curls can not only cancel out magic but also borrow it? Do keep her secret, though, sugar. If she's harassed and harmed, you won't see me again."

I had to give Rowan something to ponder to throw him off the track. I was a pathological liar like Barbie.

Rowan pulled out of me. Just as I wondered if I'd turned him off, he flipped me over and gathered me into his lap.

"Who are you, Sy?" he asked, looking into my golden eyes. "Why weren't you enrolled in the Selection? The realm rounded up all the eligible candidates, yet you aren't in the system." He cupped my face. "Did you come from Crimson-Tide? Are you running away from someone?" He growled at that. "You can tell me. I'll protect you."

I couldn't tell him how much I craved to be able to tell him everything, to have my own life, even to be a bride candidate and rise above all the others, but my life wasn't just my own. I could only fuck him and spend brief moments with him. I wouldn't put Barbie in danger again.

"What about you, princeling?" I challenged him instead. "You don't tell me your secrets either. In fact, you don't say much when you aren't fucking me. Have I complained?"

He considered me darkly. "Then I'll tell you my most-kept secret that only my queen mother knows. Can I trust you to be discreet?"

I spread my arms, showing my fangs. "Whom am I going to tell, sugar?"

Barbie stopped thinking about diamonds and moved to the front row, pricking her ears.

"I'm not my father's son," Rowan whispered. "I'm a bastard."

My giggles dropped just as soon as they came at Rowan's serious expression.

"You're not joking," I said quietly.

"Never to you," he said.

My heart raced, and Barbie inched closer, her two-toned eyes widening. We knew what this secret meant. If it got out, Rowan would be stripped of his heir status. He'd be shunned even if his king father didn't exile him, or worse, have him killed.

He'd entrusted me with this dangerous secret that he'd never told anyone else. My chest ached and warmed. At that moment, I realized that I was falling for him, irrevocably, though I knew I shouldn't. It'd only end in disaster if I kept falling for him and grew too attached. The fight between Barbie and me last time nearly undid her.

If she died, I died too.

"I—" I gazed up at him. But I couldn't share my secret with him despite his trusting me with his. It hurt my bones to be unfair to Rowan, but it wasn't just my secret. I'd need Barbie's consent. I touched his face gently. "Your secret is safe with me, heir."

At the same time, I demanded Barbie to swear secrecy as well, and she made a sign of crossing her heart. *Will you still ask him about diamonds?* she asked sheepishly. *It's also important that we must gather wealth.*

That chick didn't have a single sensitive bone in her.

"Make me come again, my sugar Rowan," I said, rubbing my cunt against his erection.

I didn't have a lot to offer, but I could give him the best lay and let him feed.

He heaved me up, nudged his thick crown at my entrance, and plunged into me with his massive cock until it impaled me. I clasped my hands behind his neck, and we started to move together.

I threw my head back at the pleasure, moaning, my need for him burning in me.

Rowan stilled, holding me tightly against him.

A second later, a broadcast rang through the academy grounds like a tremor. The sound, though faint, reached Underhill through magic. Rowan and I caught every word with our superior hearing.

"This is the final call!" Headmistress Ethel's voice carried in the wind. "All bride candidates must go to Skyward now. The first trial of the Brides Selection will start in thirty minutes. The kings and queens of the five kingdoms and the Council have decreed it."

Skyward, the ivory tower, was the symbol of Shades Academy. It had never been opened to the public before.

"Fuck!" Rowan cursed. "This isn't a normal course of action. They were supposed to inform us heirs first, since this entire Brides Selection is to make sure one of us finds his fated mate and produces the chosen one who will bring back old magic to the realm. The Council fucking changed the rules of the game." He paused for a second. "I wonder if it has to do with Medea's death, and that all five heirs have challenged Ethel and banded together to shield Barbie. But Barbie isn't just any bride candidate.

"We've all sensed how special she is, and she might just be

the one who will change the realm for the better. Some of the old foundations are rotten. The Council hate changes and cling to power at all costs. I have a feeling that they drew Killian, the most lethal and ruthless among us, out of the academy, then they announced the start of the Brides Selection while he's deep in his kingdom fending off his queen stepmother. Fuck!"

Barbie grew agitated, fear brewing in her middle. Anxiety twirled in my middle as well. Barbie was the target! This was the reckoning that old crone Ethel had promised. All the princes had gone out of their way to protect a lowborn against a powerful princess, which had never happened before in Shades Academy or the realm. Ethel would never let the matter rest. She must've gotten through to the Council and had them back her up.

Pucker said that the Brides Selection was actually a culling. And who would Ethel and our foes want to cull the most?

Barbie, of course.

Send your prince away, Sy, Barbie said. *We need to get ready.*

We'd need to shift back, and then she'd have a quick bath in the icy lake to erase Rowan's scent, though one of my deepest wishes was that one day I could wear his scent to sleep and wake up to the memory of him fucking me nice and hard.

"I shall go," Rowan said before I could persuade him to do the same.

"Go now, my sugar," I said.

"Will you be okay?" he asked.

I beamed at him, showing him my fangs. "I'm badass."

"Will you wait for me here?" he asked.

"I'll try, but I can't promise you anything," I said.

My heart ached for him while fear lodged in my throat for Barbie.

"Thank Barbie for the cabin in Underhill when you see her, will you?" I said sultrily. "Also, she mentioned that the diamond you brought her was for six messages, not ten."

24

Barbie

Just as I crept up on the House of Chaos, dozens of students poured out of the violet building of steel and glass. I spotted Cami and Rock right away. Everyone parted to make a path for them.

"Team One-Hit Wonders, head toward Underhill!" Rock barked at the warriors who stayed behind to babysit me. Judging from the tightness on their faces, they must be mad at losing me. "Team Unhinged Copycats, search the courtyard—"

"Barbie's there!" Cami shrieked, pointing in my direction just as I was about to blend in with the other students.

I smiled at them sheepishly and waved a tentative hand.

In a second, the teams reached me.

"How did you even get out?" Rock demanded furiously.

"We shouldn't have let that guardian distract us!" Archer complained.

Pucker had zipped to me to inform me of the trial while I was bathing in the icy lake to get rid of the scent of the fae prince on Sy. It always leaked to my skin too after they fucked.

Over my dreadful look at the culling, my ghost familiar had rubbed his phantom hands in excitement. "Finally, we're going to get some action!"

"That's not important now," Cami said, grabbing my elbow. "Go change, and I won't let you out of my sight even as you undress."

All the students were heading toward Skyward in their uniforms. I was wearing my casual clothes—a long-sleeved shirt and a pair of yoga pants.

I protested, "But I'm shy!"

"Who cares?" Cami said, dragging me up the stairs. "Hurry up! We're running out of time."

"Then you should run, and I'll catch up with you later."

Cami jutted her jaw out. "Not a chance. I don't trust you!"

"Well, I don't blame you, but I don't think the Brides Selection is for me, Lady Cami," I said, slowing down before we reached the top of the stairs. "I think I should skip the trial."

"You aren't getting out of it!" Cami snapped. "They're already after you. Staying in the Brides Selection is the only way for you to stay safe and stay in our house so my cousin can protect you. Don't you know that he went to the Chaos Court that he hates for you? Now that he's away, you take orders from me. You hear me?"

"Yeah, I'm not deaf," I said. "And you're unusually loud. But I just have a bad feeling about this trial."

"Feelings come and go. And what can go wrong in the trial? Everyone's doing it. So get moving, Barbie."

Under the lady's uncompromising supervision, I changed into my uniform swiftly, and then we merged into the flow of students and headed toward the ivory tower.

THE TOWER WAS SITUATED in the middle of a river up north under a brilliant moon that lit the entire area.

Academy sentinels with stony faces lined either side of the bridge as the bride candidates crossed it in groups.

A dark feeling deepened in me.

"Where are all the guys?" I asked Cami, who strode beside me, true to her word about not letting me out of her sight.

"This is the first trial of the Brides Selection," she said. "It's for the candidates, so no males are allowed to enter Skyward, expect for the prince heirs."

"Then why do we have male students in this school?" I asked.

"They're here to study magic, like everyone else," Cami said. "Did you even pay attention to the orientation?"

"I didn't attend the orientation. I came later," I said. "But I heard Professor Longweed saying that the purpose of joining Shades Academy is for at least one of the princes to find his fated mate and produce the One to bring back the old magic, or whatever. And Pucker said all the princes have been under great pressure to perform in bed since then."

Cami gave me a chiding look. "It's not that. Magic is fading faster in the realm now, so the kings of the five kingdoms and the Council decided to move up the timetable for the Brides Selection to this year." Her brow furrowed in worry. "But no one expected the first trial to happen now. It isn't supposed—" She stopped herself. "My cousin is away.

They should've waited for him to be present to start the bride trials. Even though he's the only heir who isn't going to select a bride from the pool of candidates, he's still the heir of the House of Chaos and represents the king and chaos kingdom. Something doesn't add up." She snagged her gaze on me. "You'll stick with me the entire time, Barbie. Don't stray away from me. Got it?"

I smirked. "Got it, Lady Cami. Don't worry, or you'll go gray early."

I was touched to realize that she was worried more about me than for herself.

I thought of Princess Medea. If I hadn't burned her to nothingness, she'd be here. She'd have sneered at me and led her army to make sure that I wouldn't pass the first trial.

We walked amid the nervous and excited candidates as everyone kept moving toward the radiant ivory tower at the end of the bridge.

No one was giving me a hard time for once, as everyone was worried about their own fate. Either they passed the first trial and moved on to the next, or they were out of the race.

And none of us knew what to expect.

Magic grew stronger as we approached the tower. It smelled like aged wine and cold autumn rain and bore the signature of all sorts of species in Mist of Cinder. It was quite different to the wild magic in Underhill.

The magic here sensed me right away.

As I felt it studying me, I reached out. Unlike the magic from all five houses on the academy grounds, it withdrew from me. It feared me and didn't want me here, which was new. I'd taken it for granted that magic, dark or light, always welcomed me. As I probed the magic here further, I felt a deep wrongness lying beneath it.

Fury shot into me.

Someone had implanted black magic in it. The corruption hadn't reached its very root yet. If it spread to its core, this magic should be destroyed instead of preserved. Maybe that was why the magic here withdrew from me in fear, as it sensed my power and intention.

Yet this magic was the power source for the entire academy. If it was destroyed, the ripple effect would be terrible.

No wonder Underhill had declared its independence and separated from the rest of the realm.

When Sy and I first came to Shades Academy, all we'd taken in was thriving blossoms, shining buildings, prosperous shops, a verdant forest that stretched far east, and a crystal lake glimmering in the west.

I'd never expected a worm beneath the wonder, creeping toward the center of the magic in the academy.

I filed a decision away and looked up at the spire of the ivory tower glinting in the moonlight, adding pureness and splendidness to Skyward. Yet I was the only one who could see it was tainted by black magic.

I halted my steps. Everything in me screamed for me to turn around, run to the other side of the bridge, and never look back.

Cami stopped with me as the rest of the students kept moving forward like drones, as if they couldn't help it.

"Why are you stopping, Barbie?" Cami tugged my sleeve. "Get going."

"It's a trap," I said.

"You'll be fine." She snorted. "You're with me. No one will dare to touch you now that I've stood by you on my cousin's behalf. Come! Every candidate in the school must go through the trial."

We crossed the bridge and stepped through the vast ivory door at the rear of the candidates.

A GOLDEN MARBLE floor and gilded columns extended before us. The moon shone through the tower's skylight, illuminating the interior as much as the tower's magical light.

Symbols of five houses on a variety of gemstones shimmered from the back wall. Candidates from each house lined up in the lane under their own house crest, facing a podium on the dais.

I followed Cami to our house lane under the symbol of seven arrows in a radial pattern on a blue diamond as big as a fist.

The five kingdoms were all about flaunting their wealth and magic. Each house had its own gemstone. House of Vampires was linked to black opal. House of Shifters chose emerald. House of Fae had ruby. I craned my neck to look for Bea under a glowing sapphire, the mage house's gemstone.

Neither Bea nor I was tall enough for us to spot each other. After a few tries, I gave up and sent a silent prayer for her and my other geek friends.

Other than footsteps and shuffling from the candidates as we all tried to settle down in our lanes, the enormous hall was quiet. It was then the stench hit my nostrils.

"Did you smell that?" I whispered to Cami.

"Skyward is a thousand-year-old building, sustained by the remnants of old magic," she said. "Only the royals, headmistress, and the druid were allowed to enter the tower before this day. I don't think any of the princes like to come here." She let out a low chuckle. "They don't like traditions or anything old. They're the rebellious new generation."

I bet the princes could sense the wrongness here too, but I doubted they'd dug deep. They simply stayed away, dismissing the ivory tower as too ancient for their liking. Their absence gave the bad actors room to work their black magic here.

The longer I stayed in this hall, the more stifled I felt. The feeling of being trapped increased.

When had the corruption started? How long had this deep wrongness been going on?

Cami still had a hand on my arm, as if she didn't trust me not to bolt at any second. But she shouldn't worry. The enormous door had sealed behind us, a dozen sentinels standing guard in front of it.

Since I couldn't get away, not until after the trial, I might as well try to figure out what the black magic was all about here. I took a deep breath, reaching out with my senses. The foulness hit me right in the center. The tainted magic carried the signature of the druid mixed with unknown witchcraft powered by blood, bones, and the pain of the sacrificed.

The agony of the victims' tormented souls cried out to me, so strong that it made my teeth chatter. I swayed with dizziness. The fear in me faded as rage seared my blood. I smelled the residue of their recent ritual of horror, of human sacrifice. It was still fresh.

A dreadful realization sank its claws into me. The druid had been so keen on getting his hands on me. Sacrificing a demigoddess would give him power beyond his wildest dreams. He'd mentioned once that he'd been tracking a demigod, and I was more than a demigod.

I'd seen a few nasty-looking witches and mages around

the druid on campus. Did they work for him, or did they belong to his cult coven? Were they all behind the human and supernatural sacrifice?

The druid loomed in front of a long desk of glass beneath the raised dais where Headmistress Ethel stood tall behind a gilded podium, ready for an opening speech. Behind her were the royal balcony seats. Cade, Rowan, Silas, and Louis took the front row. Killian's seat remained empty.

Sy peeked out, training her lustful gaze on Rowan.

He wore a fae royal military uniform in wine-red and blue tones. The vampire prince wore black and dark red, the mage prince wore gold and sapphire, and the shifter prince wore green and blue.

Anxiety and a hollow feeling expanded in my chest at the absence of the chaos prince.

My icy gaze landed on the druid as I felt his ink black stare on me. Amid thousands of candidates, the fucker still singled me out. I didn't look away.

I'd pondered slitting his throat, or setting Sy on him and letting her eat him, as I realized that he was so fixated on me that he wouldn't rest until he had his filthy hands on me. And now, knowing what he'd done to other victims, I was determined to find a chance to erase him for good.

An evil smile ghosted the druid's black lips at my challenge, and my stare told him clearly that he was a marked man. He just didn't know yet that he was a dead man walking.

Don't engage with the druid. Not now, Sy warned. *Don't let him distract us and make us lose the game. We need to get through the first trial and win, and then we'll take the first opportunity to off him.*

Talking about games, I didn't care about the trial, but Sy took it to heart. She was always competitive.

"Good evening, bride candidates!" Headmistress Ethel raised her arms in a big welcome gesture under the banner of the star charts of Mist of Cinder.

She wore an elaborate white gown, the height of fashion for mature noble fae ladies, with a collar high and tight enough to choke her if she wasn't careful. Her hairdo was meticulous, every pin in the right place, and her makeup was flawless. I was more interested in her ruby earrings, amazed that her pointed, elegant ears could sustain their weight. It was all show and vanity, right?

I can eat her too after we slay the druid. And we'll take her rubies for ourselves, Sy said. *You can put those rubies with the diamond Rowan gave us and the other gemstones the house got us in that shoebox.*

Sy knew all my hiding places.

"Today, we're gathering in our beloved Skyward, as the time has finally come!" the headmistress called, her silver eyes shining with tears. What an actress! "The kings and queens of all five kingdoms and the Council of Mist of Cinder will be watching the livestream of the first bride trial from their palaces. Let us honor them!" She raised a fist and pressed it against her heart. Everyone followed suit. I hesitated for a beat, looked around, and did the same. Whatever.

"Unfortunately," the headmistress continued, "the House of Underworld, the new gem of the realm, will be absent from the Brides Selection. As we all know, the heir of the House of Chaos has found his mate, Queen Lilith of the House of Underworld. At this moment, instead of gracing us with his presence, Prince Killian and his beloved are celebrating their bond..."

The rest of her words passed by my ears without my registering their meaning as "Prince Killian and his beloved are celebrating their bond..." echoed in my head over and over, piercing my heart.

What did I expect? Even if the chaos prince offered me a future, what could I give him back? I'd known right from the beginning that he was taken. Spoken for. Betrothed. But in the middle of it, as our relationship progressed, I'd thought he was mine. The next second, I knew it was impossible and decided not to ask him for what he couldn't give. I was living on borrowed time anyway.

Yet when the reality of his being with another woman slipped into my mind, I still couldn't deal with it.

A riot of angst hit me like a dark storm, chasing me, shattering the reason that held me together, until I felt my chest grow too tight and my lungs close up to stop air from coming in.

Shit!

My lips parted in terror as I felt my core power emerging from my dark abyss, ready to meet the storm. If they merged, I'd lose my shit. I'd torch everyone here, along with the tainted ivory tower.

I needed to get the fuck out of here before I went supernova.

Then an arm wrapped around my shoulders.

"Lean on me," Cami said in my ear. "I promised my cousin that I'd be in your corner during his absence. Just remember, he won't abandon you."

I shivered in her arms. While her skin felt icy, mine was burning.

"Breathe," she said. "I got you, Barbie."

I let out a breath, and my core power sank back down. My temperature returned to normal. Then Cami's hand left my shoulder.

"Killian won't leave you to the wolves," Cami said.

"Wolf?" I asked. "You mean the big, bad wolf Silas?"

She let out a low laugh.

As if on cue, we both peered into the royal seats. Silas was looking back at us. He threw me a thumbs-up, a goofy smile on his handsome face. Louis scowled at him.

Headmistress Ethel had stepped aside, and the druid took center stage, barking instructions. "Each student must drink the potion. There'll be no exceptions." His inky eyes fixed on me again. Cami squeezed my hand to show her support. She'd also noticed the druid's unhealthy interest in me. Every student shivered in front of the druid, as he just crept everyone out.

"After you take the potion, the crystal ball will show if you're worthy and chosen," the druid explained emotionlessly. My heart skipped an icy beat at the mention of his crystal ball. "If it glows red, you'll join the next trial of the Brides Selection. Should the crystal ball turn green, you'll be sent home. You may choose to stay and study at Shades Academy, but you won't have any of the privileges of a bride candidate anymore. You'll also have to pay for tuition and your boarding expenses..."

The druid moved his hand over the glass table, and a crystal teapot with pale blue liquid inside appeared on the table. At the same time, the crystal ball that had attracted my father's attention materialized in midair, spinning slowly.

My blood turned to ice at the sight of the fucking crystal ball. I'd lose my shit if Ruin showed up in it again. I sank my fingernails into my palms to keep my panic at bay. I had to hang in there until the trial was over.

"Any questions?" the druid asked sternly, darting a dark glance at me, as if he expected I'd raise a hand.

"What's in the potion, Professor Druid? How does the

potion tell who is worthy to enter the second round?" America asked from the ranks of the House of Fae, sounding worried.

"The potion contains a drop of old magic," the druid said. "It reveals your very essence. Only the brave who can face their fear and true self will be allowed to stay in the Brides Selection."

My heart pounded. This was bad. All my life, I'd been running from my true self and fear. This wouldn't end well for me.

Don't worry, Sy said, cheering me up as she always did when I was near panic. *If we fail, they kick us out of the Selection. Isn't that what you want? We'll have more freedom. I bet Rowan and Killian will still feed us even if we aren't a bride candidate.*

`That was the plan, then. What worse could happen? They'd just kick me out. Besides, no potion worked on me. But what would they do if the crystal turned neither red nor green?

Yet my heart still rammed into my ribcage, as I couldn't expel this foreboding feeling that I was a target here. That fucker druid wouldn't go easy on me.

"Let the first bride trial begin! May the odds be with you!" Headmistress Ethel shouted with fake cheer, and half of the students applauded, confident that they'd be chosen.

Cami darted a worried look at me. She'd pass to the next round for sure, but I was the wild card. I beamed at her to try to convince her not to worry about me. Again, what was the worst that could happen even if I was the target in this ritual? The druid wouldn't be so stupid and ruthless as to drag me to his dark altar to sacrifice me in front of everyone, would he?

I chuckled nervously to myself at the absurdity while Sy stayed alert, watching my six like a hawk.

The long lines started moving forward. America from the House of Fae was the first to go up. She stood in front of the druid, who chanted something. A crystal teacup materialized beside the crystal teapot, and the teapot tilted all by itself and poured the pale blue liquid into the cup. The first teacup floated to America. She took it with a shaking hand. Then, with a determined look, she lifted it to her lips and downed the potion.

The cup in her hand vanished.

Everyone held their breath while staring at the crystal ball. It was so quiet that we could hear our own heartbeats. The crystal ball spun, humming, before it pulsed red.

America cried in joy, "I'm in!"

"That's your destiny, Lady America!" Headmistress Ethel beamed in pride as she congratulated her niece. "May you shine like a star!"

A sentinel in a gray academy uniform escorted America to the right side beneath the flowing banner of star charts. The fae chick stood tall with her chest puffing out and her chin lifted.

A student from the House of Vampires moved toward the druid to receive the potion. She drank it, and the crystal ball turned red. Then candidates from each house took turns taking the potion, and a dozen students were escorted to join America after the crystal ball beamed red, deeming them worthy.

"This is the fucking first trial?" I asked Cami in a whisper. "Pucker said it was supposed to be a culling."

Headmistress Ethel stared hard at me from the raised dais where she could see everyone, and I zipped my lips.

A short girl from the House of Shifters wailed after she

received green from the crystal ball. She begged for a second cup of potion, but she was denied. A few more students also melted down when the sentinels half-dragged them out of a side door to where a boat was waiting to cart them away from Shades Academy.

The princes in their royal seats looked bored, not slightly impressed by anyone who passed through the first trial, without a care for the crying and whimpering of the rejected.

Then it was Cami's turn.

I smiled at her encouragingly. "Break a leg."

She narrowed her eyes at me.

"It means good luck," I explained. "Now go knock them dead, she-tiger."

She shook her head. "I'm not even a shifter."

She strolled toward the druid to take her potion, and the crystal ball beamed red instantly. I wasn't a little bit worried for her. Of course she'd pass. She was a royal.

More candidates streamed toward the druid to drink the potion. Some passed, and some failed. I grinned as I watched my geek friends get in.

Then it was Bea's turn, and my heart pounded. She was an oddball like me, but then she also got accepted, and my breath eased.

The line moved faster. Before I knew it, I was pushed ahead for my trial.

I STROLLED toward the glass table and paused a few feet further from the druid as I eyed the crystal ball overhead. My heartbeat calmed in my ears when I didn't see my father pop up in it.

I could feel all the princes' intense, expectant gazes drilling holes in my forehead. I slanted a glance at them, my jaw locked stubbornly, as I was determined not to cause drama to entertain them.

A new teacup appeared in the air, the crystal teapot poured the liquid into it, and the cup floated toward me. It seemed nothing was out of order, as it was the standard procedure. Yet my shoulder blades tingled, and my sense of danger flared.

I snatched the teacup and peeked down.

Shit!

There was something at the bottom.

"Drink the potion, Barbie!" the druid called. "You're holding up the line!"

"Wait!" I called.

"What is the fuss this time, Barbie?" Headmistress Ethel scolded.

"Why is there a pill in my cup?" I asked nervously. "Did everyone else have the same shit in their potion as well?"

I had to make sure. The candidates who had been accepted into the next round shared confused glances.

"I didn't see any pill in my cup," Bea blurted out before she was given permission to speak.

Headmistress Ethel glared at me, as if I were a certified troublemaker.

"There's no pill in it! Your potion is just like everyone else's," the druid barked. "Drink it, or you'll be disqualified!"

"Then disqualify me," I said, lifting my chin in defiance.

It was better to be disqualified than to be drugged. Who knew what was in that fucking pill? The more the druid denied it, the more suspicious I grew.

"You won't get out of here until you drink the potion!" the druid snarled, playing tough.

The princes all stood up, ready to walk over to investigate, but the headmistress beat them to it and reached me at a brisk pace.

She stared down into my cup. "There's no pill!"

I peered down. There was just potion now.

"It dissolved!" I looked up at the headmistress before regarding my potion again. "I know what I saw. I wasn't lying!"

"Stop stalling, Barbie!" Headmistress Ethel hissed.

"May I have another cup, then?" I asked.

"Request denied," the druid said. "Every cup is being counted. Drink the potion just like everyone else, girl! We don't have time for your shenanigans!"

"But I don't have a good feeling about this one, since the potion in it was tampered with." I raised my head and looked straight into the druid's eyes without flinching. "I don't trust you! You've been practicing black magic by sacrificing the innocent in this tower. I won't be your next victim!"

Gasps rose across the hall at my boldness. No one liked the druid, but no one dared to openly support me either.

A vein throbbed in the druid's temples, unholy fire in his eyes. "How dare you!"

"Be careful of whom you accuse!" Headmistress Ethel said. "All you've done ever since you came to Shades Academy is to stir trouble, you little hellion!"

The druid's power slammed into me, alien and foul, while I was distracted. I opened my mouth and yelped in alarm. The potion shot through my lips, poured down the passage of my throat before I could stop it.

The empty teacup vanished from my hand.

The princes shot to their feet, but it was already too late for them to intervene.

"What the fuck?" I cried out, rage and fear pounding in my veins.

The milky-white crystal ball started to spin, turning neither red nor green. This was a first. Whispers and gasps filled the hall as everyone waited for the ball to settle.

Humming louder than ever, the crystal ball spun faster and faster, as if it had gone nuts.

"What is happening?" Headmistress Ethel demanded in alarm.

The crystal ball turned pitch black.

"What does it mean?" Cade frowned.

"Shouldn't it turn red or green, likely red for Barbie?" Louis questioned.

"Evil incarnate!" the druid shouted, pointing his black-nailed finger at me. "The crystal of the oracle has recognized Barbie as the evil prophesized to bring blight to this realm." He sliced his pointing finger in my direction. "Seize her! We must contain the evil."

A burn erupted in my stomach.

Shit! The effect of the potion that the druid had forced down me had just kicked in. No potion could get to me before, but the pill in my cup must've targeted me genetically. It dawned on me that the druid might've known about me all along.

He'd mentioned something about tracking a demigod when he tried to take me captive in the ice rink. If he sacrificed a demigoddess like me, he would harvest great power. Was he behind hiring the mercenaries from CrimsonTide to kidnap me?

Framing me as a monster that brought blight to Mist of Cinder was a clever way to get his hands on me, especially since he had waited until Killian was out of town. Who would stop him from taking me now?

As the burn spread in my veins, I stretched a hand out to grasp his druid magic. I'd siphon it then turn it against him. I'd kill the fucker before he laid his hands on me or anyone else.

Yet my dark wind couldn't grab his power, incapacitated by the potion he'd slipped into me. I'd break through the venom of the potion eventually, but I was running out of time.

Burn the motherfucker! I roared at my core power, the darkest flame that had proven hotter than heavenly fire and hellfire. It was the only power that could help me take down the druid.

My dark flame lashed out. Instead of toasting the druid, it slammed into his crystal ball, which exploded into hundreds of pieces. The druid staggered back and screamed in pain. A second later, it dawned on me that the crystal ball had been his magical shield and he'd infused part of his essence into it.

My flame had destroyed his shield, but now it had no fuel to keep going, as something in that pill had taken root in me. It couldn't kill me, but it rendered me immobile.

I collapsed, falling at an odd angle, my numb limbs unable to move an inch. Sy roared, trying to break out to defend me, but she was also crippled alongside me.

I stared up as the druid stalked toward me, ready to claim his prize.

25

Barbie

The druid tossed his black mesh net toward me. Once he trapped me, he'd drag me to his lair and deal with me however he wanted. I was his ultimate purpose, but he didn't know that I'd be more than he could chew.

I didn't even struggle to get up to fight. I had to save my strength to fight off the poison in my bloodstream. My core magic was already working on purging the alien poison in me.

So, I'd allow the druid to take me as his trophy, but I vowed that he was done.

"Not so fast, druid!" a powerful voice snarled, and a figure jumped across the space in one leap, slashing through the net before it landed on me, and positioned himself between me and my hunter.

My head still swam, my body raw with pain and numbness at the same time, yet my heart leapt in relief and gratitude.

Killian had reached me again. He'd come!

A second later, I realized it wasn't him but Prince Silas. Of all people, the heir of the House of Shifters had come to defend me in front of thousands.

"You'll not take Barbie, druid," Silas said firmly.

"You should not meddle, Prince Silas," the druid reproached. "She doesn't belong to your house. And since the heir of the House of Chaos isn't here, the academy has every right to step in and deal with a sinner in his house."

The fucker had planned this. They'd planned to take me after luring Killian away.

"Barbie is only temporarily assigned to the House of Chaos," Silas insisted. "She was taken from my house unlawfully. I've been trying to use the legal channels to get Barbie back to my house, since she's a dormant shifter. Some might've called her a chihuahua, but I bet that she's a little wolf. She has claws. Now that Killian isn't even present at the most important event, I'm exacting my right and reclaiming Barbie back to the House of Shifters."

"If I were you, Prince Silas," the druid said as if facing a toddler throwing a tantrum, "I wouldn't take such a creature into my house. Haven't you seen what chaos and unrest and darkness she's brought? Look at her lying at our feet, crumpled on the ground without any dignity. She can never be a potential mate to any of you. Let her go, Highness, I urge you, and let me take this dark creature to where she belongs so she'll never cause harm again."

"Now that's bullshit," Louis called. "And everyone can smell it."

The vampire prince had snuck over to park himself behind the druid at a strategic angle. Rowan and Cade had also come forward, letting out their predatory sides and standing on either side of the shifter prince. The trio formed a barrier between me and the druid.

Their formation illustrated how the princes knew how to work with each other.

"Have you all forgotten what happened to Princess Medea and how this creature burned one of royal blood with her unholy fire?" the druid asked. "Do you think the five kingdoms would just let it slide and there'd be no reckoning for this foul creature?"

So, the kings of the five kingdoms or the Council had plotted to push up the timetable of the first trial and use the druid to do their dirty work to clean house when Killian wasn't around. They'd lured him away, hadn't they?

A dark thought churned in my mind. Maybe I wasn't the Council's target, since I was nobody, but they were showing Killian who really called the shots in the realm by punishing me as collateral damage.

The power struggle in this realm was as real as it was in the human world.

Politics were dirty in every corner of every world.

"Stop calling her creature!" Silas snarled. "She's Barbie, one of the candidates, so treat her as such."

"And Medea was a traitor!" Rowan chimed in coldly. "In case you choose not to remember, she used a forbidden, dark artifact to try to murder Barbie."

"You're infatuated with her," the druid said. "Barbie bewitched you all, including Prince Killian. All the more reason I need to put her away so everyone will be safe."

"Careful, druid," Cade growled. "No one can bewitch us. No one is more powerful than us heirs."

"Barbie isn't just anyone," the druid said. "We all underestimated her. Ever since she came to the realm, chaos, darkness, and death have followed in her wake. The potion was designed not only to weed out the weak but also to keep evil out of the Brides Selection. The crystal ball has never been wrong. You all saw it turn black, showing Barbie's true colors, so she destroyed it. We must remove her while she's incapacitated. It's my duty as one of the Council members to protect the realm."

Despite the druid calling me evil, Cami and Bea had dashed toward me. Cami propped me up against her, and Bea waved her wand in front of my chest, trying to ease my breathing. While feverish—fire burned in my veins and ice clogged my airway—I gazed at them in gratitude.

"Right before Barbie took the drink," Cade drawled, "she said there was a pill at the bottom of her teacup. What did you give her, druid?"

"There was never a pill," the druid said. "That evil girl loves to make a scene."

"Then why did you deny her a new cup of potion?" Cade asked.

"As I said, there's limited potion," the druid said.

"One more cup would be too much?" Silas snorted.

Cade stalked to crouch by me.

"Your Highness." Bea bowed at Cade. "I can tell the potion Barbie took is different than ours. There's something in it! I can still feel the residue of the spells, unlike anything I've encountered or read about in the Book of Shadows."

Cade wielded his wand above my face, chanting in an ancient tongue. Before he even finished it, he stood up abruptly and leveled his wand at the druid. "What the fuck did you give her?"

"He poisoned Barbie?" Louis asked, his eyes on fire. "He dared?"

"What's all this?" Headmistress Ethel had come closer

but was careful not to place herself in the potential crossfire between the druid and the princes.

"This is a bad case of trusting everything in one corrupted man's hand!" Silas barked. "We, as heirs of the five houses, should've been informed of this trial ahead of time, and we should've monitored the process to prevent any illegal operations!"

Pucker popped out beside me. I'd sent him to patrol the Veil, for fear of any Shriekers sneaking in while we were stuck in the middle of the ritual.

Barbie! Barbie! he screamed in my ear. *I came as soon as I felt your distress. If you can hear me, blink!*

Instead of blinking, I started to convulse on the cold marble, like a seizure. The poison was coursing in my every vein, burning too fiercely even after Sy had taken most of it into her and passed out. It spread faster than my dark flame could purge it.

Genetic knowledge sparked in the depths of my memory. The druid had slipped me the Seed of Heaven, and I related the information to my familiar.

Pucker materialized by my side. The crowd stirred and cried out in alarm.

"That's evil Barbie's companion!" the druid shouted. "She summoned him!"

"He's the ghost guardian of the House of Chaos," Cade said, raising his wand to stop the sentinels from charging Pucker. "We've all met him. He's harmless."

Pucker thrust three fingers at the druid. "The druid slipped the Seed of Heaven into Barbie's potion. It was not only illegal. It was shockingly criminal!"

The princes snarled. I could feel fear and fury rolling off them, all for me.

"The Seed of Heaven?" Headmistress Ethel sucked in a breath. "You must be mistaken. It can't be!"

"The Seed was brought from Heaven but grew in Hell," Pucker explained, his expression grim. "Even a tiny drop from it can paralyze a god. The angelic beings once served drinks with a seed in it to the old gods in a feast to take out the competition." He swept two fingers at Headmistress Ethel. "Anyone of lesser power, including you, headmistress, would die instantly at a sip of the potion that Barbie was forced to drink."

Yet I was still here, though crippled. There was no hiding my power anymore.

"Give Barbie the antidote, druid!" Rowan roared, his hands raised, his powerful fae magic at the ready.

"Now!" the other princes demanded, seeing red.

"There's no antidote to the Seed of Heaven," the druid sneered. "The evil incarnate is done!"

"Take Barbie to my house and call the healers," Silas said, never taking his eyes off the druid.

"No one shall take that creature from me!" the druid said. "I'm sick and tired of your meddling, you spoiled brats!" He raised a fist and shouted, "Now!"

A deafening crack boomed across the hall, then glass rained down from the ceiling.

A death squad dropped from the top of the ivory tower, breaking through the skylight.

26

Pucker

T he death squad, wearing visors and armed to the teeth, besieged Barbie and the princes.

"What is this?" Ethel screamed at the druid.

The squad of mixed species, some with scales and others with horns, was led by two giant angels, or fallen angels. Who could tell? They were mercenaries now.

I wasn't much as a dead man, but I was determined to defend Barbie from the force that had come to take her with all I had.

"They're the Legion of the Brotherhood!" the druid pronounced proudly. "This is but a section of the Brotherhood."

"Angels and demons?" Louis growled, his fangs flashing. "Are you fucking kidding me?"

"So, the myth is true," Cade mused.

Rowan nodded. "The secret force of the Brotherhood exists."

Among the princes, Rowan and Cade were pretty much an encyclopedia on all things regarding spells, runes, artifacts, and magic.

"Of course," said the druid while Ethel's mouth still hung open as if she couldn't believe her eyes and ears. "The Brotherhood has existed since before the five kingdoms. Now step away, princes. We'll take Barbie off your hands. We're the good guys. We do this to preserve the realm. Stop me, and there'll be bloodshed!"

Silas and Louis snarled at the same time, baring their fangs. The two princes didn't care for each other, but they had more in common than they'd admit.

"You'll not take her, dick!" Silas said murderously.

"Surrender yourself to justice, druid!" Louis called.

The druid laughed coldly. "Take the girl!"

Louis zoomed toward the druid, his claws out and fangs showing, no mercy in his eyes. His killing strike, however, didn't land on the druid, as our foe turned to smoke and vanished from where he had been. A second later, the druid appeared behind the vampire prince.

"Watch out!" Cade shouted, flicking his wand. A shield materialized behind the vampire prince just as the druid tossed a potion at Louis. The potion ate a hole in the mage's shield, but it bought time for Louis to dash out of range.

Louis nodded a thank you to Cade and lunged at the druid, but his opponent turned to smoke again. He growled as his claws swatted at empty space. Then Rowan and Cade were up, one conjuring a web of thorned vines to trap the smoke, the other tossing dark spells at the fading smoke.

"Fucking coward!" Louis spat.

The druid wouldn't engage directly with the powerful

princes, since I'd destroyed his supposedly unbreakable shield—the crystal ball. He popped up a dozen yards away with his army between him and the princes. The left sleeve and a corner of his robe frayed away where he stood. Cade's spells had grazed him after all.

Silas had engaged in a fight against three cult brothers, one sword against three. When they broke apart, all four of them were bleeding. A beastly growl tore out of Silas's throat as he shifted to his warrior form—half-wolf and half-man—and added two feet to his formidable height.

The shifter prince leapt into the air, his broad blade finding purchase and swiping a cult brother's head clean off, but another cult brother shot an arrow into his thigh. Silas roared in rage and pain, throwing his hand up, and a stream of water forced its way into the archer's mouth, not stopping until he was down.

The rest of the princes formed a protective triangle around Barbie, watching each other's backs while guarding her as waves of cult brothers charged them. There were too many, dozens of them. Surprisingly, Headmistress Ethel joined the princes, tossing her wind and fire at the legion to try to push them back.

Rowan's lethal, thorny vines shot out from the ground and burst from the walls, but too many students got in the way. Some students, mostly first-years, ran like headless chickens, trying to duck the magical fire, water, vines, arrows, and spells that flew everywhere. There were casualties, of course, the innocent caught in the crossfire.

"Get the bride candidates out of here, Lady Ethel!" Rowan shouted. "That's your duty!"

Headmistress Ethel darted to clear a path and led the students out. America rushed to assist her. The death squad didn't stop them, as the bad guys were only interested in Barbie.

Amid the chaos and clamor, quite a few students fell and were trampled by the other students as they all shoved forward to flee toward the exit. Cade let his spells fly toward the windows and shattered them to create more exits for the students to get out.

A group of candidates from Barbie's underdog cult rushed to join the princes' team instead of fleeing, tossing fire, wind, and water at the Brotherhood members. I was proud of them.

The princes' guards, including our chaos house warriors, hadn't been allowed to enter Skyward when the trial started. And now they couldn't get to us through the exodus of the candidates. The bridge was packed with panicked students trying to get to the safety of the other end. Some students fell off the bridge as a result. The warriors at the end of the bridge were yelling for the candidates to be calm and hurry the fuck up. They were anxious to get to us and join the fight.

Jinx, one of Barbie's friends, got hit in the shoulder and cried out in pain. Bea flew to her side to tend to her. I appreciated their bravery and loyalty, but they weren't ready to fight against the death squad, who were all professional killers.

Get my friends out, Pucker! Barbie said weakly in my head as soon as she stopped thrashing around in a violent fit. *Tell them to leave me. Send them to safety.*

I related Barbie's urgent message.

"Let us be part of this fight!" said Drusilla, the half-vampire. "We won't abandon Barbie. She's the voice and hope of the underdogs."

They won't leave. They're loyal to you, and they need this, I told Barbie. *If you want to protect them, fight the Seed of Heaven and get up!*

I'm trying, she whimpered, beads of blood dotting her forehead, pain filling her eyes.

Try harder!

The druid had disabled Barbie first so she couldn't join the princes in the battle and tilt the odds in our favor.

I held her hand for moral support. She was fighting to stay conscious. If she blacked out, it'd be game over for her.

I needed to go get Killian. No one could reach him faster than I, yet it wasn't in me to just leave my mistress while she was mortally wounded. I was terrified that once I was gone, I'd never see her again. I knew a goddess wouldn't perish like a mortal or even an immortal, but when you cared for someone so much, you didn't follow all the facts and cold logic.

The battle raged on in the hall. The two sides hurled offensive magic at each other. Blades flashed. Claws sank into flesh. Screams of pain met battle cries.

Cade brandished his wand, chanting rapidly. Where the spells from his wand landed, fireballs exploded and flesh burned. Silas, in his formidable warrior form, led with his long claws, his sword a sidekick. He was very much into tearing out throats and beheading his opponents as he leapt into the enemy ranks, ignoring the silver arrow still buried in his thigh. Actually, he had a new one piercing his shoulder.

Rowan and Cade fought near Barbie to safeguard her. Louis charged into the enemy's ranks to thin the herd. He was missing an ear and had a long gash across his forearm.

Fire, smoke, fallen beams, broken glass, and blood were everywhere. There were heavy casualties on both sides.

"First the kidnapping, then this. Why do they want

Barbie so much?" Rowan asked, his thorny vines piercing the heart of a cult brother.

"Why do we all want her in our houses, Rowan?" Cade answered. "Her power calls to everyone."

Louis retreated to join Cade and Rowan, cursing. A second later, Silas also returned after he'd dealt with a half-demon, half-shifter. The princes fought back-to-back, with Barbie in the center, guarded by Cami, Bea, and me. Drusilla, Jinx, and the other geeks fought between the princes as the first defense.

The enemies' numbers were too many.

"Barbie could be the answer to our—" Louis uttered.

She could be a mate to only one of them.

The princes didn't finish their discussion as Cami shouted in urgency, "Barbie can't hold on any longer. We need to get her to the healers!"

"Let's fight our way out!" Silas growled.

Cami carried Barbie over her shoulder, Jinx, Bea, and me guarding their backs. Cade and Louis led the retreat, Cade deploying spells and fire and Louis using a blade and wind to clear a path. Silas and Rowan brought up the rear. The shifter prince's strong water shot into the ranks of our pursuers while the fae prince wove the thorned vines as a barricade between us and the enemies.

Fortunately, the students had mostly exited Skyward and crossed the bridge. The warriors from five houses poured into Skyward as our reinforcements.

Just as I was about to zip toward the chaos kingdom's court to find Killian—I hadn't visited the kingdom for two centuries—a company of cult brothers, with the druid and two winged dark angels in the lead, blocked the middle of the bridge, cutting off our retreat.

We were boxed in by the Legion of the Brotherhood.

The dark angels took off and dove toward Barbie, who was half-conscious on Cami's shoulder, blood dripping from her nostrils. Bea begged Barbie to stay with us. While all the geeks stuck with Barbie and fought bravely, I could still feel fear pulsing off them.

All four princes hurled their strong magic at the winged angels, but it wasn't enough, since our enemies came at us from all directions, overwhelming us with their numbers.

I hovered above Barbie, trying to shield her, as if that would help. The dark angels could pass through me easily, even if I had more juice to go solid.

Rowan sent his vines high into the sky to trap the angels. He got only one of them, and I cheered. But then a third winged being appeared, slashing clean of the fae prince's thorned vines with a flaming blade.

With a battle cry, Silas charged into the ranks of the legion that pursued us, a lone wolf snapping his teeth. He wheeled, his blade piercing the visor of an enemy solider while he booted away another foe.

Blood dripped from his blade as he yanked it out of the soldier's face. A female bear shifter appeared by her prince's side, roaring as she hammered her axe into a cult brother's chest before he could put his spear into the base of Silas's spine.

"Go. Go! Bring Barbie to safety. I'll hold them back!" Silas shouted.

The shifter prince already had three arrows in his flesh. He was determined to sacrifice himself to preserve Barbie.

And just two months ago, he'd backhanded Barbie for her attitude in his house.

Two more shifters in their wolf forms dashed to their prince's aid. Rock and Archer joined their ranks as well, wielding their swords in a lethal dance. Together, they gave their all to push back the waves of enemy soldiers to give Barbie a chance to escape.

Cade and Louis fought hard in front of the group on the bridge. Both princes were wounded, their royal uniforms tattered and bloody.

Louis leapt up, his longsword cutting down a dark angel before it could snatch Barbie. A female dark angel shot a flaming arrow into Louis's chest, pinning him to the ground.

"No! No!" Cade roared, sending spells to vanquish the flame on the arrow before it burned the vampire prince to a crisp. He crouched beside Louis, chanting, and yanked the arrow out of Louis's chest.

Louis bellowed in agony.

"Hang in there, brother!" Cade shouted. "You hear me?"

Three vampire warriors, one of them Barbie's nemesis— Gunther—took the front position along with two chaos warriors and one fae. One of the vamps was soon cut down by the druid's spells, which also shot into a chaos warrior's chest, the impact throwing him off the bridge.

Fuck, we were on the losing side! Soon, Barbie would be taken, and there wasn't a damn thing we could do.

No! I refused to accept defeat.

I'll be back! I sent a thought to Barbie, not sure if she could hear me while she was fighting the biggest battle of her life to stay conscious.

I zoomed toward the chaos kingdom in a streak of light, praying I'd find Killian.

Maybe he could save the day if it wasn't already too late.

27

Barbie

ard, cold rain fell from the sky. Wasn't it supposed to be a warm night?

While my skin froze from the fever chills, my insides were boiling alive. The Seed of Heaven was bad news to old gods, and I was a direct descendant. The poison hadn't killed me, but it was damaging me on a cellular level.

It hurt. Fuck, it hurt so much.

For a moment, I forgot where I was until I found myself bumping on Cami's shoulder, shrieking in pain, as she tried to cross the bridge as fast as she could, protected in the center of our small group.

The princes and their warriors were fighting our enemies in all directions, cursing profusely. They should just leave me to save themselves. It was me that the Legion of the Brotherhood wanted.

Let them sacrifice me on their heavenly altar. My father

had done the same to me and would do it again and again. The future was never supposed to have me in it.

Yet the princes kept fighting, not giving up on me, as did my friends who guarded me.

"You'll be okay, Barbie," Bea kept saying like a prayer. "You'll be okay!"

But she couldn't know that. I didn't care about my fate, but I couldn't bear to lose any of my friends. From upside down over Cami's shoulders, I helplessly watched our team members go down one by one.

The princes could barely stand. Yet they still defended me. If I let this continue, they'd die here today.

I wouldn't allow it. Now it was my turn to defend them. I'd give my last breath for them, for my friends, and for my new home.

I wouldn't let them be doomed.

Today wouldn't be the end of them!

A war song drummed in my bloodstream, battering my core magic over and over. It'd broken through the runes and spells laid out by my god father and defended me once. I needed it now more than ever. Even if it couldn't purge the Seed's death lock on me, it could still aid me one last time.

I was like no other. My power was like no other.

I summoned the dark flame, not reasoning with it but commanding it.

An unnatural sound tore out of my throat. I pulled away from Cami, levitating in midair above the bridge. My friends shouted my name in alarm, but I ignored their calls.

For a breath, the fighting all around the bridge froze, every eye on me.

"What is she?" A fearful murmur rose from an enemy soldier.

"An abomination!" the druid shouted. "Throw all you have at her. Don't let her manifest!"

I flashed him a sugary smile. "Too late, babe."

Give them hell, babe! Sy cheered. She'd come around from blackout when a rush of adrenaline pumped into my blood.

Jets of dark flame blasted out of me like an atomic bomb. It was so bright and so dark all at once that everyone shielded their eyes and staggered back. Their shouting increased.

The druid leapt over the railing of the bridge into the river, abandoning his brethren. A trail of smoke rushed away from the waves caused by the shockwaves of my dark flame.

When the flame vanished like the wind, every enemy was vanquished without a trace, just like what had happened to Medea.

"She erased the Legion of the Brotherhood with one blast," someone said in fear and awe.

"Barbie has magic after all," said Cade.

"She's indeed something," Silas said in satisfaction. "I was never wrong."

"Really?" Louis retorted. "Didn't you call her a chihuahua, mocking her 'low magical grade'?"

"That stupid name for her came from your house in the first place!" Silas snarled.

I plummeted to the ground like a burned phoenix that had no wings anymore. Silas and Louis both lunged toward me, but the shifter prince caught first, and Louis growled.

"I gotcha, Barbie," Silas said.

"But she's burning up!" Louis shouted beside me, his hand on my forearm.

Cade was at my side in a blink, feeling my neck with his finger. "Her pulse is very weak. We need to—"

"Clear a path!" Rowan roared.

As I struggled at the edge of unconsciousness, I tried and failed to smile at the princes and my friends. I was thankful that they had survived. They were alive.

But my relief was short-lived.

A portal opened in the sky before we reached the end of the bridge. A new death squad poured out.

The cheers of victory died on everyone's lips.

The princes were all injured, and I didn't have a drop of energy or power left. The Seed of Heaven had reclaimed me, tormenting my every cell. Sy lay coiled in a corner, fighting not to pass out again.

"Save...yourself... Let me be taken..." I managed to tell the princes.

"Never!" Silas said.

"Please do it," I begged.

If they refused, they'd all die.

WE GOT THIS, Barbie! Pucker had returned. *Help has come!*

A roar from a pissed-off dragon thundered, so powerful and full of rage that it rattled my bones. Everyone on the battlefield froze in apprehension.

I smiled. Killian had come.

I could rest now. I could sink into oblivion, as I was bone tired. I hadn't saved the day, but I'd bought enough time for the chaos prince to save it.

Lightning and starlight surged toward the open portal in the sky, the mightiest I'd ever seen. Several Brotherhood soldiers plummeted into the river, and the raging water swept their corpses away.

The next moment, Killian reached my side. He held my dimmed gaze and squeezed my hand to assure me that he'd protect me before nodding at Silas. The shifter prince didn't argue and reluctantly handed me to Rock, who had fought his way to our side.

Now Rock was responsible for carrying me, as he had a lot more experience than others in that department.

"Brothers, will we guard what's ours?" Killian roared.

"Always!" the other princes roared back.

"You have to ask, asshole?" Silas snarled. "And you're late, as usual."

Killian ignored him and called, "Let's end this, shall we?"

All five princes held hands in a circle, their powers merging. Lightning, light, wind, fire, and ice formed a vortex, shooting toward the legion reinforcements. The enemies dropped like locusts before the portal sealed.

The last sight I saw was the raging river crashing into the ivory tower.

You've gone soft, Barbie. Sy gazed out weakly, her golden eyes alighting on the fae prince. *Our foes will know your weakness now. You care too much. And you feel too much. It is starting to rub off on me.*

We're two peas in a pod, I offered before darkness took me over like a vast blanket.

But I wasn't worried, since I wasn't alone. Sy would be watching my six. And we had Killian, the other princes, and our friends.

28

Barbie

A blink, and I found myself perched on a comfortable chair in a banquet room, a feast spread out in front of me.

Hunger roared in me, as did an acute sense of danger. For the first time, I didn't descend on the food like a locust.

Something wasn't right here.

My shoulder blades tingled, confirming my suspicion.

A memory flooded back, though foggy. The last thing I remembered was Killian and the other princes merging their powers to take down the legion. I'd thought I was finally in safe hands, but obviously I was wrong. I wasn't out of the woods, and thus I was here. I scanned the hall lit by artificial light coming from the black marble ground that stretched far into the distance. The ceiling was open to the night sky, but there wasn't a single star above. Black gemstones adorned three walls, a full glass door overlooking a dark lake.

I wasn't on the Shades Academy grounds, as I was supposed to be after the battle.

Sy! I shouted. *Sy!*

She didn't come, and I couldn't feel her.

I stared down at my wrists. There were no chains like those mercenaries from CrimsonTide had used on me. There was no torque around my neck either.

Yet my link to Sy was cut off, as was my connection to my familiar. As I searched deeper to reach for them, only an empty echo returned. But then I noticed another link deep down, fluttering yet veiled. It took me a long minute to realize that it led to Killian. My breath caught in my throat.

I hesitated for a beat, then left it alone. If it was hidden, there must be a good reason. I needed to draw attention away from that hidden bond, so our enemies wouldn't fix their eyes on it.

I regarded my wrists again. I had no chains on me, yet I couldn't reach Sy.

I nodded an understanding of my situation. It didn't take a genius to figure out that I had been hijacked. My mind was compromised.

This wasn't the realm that Killian created to dream-walk to me. This was a different place from a different time, fabricated by someone else. This banquet hall appeared more splendid than Shangri-La Paris, but only a single table was set, where I perched.

A variety of cupcakes, puffs, donuts, and fruits—all my favorites—packed every inch of the table. Whoever had brought me here was very powerful, and they'd studied me, knowing my undying love for food.

Hunger gnawed my stomach. I desperately needed to

replenish myself. A voice in the back of my head urged me to take a bite and make myself feel better.

I picked up a puff, but before I inserted it into my mouth to quench my hunger, I spotted a slice of fruit between the cream filling. It wasn't orange but something else. I narrowed my eyes, and my innate knowledge flashed.

Shit! It was ambrosia, food for gods and goddesses. There'd be a heavy price to pay for a mortal or an immortal who consumed it. I was neither. Ambrosia couldn't harm me, as I had goddess blood, but there would be strings attached.

As I studied the fruit, my senses spiked, and my shoulder blades tingled again. Someone was watching me. The ambrosia offered to me was local, grown from the soil of the Underworld.

The mythology told the story of Hades, Killian's grandpa, kidnapping Persephone. He offered her a pomegranate. She tried to be polite, so she ate six seeds. Fates showed up right after saying that she could never return to the land of the living.

Whoever offered me food had tried to trick me, as a slice of ambrosia could easily be mistaken as a slice of blood orange. Once I ate it, I'd never leave the Underworld.

I had a hunch who had set the trap, but she had no idea that I'd been training my mind since I was a child. Who wouldn't when her father was a sadistic god? When I reached age seven, even the original god couldn't penetrate my mind, my most-protected asset.

I had to give the queen credit, since it wasn't an easy task to even bring me here. Now, I'd just wait, maybe even get some shuteye to preserve my energy.

One thing did worry me, though. No one, not even Pucker, knew that my mind was being hijacked. No one could help me if I didn't get out of this. I'd end up in an eternal coma.

As I propped my feet on the table on top of the cupcakes and ambrosia while shutting my eyes for a fake nap, I felt pressure pricking against my mental shield. A force was trying to pierce my mind. The pressure kept increasing, and my head pounded in pain.

After a while, I caved in, weakened and compromised by the Seed of Heaven, and then my first shield was breached. I clenched my teeth as it dawned on me that the Seed of Heaven, the torque, and the chainlock were all connected. The druid might want to get his evil hands on me, but he'd received the tips about my perceived weaknesses from someone else, someone who knew my origin.

Had my father made a new ally? But he wasn't one to share power. He was a conqueror and an eater of the world. He didn't require allies, only slaves.

I clamped the second shield down, ready to swing at whoever came along. My opponent clawed at it, rammed into it, hacked at it, but my second shield was firmly in place and unbreakable.

Who are you, girl? a feminine voice asked, carrying seductive and persuasive power stronger than a siren's.

She knew who I was, I was damn sure, but she needed confirmation. If I answered her truthfully, I'd give her power over me.

Huh? I offered, playing dumb.

Tell me who you are and where you are from, her voice commanded, carrying compulsion that was much stronger than Silas's.

If you answer my question first and correctly, ma'am, I'll tell you everything. I smirked, ignoring the headache her compulsion caused me.

Fire away, she said with a hint of humor.

What came first? The chicken or the egg? I asked eagerly.

What? I couldn't see her, but I felt her frowning upon me. I had that effect on a lot of beings, especially superior beings.

Did the chicken come first, or the egg? I repeated slowly.

She sighed, then decided she no longer wanted to play nice as she hammered at my head. If I were a mortal, it would've cracked.

I started a heated debate about the egg and the chicken with myself, aiming to drag her down with boredom while I strengthened my mental shield.

"*Let's solve the chick and egg situation,*" I called. "*Some think it's an impossible argument in a scenario of infinite regression. However, the truth is out there. Barbie A, you're up.*"

I shifted my voice to a high-pitched, girlie type. "*The egg came first, since if there'd been no egg, there would've been no chicken. The first chicken was hatched from an egg.*"

I changed my voice. "*Barbie B, do you agree? Speak up.*"

I gave Barbie B a low, husky voice. "*There had to be a chicken first to lay an egg. I'm dying to know what the first chicken looked like. White? Black? Yellow? Brown? Or even green?*"

The force pounded my second shield, yet it couldn't get in, as I didn't give an inch while looping my tiresome debate over and over, broadcasting on all frequencies to anyone who was willing to listen. I could do this not only for hours but months, nonstop, like the training I'd gone through as a child.

I didn't even need to stab her. I'd bleed her with boredom until she was fucking bored to death.

"*Humans think they evolved from monkeys.*" I started a second round of my loop, as I had endless uncut material.

Good thing I didn't need to be original. *"But the supernaturals laugh at that shit. Why are the apes and monkeys from the jungles still apes and monkeys? Should they visit their human cousins for a recipe?"*

Not for a nanosecond did my thoughts drift to anything —not to my father, not to Sy, not to Killian—other than chickens and eggs.

"My, my, tell me," I said, starting over. *"Did the chicken come first, or did the egg?"*

It might've been hours before the pressure in my mind eased, the probe withdrew, and my pounding headache lessened.

Sensing someone entering the hall, I slowly pried open my eyes.

A regal woman. An immortal. A queen.

Instantly, I knew who had just walked in.

The Queen of the Underworld, Killian's betrothed.

QUEEN LILITH WAS A GREAT BEAUTY.

She looked only a couple of years older than me, but I knew she was at least centuries older. I was twenty going on twenty-one. She was almost as tall as Killian and had a ruthless air like him. I hated to admit it, but the two would look great together.

The queen's golden hair, two shades darker than mine, flowed down to her slender ankles. While my face was pale gold, hers was creamy and radiant. She shone brighter than anyone on this planet, yet somehow, I knew that she couldn't outshine me, and I didn't even shine.

There was a lot of gossip and rumors about her. Mostly, they said the Queen of the Underworld came from a fallen star, one of the brightest before the fall, like Lucifer.

I sent out my dark wind to feel her power, but in this world controlled by her, she called the shots. When I stopped trying, the familiarity of her power rippled toward me. Could my father have had another daughter before me?

I shook my head and scratched the ridiculous idea. If he had one, he'd never have let her go. He'd have sucked her dry as well, like he'd done to me.

I couldn't explain it, but I felt connected to the queen, drawn to her like a fly to a spiderweb. A voice tried to convince me that I could trust her.

But I wouldn't trust her. Sometimes you could judge a book by the cover, but most of the time, you shouldn't. Trust me on that.

"Hello, hello," I said with a smile aimed toward my adversaries. "Are you also responsible for my kidnapping not so long ago?"

She tilted her head to regard me. "So, you're the girl whom my beloved took into his house against objections?"

A fit of jealousy shot to my head. I didn't like her great beauty and perfection. I liked even less her lyrical voice infused with cold power.

Multiple voices from myself churned in my head.

Break up her and Killian.

Send Sy to eat her.

Drag her down by her golden hair and maul her gorgeous face!

But will Killian get upset if I maim her? In the end, he has to marry her.

Tears suddenly gathered behind my eyelids. I could never give Killian anything. I had nothing to offer him, or anyone, except disaster, curse, or even death.

No, it wouldn't come to that.

When my borrowed time was over, I'd leave of my own volition and draw Ruin away from Mist of Cinder and everyone I cared about.

So, I should protect Killian and his interests, including his engagement to the queen, while I could, even though it felt like acid dripping through my stomach. At least, I would not cause shit for Killian by letting his betrothed suspect that I was the other woman.

"Sir Killian is known for his charity," I said. "I guess I'm his new project."

She smiled at me, and that smile had teeth like blades.

"Hmm." The queen tilted her head. "Do you understand what you consumed?"

There was no need to beat about the bush and pretend that I had no idea what she was talking about. I bet she'd studied me extensively before she hijacked my mind and brought me here.

"Seed of Heaven," I said, "brought from Heaven and grown in your garden. Are you the drug dealer or the supplier?"

"You're young and green, yet you possess such knowledge," she said, her seductive voice the music of the dead and living. "You've never been to my realm, yet you figured out right away you're in my Underworld."

I felt the strong urge to pour out my guts to her under her power.

"I have my moments, ma'am." I smirked, then corrected myself. "Your Majesty."

"Both Heaven and Hell have been conducting experiments to find ultimate weapons against the old gods for an eon," Queen Lilith said. "But it's impossible to get their hands on the three originals. We believe two of them are gone, but one is making a comeback. So Heaven has been hunting for the direct descendants of any old gods." Her brilliant green gaze fixed on me as if I was the shit. "The Seed has taken root in you. All involved parties are eager to see the development. The Seed of Heaven might be the only thing that you can't absorb."

"Thanks for the update," I said. "People suck. Gods are worse."

She arched an elegant eyebrow. "Do you have other questions?"

"Are you truly a fallen star?" I asked.

She laughed, full of the promise of the star and the power of the Underworld.

I'd never heard any laughter so enthralling. The more she talked, the more I was drawn to her, addicted to her voice. She was the speaker of the truth. I put my chin on my palms like a puppy laying its head on its paws, gazing up at the Queen of the Underworld in utter admiration.

It seemed that we'd been talking for eternity, though I didn't mind it one bit. Only I couldn't remember the subjects we'd visited, as I felt time slipping through my fingers. And then I started to forget more of myself, my past, and my friends.

"You should eat the fruit," the queen said.

I beamed at her, aiming to please. "Maybe I should, but something tells me that I shouldn't. I wonder why."

"Just try," she urged. "Once slice of the orange will do you good, and then you won't be hungry anymore."

I picked up the puff with the fruit in it that I'd put down before.

"But this isn't orange, Your Majesty," I said. "This is ambrosia. You think I should really eat the gods' food in the

Underworld? If I do, I won't be able to return home. That's a big deal."

"Where do you think is your home?" she asked, her enchanting voice the flow of a beautiful violin.

"Uh?" I tried to think, then nodded. "That's a good question."

There was this place, but where? Fragmented images flashed before my eyelids—rare blossoms shivering in the night, a fairy lake, and a violet building of glass and steel under a starlit sky that stretched to eternity. Those images conveyed feelings, but they didn't stick. As soon as they appeared, they vanished, plucked out and chipped away by time.

I frowned in confusion and dismay. "Maybe I don't have a home?"

"You do now," she said. "This is your home. Eat the puff and the fruit, and you'll feel more at home."

Barbie! a high-pitched male voice screamed in my ears. *There's something wrong with Barbie!*

Who the fuck was Barbie? And that person was so loud and rude. I should send Sy to eat him!

Wait! Where was Sy? Why wasn't she around? Even if I forgot myself and everything, I could never forget Sy, my other soul, a beautiful savage with glowing golden eyes and a penchant for blood, gore, and porn.

I ran my fingers through my golden curls, ruffling them to make them bounce. Sy's hair was dark, lush, and straight, down to her ankles. Even her hair was a weapon that she'd used to wrap around a few rapists and choke them to death. I grinned at those memories fondly, not because of the brutality Sy had dealt to those bad men, but because I'd remembered.

And then I remembered more.

How many times must I tell you, Sy, that you can't just eat people merely because you don't like them?

Sy wasn't convinced.

We must be our better self. Plus, if you eat intelligent beings that annoy you, you'll have bad breath, I pressed. *Rowan will be turned off, and he won't give us diamonds anymore.*

I won't eat people raw, then, she pondered. *We can cook them well done with pepper and garlic. Those are good seasoning.*

Rowan? Who was he?

I cocked my head. A gorgeous, formidable male came to my mind, with a body built to kill and fuck. His storm-blue eyes gazed at me, containing scorching heat that expelled the cold winter in them.

As I recalled this male who had made me shiver down to my toes in lust, his scent of pine and clean, powerful male followed me to the Underworld, enveloping me in protection. But he couldn't be Rowan. That name didn't fit.

I blinked hard, desperate to remember him. The core part of me also told me that it was uber important to find out his name, but an outside force was hellbent on erasing him from my mind.

Sy! Earth to Sy! I shouted, peering into the deep well within me. *Do you copy?*

I heard a faint echo, and I called her again and again, sinking all I had into my search. *We're two peas in a pod. Sy, do you copy?*

Roger! In the distance, a roar came. *Mars to Barbie, we're in danger!*

No shit!

29

Barbie

"You are home," the Queen of the Underworld said, her icy hand cupping my cheek.

Her power tore into me, trying to sear a path to my mind. Her touch conjured an unfamiliar longing, almost as if I was looking for a maternal figure.

A mother.

At that moment, I wanted to please her more than anyone else, yet I bit my tongue. I just couldn't let her know about Sy, or she'd take Sy away from me, as powerful as she was. This was her territory.

I flung out my core magic by pure instinct. It rose from ashes and embers. With one precise slash, it severed the nearly complete connection between the queen and my mind.

Queen Lilith jerked her hand back as if burned.

"Why? How?" she demanded, menacing light glinting in her darkened green eyes.

Come back to me, little scorpion! a rich, familiar voice boomed in my head, making me shiver with longing.

Should I answer him?

Answer him! Sy said. *Let's go to him and get a good lay.*

I felt a warm mouth pressed to mine, full of carnal need. I blinked to find Queen Lilith staring at me furiously, her long golden hair flowing wildly in the phantom wind.

What the fuck was going on?

But I liked being kissed like that.

Killian is kissing your real lips, dummy, Sy said. *Feed on the energy he gives you and get the hell out of here.*

It dawned on me that while my mind had been taken here, Sy stayed with my real body. That was why I hadn't felt her until she came running and joined me here. While I was lost, she guarded me.

Killian's kiss deepened, and I parted my eager lips for him. The chaos prince thrust his possessive tongue between them, pouring his lust energy into me, purer and more potent than ambrosia.

A primal hunger in me swirled to life, although I felt torn for betraying the queen. But it couldn't be helped, could it?

The chaos heir lavished more of his power into our kiss. With each stroke of his tongue, I remembered him and us a bit more. My desire to go back to him overwhelmed me.

"Who's with you?" the queen demanded. Her dark power struck me.

But the shield forged by the combined powers of Killian and me held.

Shit!

Now everything flooded back to me. Killian was her betrothed, and I was the other woman!

I needed to get the fuck out of here before shit hit the fan.

"Uh, I'd love to chat more, but I gotta go." I fumbled for excuses. "Kind of busy."

"No one departs my realm unless I allow it!" she spat icily. "No one has ever succeeded, child!"

I waved at the furious Queen of the Underworld. "Sorry. Ciao."

My dark flame burned the tendrils of shadow power that had pinned me in place, and then wild magic from Underhill came to aid me. I shoved the phantom realm of the Underworld away and dove toward the portal Killian's lightning and starlight had torn open.

"Here I come!" I roared like a sailor.

California! Sy roared with me.

But we'd fled the City of Angels years ago, not only because of the high taxes and bad policies. No angels lived there.

We were going home now that I remembered where home was.

30

Barbie

I flashed open my eyes and smiled at the chaos prince.

Blossoms fell like little stars. The wind rippled across the icy lake. The shadow beasts howled, assuring me that they were taking their sentinel duty seriously.

I'd returned to Underhill, the safest haven for me.

Killian's mouth departed mine, yet warmth lingered on my lips.

"There you are, my little scorpion," the prince said.

I blinked at him, taking in his handsome features greedily. I could look at him like that forever.

"Barbie!" Pucker materialized beside us, floating above the lake, grinning like an idiot. "Glad you're okay! I helped, didn't I?"

"I chose you for a reason." I smiled at him. "I know you'd never let me down."

"Of course," he said, rubbing his hands in appreciation. "I'm now one of the elites Underhill lets in! To give you a brief, you were in a catatonic state before we got you here. You're in safe hands now, but many candidates and sentinels weren't as lucky." His voice remained gleeful. "It was the worst casualty rate in the history of Shades Academy!"

My heart sank with grief, and tears burned behind the curtain of my eyelids. If I'd never come here, no one would have died.

It's not true, Sy chided. *Ruin will find this realm sooner or later. Magic is already fading in Mist of Cinder. Our coming will change its fate. In the course of history, whenever a revolution happened, death was inevitable, but it paved the way for a new future. War, though not for the faint of heart, is the way of things. And know this: we're the protector of the realm.*

I blinked. Sy was evolving at rapid speed.

So, you won't eat other intelligent beings anymore, right? I asked, but she refused to make any commitment.

"Are the other princes safe?" I asked Killian.

My sugar Rowan is safe. Sy preened. *He'll be looking for me soon. You need to check your messages as soon as you get out of here! I need to feed for both of us. The Seed is still in you. We aren't out of the woods.*

"The other heirs are fine," Killian answered me. "The healers have tended to them, and they've returned to their own houses to take care of house affairs. There's a lot to do, and we all need to strengthen our security on academy grounds."

"Shouldn't you go back to the house too, high sir?" I asked.

He pressed me closer to him. "Cami is keeping the house in order during my absence. Rock can take care of security without me. They're capable, and I'm where I'm needed the most." He slanted a glance at Pucker. "Return to the house, guardian. Come back only if there's an emergency."

Pucker smiled at me, bowed at Killian, and vanished.

"You came for me again," I said.

"Always," he said softly. "You knew I would."

"Do you know your—your betrothed skyjacked my mind to her Underworld?" I asked.

Killian's face turned grim. "Queen Lilith has strong mind-bending power." His throat moved up and down. His eyes grew colder. "I'll warn her away from you."

"No need," I said. "I can handle her. She tried to make me forget about myself, and you as well. I almost did, until I didn't want to forget." While I was in the Underworld, it was almost blissful not to remember the horrors of my past and to push away the worry for my future. "I don't want to not remember you."

He cupped my cheeks, pride in his eyes. "My brave little scorpion."

I beamed at him. "I don't stay down, sir. I always get up swinging."

"I'll train you in shielding your mind," he offered.

"I don't need more training, sir," I said. "I don't have time."

He chuckled. "Make time. It's important."

"She's very powerful," I said, not happy to admit that Killian and Queen Lilith were well matched in every aspect. "Is that why"—I took in a breath—"why you two are going to get married?"

He sighed. "It's complicated."

"I tried not to let her know I'm the other woman."

He arched an eyebrow. "Should I be proud?"

I shook my head. "Men are fickle anyway."

He inserted his large hand into my tangled golden curls,

pulled my head back, and slanted his mouth onto mine. I threaded my fingers into his thick mane as well and kissed him back fiercely until my lungs demanded air.

Who fucking needed air when one could get a kiss like this?

Sy purred. *Are we going to get laid for real this time?*

Why must she always spoil a romantic moment with her insatiable need and vulgarity? But my pussy throbbed with aching need and heat nevertheless.

Killian pulled back, and I chased air.

"How's that being fickle?" he said, his eyes laughing at me before becoming serious. "You need to feed now."

My breath hitched, and my blood raced madly. I had never sex-fed the way Sy did. I'd always held back.

Somehow, Killian knew about my true nature, yet he wasn't flinching. Warmth and desire coursed through me, my dark flame dancing in my bloodstream. Maybe we could start a new chapter? Hope was a dangerous thing, but I clung to it.

"But..." I said hesitantly. "I might not be able to stop once I have a real taste of you. I might even hurt you."

An image of promise flashed in my head—I'd fuck him raw and hard until he begged for me to stop, but I wouldn't oblige. I'd mark him as mine, and no other woman would ever touch him again.

"You'll always hurt me, as I'm only vulnerable to you," he said. "Yet at the same time, you can never hurt me, just as my power will never harm you. Hurting you would be like harming my own, and my dragon will never allow it."

He'd just admitted to me that he was also a dragon!

"I want to see your dragon," I said.

A growl rumbled from his chest. His dragon wanted to come out to meet me.

"Stop it. Not now!" Killian growled at his beast, his face distorting for a second with the effort of reining in his beast.

"Feed on me, little scorpion," he said, his intense, heated gaze on me. "Take all you need to uproot that fucking Seed of Heaven."

"But sir, how should we proceed—"

Killian pounced before I could finish my question. His mouth crashed down on mine with impatience and raw need. Our breaths mingled, his scent of powerful male with starlight and winter pine enveloping me. My grip on his hair tightened.

Fuck! This was too good to be true. The chaos heir was so hungry for me!

Our tongues tangled. He led the dance and I let him. When he became even more dominating, I bit the tip of his tongue and tasted his rich blood.

His power poured into me, and I sent it to Sy first. When the Seed of Heaven seized control of me, damaging my cells, Sy had taken most of the poison into her to give us a fighting chance. I'd watched her burn and writhe in pain, yet I couldn't do anything about it.

Pleasure rocked through my body and buzzed on my skin as Killian kissed me deeply, feeding me his energy. The lake we floated on was no longer icy. Killian's dragon fire heated the pool for us, and steam rose into the air.

A moan escaped my throat. Without breaking our carnal kiss, Killian picked me up, with my legs wrapped around his waist possessively, and carried me to the shallow water. He freed a hand to cup my breast.

I didn't remember when my uniform had been stripped, but I didn't mind at all that both of us were as naked as the day we were born. My skin burned for him; my body hummed.

Shit was getting real!

Prepare yourself to get royally fucked, Sy chimed in with glee.

I hissed at Sy, wanting her to shut up, but Killian took it as my challenge toward him and growled in answer. His fingers kneaded my nipples roughly, and my toes curled at the sensation.

I rubbed my slick pussy against his front as he kissed my lips, then my throat, then my lips again hungrily. His hand slid down to rub my swollen clit. I cried out in pleasure at the incredible sensation and wiggled my ass to demand more.

His scorching touch made my every cell come alive.

"This little, tight cunt has been waiting to be fucked," the chaos prince said coarsely, making my blood heat and my face flush.

I let out breathless moans in answer.

The chaos prince placed me on a wooden counter by the lake, courtesy of Underhill. I propped my feet on the edge, my knees apart, baring my pussy for him.

He stared at my golden cunt, my plump folds parting in invitation, wanting to be impaled, wanting to be invaded, wanting to be claimed. He'd seen my naked flesh in the dream-walk realm, yet he stared at my sex as if seeing it for the first time, dark fascination brimming in his eyes and making me shiver.

My gaze dipped from his face to his cut chest, his six-pack, then farther down to his huge erection that was so silky and hard.

He smirked. "What do you think?"

"Come here!" I demanded.

With a low chuckle, he stepped between my legs. "Want to have your way with me, little scorpion?"

I reached out, wrapping my fingers around half of his massive shaft. His cock jerked in my palm. I squeezed it, and Killian gasped, his lustful eyes going two shades darker.

I held back a smirk as I glided my fist up and down his length, experimenting a little. This was the first time I had truly held a cock in my hand, so I was planning to take my time with it.

"Enough. Quit playing," he hissed. "I need to fuck you now."

"But," I gasped, staring down at his cock, "it's too big and I'm petite. I don't think it'll fit, sir!"

"It'll fit," he said. "Your pussy is soaking wet for me."

"Yeah? But it's not large enough to accommodate you. I don't like pain."

He let out an amused and frustrated chortle. "We've done it a few times in my dream walk, and you couldn't get enough of me."

"It's you who couldn't get enough of me."

"That's true too."

"It'll be real this time."

He chuckled. "Those times were as real as this. Relax. Stop hissing and huffing. I'll ease you into it, and you'll enjoy it just like before."

He palmed my pussy, and I gasped at the scorching touch and incredible sensation. He started to rub my sex up and down, sending shivers of pleasure to my nerve endings.

"You're so wet. If you don't take in my cock soon, your cunt is going to weep," he taunted me.

I pumped my fist along his length harder in retaliation. He slanted his mouth over mine, his tongue thrusting between my parted lips. It was never easy to resist the chaos prince. His tongue swept over my hard palate, and I shuddered at the pleasure. As his tongue thrust, mimicking how his cock would move, I was drowning in a lake of burning lust.

I needed his cock urgently. Whether it fit or not, I'd take it!

I wiggled my ass, inching toward the edge to urge him to get inside me. Killian growled at my desperation. Nudging his hard cock at my entrance, he slid in smoothly and steadily. I gasped at the incredible feeling that was ten times more intense and pleasurable than the copulation in the realm of his dream walk.

With a final push, he embedded himself deep within me. Then pain bloomed, as his hard shaft was too large. Killian stilled, his lips leaving mine, as he gazed down at me in concern.

"I didn't feel such a burn in that world you created," I complained. "This is different."

No pain, no gain! Sy said. She didn't want me to back off. I wasn't going to back off. I was just expressing my feelings.

"Do you want me to stop?" Killian asked gently.

"No! Don't you dare stop!"

"We'll go slow then," he said. "I'm a patient man. I'll take care of my woman."

"Sure, you've had a lot of experience," I said, jealousy searing my middle.

He chuckled, but he started to thrust slowly, in and out, moving carefully.

My whole body tensed as I expected more pain, my hands clutching his massive shoulders, my fingernails sinking into his skin.

"Relax, baby, and you'll enjoy it more," he said. "You know I'll never hurt you."

"But you hurt me last time when you ripped off my breast binding in front of thousands of eyes."

"It couldn't be helped," he said regretfully. "And you still hold a grudge? Let me make it up to you, then."

He glided in and out of me, a little faster now. The pleasure increased, overriding the pain and slight burn.

I moaned. "More."

"Now she wants more," Killian purred, thrusting into me slowly and smoothly.

The feeling was delicious, but when I said I wanted more, I'd meant it. And I wasn't going to wait for him to do it for me. I'd learned never to depend on anyone to bring you stuff. Just take what you want and never apologize for it. I propelled my hips toward him, riding his length. I experimented a little at first, moving this way and that way, rocking my hips to find my G-spots.

I might not have fucked as much as Sy, but I'd watched plenty of live porn. My pussy milked Killian's cock, gloving it completely.

"That's how you like it?" He groaned in pleasure and shoved his cock deeper inside my heat. "Did you picture how I would fuck you when you lay in your bed in that little room of yours, Barbie?"

My room wasn't exactly little now, since the house magic had expanded it, but it was small compared to his penthouse.

"Sometimes." I panted in pleasure as he thrust harder into me.

"I've fantasized about fucking your little cunt every night ever since I first saw you," he confessed. "Ever since I caught your scent in the woods."

"I want you to fuck me really hard now."

"Think you can take it?" he purred.

"I'm not fragile," I said. "I just keep forgetting I'm not sometimes. Now that I'm used to you, I want rough sex so I can feed better. I need your cooperation to uproot the Seed of Heaven. Show me what you can do, princeling, and don't hold back."

"Challenging me again?" he growled, pounding into me with his immortal strength. His cock grew larger and harder as his dragon came out to play. His steel rod filled my every inch, stretching my inner walls. Intense pleasure lit my every cell and set my body on fire.

"That's more like it," I purred in approval.

"You're made for me, little scorpion."

At his praise, I let out my sexiness, more feminine charm and less predatory, as I took a different approach than Sy.

Heat engulfed me, and I fed on the sea of sexual energy. I had to purge the poison of the Seed in Sy first, then I sent my dark fire, boosted by Killian's lightning, burning through any alien elements in my cells.

Killian pounded into me relentlessly with endless stamina.

"Take all you need," he commanded.

Sy swam on the sea of energy and lust, feeding greedily. I had to clamp my mouth shut so no giggles from her would escape my mouth.

"I'll guard this little pussy like the most valued treasure," Killian said, "and my dragon agrees. He'll guard it harder. You're ours."

He thrust into my molten core with his mighty demigod and dragon strength.

I threw my head back, my hands planted on the counter, my legs wide open as he thrust into me brutally.

"More!" I called.

His storm-blue eyes growing more hooded, the chaos prince pulled me to him and drove into my depths, his cock impaling my flesh mercilessly again and again. Not many females could take this kind of strength, but I was a goddess. Kind of.

I hissed in pleasure, watching how his cock drove into my depths in a blur. His cut chest heaved. His hips propelled forward, every muscle taut and hard.

His every line spelled power and strength. His lust was mighty.

I pressed a hand to his chest, his strong heartbeat echoing mine.

My heated core clenched around his shaft, milking it mercilessly. I propelled my hips toward him, grinding my clit against his groin for maximum friction. Pleasure rocked through me in waves at his possessive, brutal thrusts.

Obviously, the chaos prince excelled at fucking. He pounded into me hard, his speed blurry and erratic, hitting every sweet G-spot like high musical notes.

I could feel he was coming. I needed to arrive before he did.

It's not a race! Sy barked.

Before I knew it, I fell apart, exploding on his cock. Killian didn't release me—he pounded into me, chasing my orgasm. His face distorted in lust and restraint, as if his dragon was about to surface. He snarled and reined his beast in. The growls from his dragon rumbled from his chest. A roar escaped his carnal lips, and he emptied himself deep within me with powerful pumps.

I cried out in ecstasy. Sy's roars and giggles echoed mine. I was quick to clamp shut my mouth, my scream of pleasure stuck in the back of my throat.

Fuck off! I warned Sy as long waves of orgasm pulsed through me.

It was inconvenient to have a third wheel when I was in the throes of heat.

Lightning, starlight, and heat all crashed into me like a tsunami, pounding in my blood, recharging my every cell. Sy and I fed on the power like two scavengers on a treasure hunt, finding too much gold to carry home.

My core magic surged with a roar, breaking through the once-unbreakable cage framed by the most potent runes and spells cast by God of Ruin, and shattered the death lock of the Seed of Heaven.

I was free.

31

Barbie

I woke up to searing lust and pleasure.

I peeled open an eye and found myself on a king-sized luxury bed with the chaos prince sucking my nipple with fervor, his other hand cupping my other breast possessively. I could get used to waking up to this every morning.

I moaned in delight, gripped his hair to pin him there, and turned my head to take in my surroundings.

Velvet curtains draped over the vast full window, leaving a crack for the morning light to shine through. Dust motes swirled in a golden beam cast on the cardinal chest across from the bed. Runes glowed faintly on the walls. The chaos prince had warded every inch of his master bedroom, so tight and potent that not even the ghost guardians could slide within the walls.

My gaze fixed on a sheathed longsword on an antique

console. Blue diamonds adorned the pommel, icy power emitting from the edge of the blade that wasn't made in this realm. That I knew. Feng shui said not to put sharp things in the bedroom, but we lived in a dangerous time.

"I'm in your room," I murmured.

Killian raised his head from my breasts and smirked. "And you're the first woman who's ever slept in this bed."

I blinked away a ray of sunlight on my heavy lashes. "So, I spent the night here."

"You were dead to the world after you came on my cock," he said with laughter. "Was I too much for you?"

"You're always too much." I pursed my lips, flushing, as I remembered that we'd fucked like there was no tomorrow in Underhill.

That had been real! I'd truly fucked the heir of House of Chaos. What would we do from here? The future felt more uncertain and complicated than ever.

"I'll have to let you get used to me, then," Killian said. "And I want you to trust me to do right by you."

"I won't ask anything from you," I said, lifting my chin, "though I know that I ask too little."

"No matter what happens in the future, trust me to have your best interests in my heart."

"In history, the worst damage was often done with the best intentions, sir. Didn't they say the road to Hell is paved with good intentions?"

"That mouth of yours." A smile tugged the corners of his lips. He was so carnal that I wanted his hot, curvy lips on me down there. I'd request it soon. "But don't fear Hell. Should you get yourself in a bind and land there, I'll always get you out."

Like he'd helped pull me out of the phantom realm of the Underworld when his girlfriend hijacked my mind. But then, wasn't he the rightful heir to the throne of the Underworld, more so than her?

"You still want me, sir," I asked, cocking my head to the side, "after you already had me?"

"Will you always call me sir?" He grinned in amusement. "Do you deem me a one-night stand kind of guy?"

I nodded as he lay beside me, pulling me against his chest. I liked to snuggle against him. "You had the reputation before you got yourself engaged."

Shadows flitted by his eyes before he shook them off. He was betrothed. He had another woman in his life. He was the forbidden fruit. But I'd tasted him, and I wanted to taste him again.

"You're different than any other woman, little scorpion," he said. "I'll always want you."

Words had power, but words meant nothing if no action followed. But I wouldn't hold him accountable for the promise that was bound to break in the end. My emotions were conflicted and raw. I wanted a future, especially with Killian, but if I let myself be a hopeful fool and expect too much, I'd not only drive myself to an unmarked early grave, but I'd also bring danger to everyone.

All I could have was now, this moment.

"Will you give me oral pleasure?" I asked sweetly.

If he refuses, you can just drag his hair and get his face between your golden thighs, Sy advised. *We don't take no for an answer. It's not our style.*

I wouldn't do that! I wasn't a bitch. And I didn't need to do that.

Killian flashed me a sensual smile before he kissed me, making me hot and cold, and then his lips traced down my jaw, my neck, my breasts, until they wrapped around my clit and sucked hard.

Shit! It felt too good.

My back arched at the sensation. I was going to come involuntarily.

Killian pulled away from suckling and let out a low chuckle at my eager reaction.

"You're so responsive, my little scorpion," he purred.

His tongue lashed out, lapping my swollen clit in a slow circle. I moaned in pleasure, amazed at what a wicked tongue like the chaos prince's could do. I spread my legs wider and let him have his way with me while I enjoyed him.

His tongue brushed open my plump folds and thrust into my heat. I writhed on the silky sheets as pleasure danced on my nerve endings. His tongue thrust deeper into me and grew thicker.

Shit, it was his dragon's doing. I didn't mind it either.

As his tongue kept thrusting in my molten heat, I came hard, and he drank my juice.

"You taste of nectar and the best honeysuckle," he murmured, lust searing his eyes and turning them to deep sapphire.

"I can't believe this is real, Killian," I breathed.

"Then I'll prove to you again this is completely real," Killian said. "More real than anything."

With one swift and smooth movement, he lifted me and placed me on his lap, his cock nudging at my entrance. Then he impaled me.

I gasped, and Sy giggled in drunken delight.

"Ride me!" he said.

He was so demanding, but I'd do his bidding for now, since I needed this as much as he did.

I heaved up and down, riding his massive shaft while he

drove up into me harder and faster. The empty ache in me eased, filled up by him.

My inner walls closed around him, my pussy milking his cock mercilessly.

His eyes rolled back in ecstasy as we fucked with our shared, savage strength. We matched in every way. I was lust incarnate, as was he.

"*Mine!*" he growled.

I slammed my butt down to his base. "But are you mine too?"

Killian's eyes sparkled with starlight, power charging in them, reacting to my goddess power. Ever since we'd mated for real, our powers had been flirting with each other. Just then, wild magic shot out of the slipstream, dancing around us in a wreath of flames. It had come to visit, attracted by Killian's and my power.

In my throes of passion, I decided that if the chaos prince offered me an utterly honest answer, I'd tell him about myself. I'd bare my darkest secrets in front of him.

Urgent knocks sounded on the door. Only his tight circle was allowed to come to his penthouse, and only three people, Cami, Rock, and Cassius the Silent Blade, dared to interrupt him.

I ignored the knocks and the prince's snarl, arching my back and riding his hard length up and down, harder and faster.

A silent beat passed, then Cami called from the other side of the door, "Cousin, I apologize for the interruption, but this must be dealt with right away."

"It can wait," Killian said, thrusting into me with a growl, and I gasped at the force and the pleasure it brought.

"It can't." Cami seemed to suck in a breath. "Queen Lilith is waiting downstairs."

Killian stiffened. I bristled, and Sy bared her fangs.

"Send her away," Killian said curtly. "Tell her I'll meet her later with the other heirs."

"She knows you're in the house," Cami said ruefully. "You'll want to take care of it to prevent any further inconvenience."

Killian's gaze drifted to me.

"I can take care of myself. I'm a big girl," I said.

"Are you now?"

I curved my fingers and dug my fingernails into his naked shoulders. I didn't want him to go. I didn't want to give him up to another woman, no matter how powerful and gorgeous she was, no matter that the queen looked a lot better standing by his side.

The chaos prince let a faint smile touch his lips at my possessiveness and passive-aggressiveness.

"You want to know if I'm yours too?" he said. "I'll tell you when I get back."

I peered at him, hope and fear warring in me. "I need to tell you something first, Killian."

"You can tell me later," he said. "We'll continue after I return."

The prince lifted me off him reluctantly and kissed me hotly on the lips. "Everything will be fine, I promise."

But why did I feel this was the end?

"Also, Your Highness," Cami said carefully outside the door, "Queen Lilith brought the Oracle, who has been searching for the lost princess, daughter of the God of Ruin."

House of Mages and Raven
Coming in August/Sept 2024

AUTHOR NOTES

Dear reader,

Thank you for reading *House of Shifters and Smoke.* This book is dedicated to you. And may joy and laughter always find you.

#TeamUnderdogs!

Meg xoxo

Excerpt of Dark Fae Kings: The Complete Series

Baron turned to me with a wounded expression. "You hurt my feelings, my lady."

My heart fluttered at that hot, puppy look. I furiously ignored it.

"Sue me," I told him.

Baron sighed, and Rowan grinned, his smile with icy fire caressing my every line. I had to hold myself still to not shiver.

"Put a smile on your face, knights of the Summer Court," Baron snapped at the six dangerous men. "Soften your expression whenever you're in Lady Evelina's presence. Your images are important as you'll represent me when I'm not around the great lady."

His knights darted puzzled looks at me, as if they didn't think I had the looks of a great lady. Then they grimaced, their version of a friendly smile.

"Drop it," I said, waving a hand at them. You couldn't force people to smile. "But don't come any closer, or you'll be sorry."

Baron nodded at his men. "Lady Evelina is jumpy today, but I don't blame her. Instead, we'll respect her every wish. The Winter King has issued a challenge, and as your king, I've responded. King Rowan thought his chocolate pleased Lady Evelina more than the immortal roses of the Summer Court, so I want you to go to the human stores and collect hundreds of the best chocolates for Lady Evelina. Empty the shelves if you must."

The six men bowed at Baron, each murmuring, "Yes, my King," and turned on their heels.

Was he for real?

"Stop!" I barked. I didn't want them to come back with hundreds of chocolates heaping outside my door. It'd be another disaster.

Baron raised an eyebrow at me. "But I thought you preferred chocolate over roses."

Was he trying to punish me for favoring Rowan's gift? I hadn't accepted either bribe.

"Candies are bad for teeth," I said. "I can't afford a dental plan for my siblings!"

Rowan whistled, and seven new men filed into my front yard.

While these men also wore menacing armor, they were different than Baron's tribe. Baron's knights seemed to appear from the warmest area on Earth, with tanned skin and short hair. Rowan's group looked like they were all carved from ice with pale skin and long hair of different shades of silver. The new group also carried longswords behind their backs, the hilt sticking out above their shoulders.

So, this bunch was called Winter Fae.

Seven against six was a statement of power and arrogance. Rowan had outmaneuvered Baron again in numbers.

"They must halt, too," I shouted. "It's already bad enough the two of you are standing right outside my door."

Rowan raised a hand, and the Winter Fae stopped advancing. The Summer and the Winter knights glared at each other. When someone in the Summer camp snarled, a few knights in the Winter group growled back. When the snarling escalated, both sides drew their swords. With a battle cry, they charged each other.

What the bloody hell?

The swordsmen crossed their steel. They swung, ducked, parried, and lunged. Every single knight was ferocious and vicious, worse than career criminals. Blades found their targets on both sides, and blood sprayed on the ground in front of my house.

As if this day wasn't bizarre enough, a freaking battle had just broken out in front of my family home, which sheltered four children and two teens.

A blaze of fury shook me.

"Fuck off!" I shrieked, my eyes burning with rage. "Everyone back off! I'm using my elephant gun with iron bullets on you assholes if you don't comply. Get out of my yard and never come back!"

"Back off," Baron called.

"Stop," Rowan ordered.

The two opposite groups immediately broke off and

stayed in their lane but still glared at each other, eager for another bloody conflict, if their Fae mafia bosses ever gave them another go.

Baron and Rowan waved their minions away. And in an instant, the Summer and Winter thugs cleared out of my yard.

"I want you two to leave my property as well, and take your roses and chocolate," I said sternly. "I don't have time or energy for all your freak shows. I have a family to look after. Leave me alone, or you'll be served with a restraining order, or suffer worse consequences."

"I can't stay away from you, Lady Evie, even if I hope to," Rowan said ruefully, his expression pained, yet the heat in his gray-blue eyes never dwindled. My body responded to his heat again, willing and ready without shame.

"What's that supposed to mean?" I hissed, annoyed when my voice sounded husky.

"It's beyond my ability as well, to not be close to you," Baron said, leaning toward me as if he wanted to bury his nose against my hair to inhale my scent. I had to leash my body tightly to prevent it from inching toward him.

"This is nuts," I said. "I don't need stalkers. Now get off my property before I call the cops."

I was bluffing, knowing that calling cops wouldn't do a damn thing. And part of me didn't want them to leave. However, my cold reason also laid out for me how bad it would end up if I entangled with the Fae. If I didn't have to look after my family, I might walk on the wild side and let hell loose.

"You're drawn to me, too," Baron said. "You can't help it any more than I can."

"Excuse me?" I narrowed my eyes at him. He spoke the truth, but I didn't want him to know that. He was arrogant enough already. I couldn't help being drawn to them, and it took every ounce of willpower I had not to pounce and have my way with them right on the porch.

"Your body summoned me with your mating call," Rowan told me.

Mating? Who talked like that?

Baron inhaled deeply. "We can smell your arousal."

Wow. Just wow.

"No one can smell that," I shouted at them, then flushed furiously as I realized my mistake by admitting it. "Just no fucking way. You should not sniff at people, which is incredibly rude. We aren't animals in heat!"

"We are now, my darling lady," Baron said, his amber eyes turning molten gold with heat, and my knees went wobbly. "Your irresistible scent is a fever song in my blood, and your carnal need—"

"—is the winter song in my soul," Rowan said. "Evie, you're my fated mate."

Utterly speechless, I did the only thing I could.

I slammed the door in their faces.

BOOKS BY MEG XUEMEI X

ABOUT THE AUTHOR

Meg Xuemei X is a USA Today and Amazon Charts bestselling author of paranormal and fantasy romance. She loves writing badass heroines and hot psycho alphaholes.

Sign up to Meg's mailing list to hear about her new releases and get newsletter only bonus scene and a special gift.

Made in United States
Troutdale, OR
05/04/2024

19653437R00155